MW00535009

Because You Needed Me

TESS BARNETT

Copyright © 2016 Corvid House Publishing

All rights reserved.

ISBN: 0692652345
ISBN-13: 978-0692652343

ACKNOWLEDGMENTS

Thanks to Michelle, my constant companion in the land of boys who touch each other, and to Addison, Ciaran's biggest fan.

OTHER BOOKS BY TESS BARNETT

THOSE WORDS I DREAD

TESS BARNETT

1

Julien was tired of waiting. He'd spent the last few days splitting his time between the hospital and a cheap hotel, reading every one of Noah's books that he could translate while the doctors tried in vain to cure the witch's magical ailment with medicine. Julien had managed to get most of their belongings out of their respective apartments and avoid the police, but it hadn't been a tremendous amount of help—much of the witch's library was in Latin or German. Some were in a language Julien couldn't even hope to name, let alone read. But Noah also had dictionaries, so the hunter had done what he could, poring over the old books in search of anything that might explain Noah's illness and how to cure it. Every time the nurses kicked him out of the boy's room at the end of visiting hours, he went back to the hotel and squinted at magical academia until dawn reminded him to get a few hours of sleep.

One of his brothers had called him to ask after his progress in Vancouver, and Julien had lied to him. If he had admitted that he had been working with a witch, who he had then convinced to work dangerous magic for the sake of killing a fairy that he hadn't been able to kill himself, he would have very quickly been surrounded by six older Fournier men eager to show their baby brother how it was done. He knew that Antony, in particular, would want to kill Noah and be done with it—the witch was an abomination as far as his brothers were concerned. He wouldn't let that happen. Noah had only been trying to help him, and Julien would do everything in his power to fix what he had done.

He had finally found a lead in the creakiest of Noah's Latin books, but the answer wasn't exactly reassuring.

"Soul sickness," he said, holding the book open in his lap as he looked across at his bedridden friend. "Everything you've said seems to match up. You've said you see visions, yes? Things you don't recognize."

Noah nodded at him. The witch was still very pale, but he had at least been conscious more often than not for the last day or two. He had even been out of bed a few times to go to the bathroom or take a short walk, but he always started coughing and trembling and had to be taken back to his room. Julien felt guilt pool in his stomach like lead to see Noah suffering because of his own selfishness. If Julien hadn't asked him to use such a dangerous spell, he wouldn't be in this state now. He could have walked away. He at least should have found another way. There must have been another way.

Julien shook his head and tried to focus on their conversation. "The spell you used—you told me it was supposed to strip a creature of its soul. The only thing I can guess is that it does that by taking said soul into the caster's body and then destroying it. But you didn't finish the spell." He glanced down at the book in his lap. "And everything that's happened to you seems to fit with the aftereffects of these soul theft spells."

"Soul theft?" Noah cringed. "I wasn't trying to steal anything, Julien."

"I know."

Noah lifted his hands for a moment and dropped them back to his lap in desperation. "So you think what this is is...that I'm carrying around this fairy's soul inside of me? What does that even mean? For me and for him?"

"I'm not sure," Julien admitted. He flipped a few pages in the book as though they might produce an answer. "But it may explain your visions. The way you've described them...Noah, do you think they might be memories?"

The witch flinched like the thought was distressing to him. He didn't answer for a moment. "I guess so," he said finally, twisting the thin hospital blanket in his fingers. "The things I see—" He stopped. "It's like I'm there. People talk to me, and I move and touch things and sometimes—" Noah paused again and pressed his lips together, not wanting to explain to Julien that some of the visions he'd had were of a very intimate nature. Noah wouldn't ever forget that frantic, panting moment in the back of a moving carriage, the scent of the other man's cologne in his nostrils and the thick velvet of his coat under his hands as he pushed it aside to reach the trembling skin underneath. If the vision hadn't felt like such an invasion, Noah would have been glad to hold onto the memory for a lonely day.

Instead of telling Julien about post-opera colonial frolics, he said, "I think you're right. But what do we do about it?"

The hunter sighed through his nose and wished he could have a cigarette. "The only thing to do is to find the fairy. Finish the spell. Kill it for good."

"Finish the spell? Julien, are you crazy? It almost killed me."

"I know," the other man answered in a softer voice. "But you can't just carry around a fairy soul for the rest of your life. It's poisoning you, Noah. I don't know if that's because it's a soul at all, and people aren't meant to have more than one, or because it's this creature, or what—câlisse, this magic makes so little sense—but you can't just keep it in you."

Noah ran his hands over his face, trying to still the slight trembling in his fingers. "So what do we do?"

"We get you out of this hospital, first thing."

"But they want to keep me. They aren't going to let me out without a fuss. I heard one of the nurses talking about telling the police; they think you must have given me something. Some kind of poison."

"Tabarnak," Julien swore, and he spared a quick glance at the door. "But that makes sense. When I started looking into it, some newer sources said it presented like organophosphate poisoning." He paused. "I suppose in a way it is organophosphate poisoning."

"Organo-what? Never mind." Noah held up a hand when Julien opened his mouth to answer. "I don't want to think about it. If I've got that fairy's spirit inside me somehow, I really don't want to think about it too much. I just want it out."

"We can't just sit around in here. These doctors can't help you. We need to get you out of here before this gets worse."

Noah gave a soft, empty laugh. "Worse than this?"

Julien shifted in his plastic seat. "You deserve to know," he said after a moment. "It seems to progress quickly." He couldn't look up at him. "If we can't get the fairy's soul out of you, destroy it somehow, it's going to drive you mad. It will devour you. Apparently it's not uncommon for the person to kill themselves once it progresses too far."

Noah slumped in the bed and looked up at the hunter helplessly. He had barely been able to cast the spell in the first place—he hadn't even finished—and it had still nearly killed him. Now he was weak from coughing and doing nothing but laying around in bed for days, and Julien expected him to do it again. He didn't like his chances. But Julien watched him with such a gentle frown that he felt calm, despite everything stacked against him. The hunter had only left his side when forced out by the nurses and had been nothing but attentive and kind since the incident. Noah almost felt guilty, but he tried to allow himself to enjoy the other man fussing over him a little. It wasn't a good substitute for what he really wanted, but he'd resigned himself to forever wanting the hunter's real affection.

"If that's what you say we have to do, then that's what we'll do," Noah said. "I guess I can check myself out against medical advice or whatever, but you know they're going to try to stop me."

"Then let's just leave," Julien suggested, as though it were the simplest thing in the world. "I'll distract them. I'll make up a story, or start a fight, or something. You can sneak out in the confusion, and I'll meet up with you afterward."

"What? That's stupid. We're doing all this to keep either of us from getting arrested, aren't we? How does it make sense for you to start a fight in the middle of a hospital?" He paused as a thought slipped into his mind, and when he glanced down at his hands, their trembling stilled. "No," he said almost without meaning to speak. "I have a better idea."

Julien watched uncertainly as Noah climbed out of the bed,

brushing aside the hunter's offered hand. He dressed himself with the clothes Julien had brought him days ago and left his thin hospital gown abandoned on the bed.

"Don't push yourself," Julien warned him, but Noah didn't seem to be listening.

The witch pulled open the door to his room and stepped outside, waiting in the hall to watch a few people pass by without even glancing at him. He took a step forward and had to move out of the way of a nurse bustling by. She must have been looking right at him, but she didn't seem to see him.

"Come on out, Julien," Noah said without looking back. "They won't see you, either."

Julien frowned as he stepped out behind Noah. He leaned forward to wave a hand in a nearby man's face but got no reaction. He looked up at Noah, but the boy was staring straight ahead, his eyes on the end of the hallway. Noah had said that invisibility was extremely difficult. He'd said he wasn't able to do it. And this wasn't just invisibility—Noah had spoken, and no one seemed able to hear him. Julien hadn't even seen him cast an actual spell. He had simply decided that no one should be able to see them, and so no one could. This was fairy magic. Had Noah absorbed so much of the creature's essence that he was able to tap into its power? The notion made Julien more than a little nervous.

Noah turned to look back at him with a calm, empty look on his face, and then he started walking toward the elevators. Julien hurried to keep up with him after pausing to make sure he'd grabbed everything from the hospital room, and they rode the elevator together in silence. Noah seemed too serene; he'd spent his time in the hospital smiling weakly and wringing his hands, but now he stood casually in the elevator with his hands still at his sides, not even coughing.

The elevator doors opened on the ground floor, and they walked through the hallways unseen, dodging the people in their way. When they reached the street, Noah took a single step away from the door and stumbled. The blood drained from his face, and he staggered to the nearby strip of landscaping and vomited behind a bush. Julien rushed to his side and managed to get a grip on his arm just before he fell forward into his own sick, but they definitely weren't invisible anymore—some people around them had stopped to look, though most only paused in mild concern and moved on.

"Noah," Julien whispered as he pulled the boy to his knees with his one good hand. His wrist didn't ache as much these past couple of days, but it was still indisputably broken. He cleaned the witch's face with a handkerchief from his pocket and tapped his cheek to try to rouse him. "Noah, es-tu correct?" Noah only slumped against Julien's shoulder, his breath coming in shallow pants. Whatever magic he had accessed to get them out of the hospital had clearly been a bad idea. They needed to find the fairy and finish this, right now.

Julien lifted Noah to his feet, drawing a drowsy groan from him, and he let the other man lean on him as they walked to the nearest bus stop. They could go back to the apartment where the fairy was staying, Noah could cast the spell and destroy the fairy's spirit once and for all, and then it would be done. Everything would be back to normal. Noah would be back to normal.

Julien let the younger man rest his head on his shoulder on the bus, and he watched him as his head lolled with every brake and turn. For the first time in his life, the hunter found himself wishing he had any kind of magical ability, so that he might lend it to Noah for this spell. The witch was growing weaker by the day, almost by the hour. He could only hope that the fairy was just as weakened. It could all be done quickly.

Julien kept a steadying arm around Noah's waist as they exited the bus, offering a quick nod of reassurance to the driver on their way out. At least Noah could pass for drunk like this, though Julien wasn't sure being this drunk in the middle of the day was much better than the truth of the situation. He helped Noah up the steps to the entrance of the apartment building and greeted the doorman as though he belonged. Luckily, it was the same man who had seen Noah collapse in the lobby a few days before, so he believed Julien when he explained that they were guests of Mr. Fa.

Once they reached the right floor, Noah leaned heavily against the wall, watching Julien with half-lidded eyes as he picked the lock on the door. He managed to walk himself into the apartment behind the hunter, but he lingered near the door while Julien searched the rooms.

The bed was unmade, the closet door was open, and the dresser drawers had been turned out. There weren't any toiletries on the bathroom counter, and the kitchen was half empty. Julien tore open every door in the apartment, checked all of the closets, and even checked the fridge, but he finally had to sink against the wall beside Noah.

"They've left," he said, trying not to let his dejection show through. Noah didn't need to feel hopeless, even if Julien felt like shouting.

2

Trent paced the length of his bedroom with his phone in his hand for almost an hour before he even managed to unlock the screen. He could have just left without saying anything. He had already called his mother and told her his plans, and he had already emptied his bank account. He could have just left. He didn't have to call. But he wanted to. He needed his father to know that he had made this decision consciously.

Finally, he touched his father's number and lifted the phone to his ear. After a few rings, he heard a familiar voice answer, and he almost hung up immediately. He steeled himself and took a quick breath.

"Fu chan," Trent began, his stomach turned to stone. "I need to talk to you."

"What is it, Trent? I have a meeting."

"I've…decided to take your advice."

"Have you?" He sounded distracted.

"Yes. You wanted me to accept responsibility. So I'm moving out," he said, hoping he sounded more confident than he felt.

A beat of silence passed. "Moving out," his father echoed.

"You were right. Everything that I have, I have because of you. So if everything that I have comes with the condition that I pretend to be something I'm not, then I...I don't want it."

"Aiya, Trent, don't be an idiot," Mr. Fa snapped. "You're going to give up all the opportunities you've been given because of this—fetish?"

"Fetish?" Trent laughed. "You think this is just something that I do for kicks? You really don't understand, do you?"

"I understand that you're throwing away everything you have for selfish reasons! You'll ruin your life for the sake of some perversion! I won't allow it. You need to focus on school and stop thinking about this nonsense. Is there someone putting all of this in your head? Why is all this coming up now?"

"It's none of your business!" Trent tried to answer, but his father continued to talk over him.

Ciaran peeked in from the bedroom door and watched Trent begin to pace again, his rapid Cantonese sounding more strained by the moment. He couldn't hear what Trent's father was saying on the other end of the line, but he could guess. Trent caught sight of him eavesdropping and turned away, hugging his arm tightly around his middle as he listened to the angry voice coming through the phone.

Trent said something that Ciaran didn't understand in response, but he could hear the defeated tone in the younger man's voice. Without hesitation, Ciaran pushed the bedroom door open and fastened his arms around Trent's waist, leaning his cheek against the taller man's back and gently touching his tense stomach. Trent seemed to relax slightly in his grip, and Ciaran listened to the quiet rumble of his voice through his back until he hung up the phone and dropped it onto the bed. For a while, they only stood silently, Ciaran brushing his fingertips over the soft fabric of Trent's shirt.

"Well," Trent said softly, "it's a good thing I'd already decided to leave, because he just kicked me out." He scoffed out an empty chuckle. "It's impressive, kicking someone out of an apartment from halfway across the world."

"Are you all right?" Ciaran murmured against his back.

"As long as you're not about to say, 'I've changed my mind, I'll go to Ireland and you stay here,' then yeah, I'm all right."

Ciaran loosened his grip just enough to slip around to the other man's front, and he leaned up to press a warm kiss to his lips. "I promise not to say that. I'm human-like now, after all; how should I pay for an airplane ticket without you?"

"Of course," Trent muttered, but then he paused. "That's a really good point, actually. I don't guess you have any ID or papers or anything, do you?"

"I haven't had much call for it, no," Ciaran chuckled.

"Well then I don't know how in the hell we're going to get you on a plane. Especially one overseas. You don't have a passport."

"Do I need one?"

"Yes you need one," Trent sighed. "They don't just let people on planes. You have to have identification. I can buy you a ticket, but they won't let you on. And you can't magic yourself one right now, right?"

Ciaran frowned at the unwelcome reminder. "Not as such, no."

"I guess we could get you a fake one, but that would take time, even assuming that I had even the slightest clue how to go about getting a forged passport."

"Really?" Ciaran chuckled, hiding a cough in his shoulder. "Rich boy like you didn't have a fake ID growing up? Getting into bars before you were supposed to, that sort of thing?"

"I just paid the bouncer," Trent shrugged. "Rich boy, after all. But I don't think I have 'bribe airport security' money. If we can't get you fake papers, maybe we can find someone who can sneak us through customs?" He sighed. "That's probably harder than just forging a passport."

"We could take a boat," Ciaran suggested. "You can just sneak aboard a boat."

"What year do you think this is? You want to stowaway on a ship?" Ciaran shrugged and nestled himself against Trent's chest. "Let's put a pin in that one. Maybe there's someone from school I can call," Trent mused, leaning his chin absently on the top of Ciaran's head.

The fairy paused. "I might have a solution, actually." He leaned back to look up into the younger man's face.

Trent should have known that when Ciaran said he 'knew someone,' he didn't mean he knew a normal sort of a someone. It was fine for Ciaran, who had no belongings in the world, to wander around Vanier Park for an hour looking for precisely the right little copse of trees, but Trent had his duffel bag slung over his shoulder and was growing slightly irritable.

"This is a real person, right?" Trent confirmed for at least the third time, sighing as Ciaran turned away from yet another tree line. "You didn't imagine them?"

"Do you ever stop grousing? Look, it's just there." Ciaran pointed out a small cluster of foliage surrounding a larger tree with long, drooping green branches that reached all the way to the ground. He led the way through the thick leaves into a small clearing dotted with pinpoints of sunshine, a tiny grove cut off from the outside world by a wall of willowy branches.

"Oi, Eveleen," Ciaran called. He stood in the center of the clearing and turned in a slow circle, watching the branches of the trees for any sign of movement. A slight breeze rustled the leaves, but he got no answer. "Oh, come on. Tá a fhios agam go bhfuil tú ann."

They waited, but there was no sound except for the quiet chirping of nearby birds. Ciaran frowned as Trent stepped up beside him.

"Not what you were expecting?" Trent asked, and Ciaran shook his head.

"Maybe she won't answer a...a human," Ciaran answered softly, sounding as though it was difficult for his mouth to form the words. As soon as he finished speaking, a strong breeze blew through the grove, and a woman appeared in front of them in a long tunic made of an airy, pale blue cloth. She was tall, at least a head taller than Trent, with thick shoulders and a masculine jaw. She had the same delicately pointed ears as Ciaran sticking out through her blonde hair, but it was difficult to think of them as the same. Trent got the impression that whatever she was, it was something darker than what Ciaran was. She watched both of them with a distant, curious expression, but she said nothing.

"Ah, there you are," Ciaran smiled, and he approached the woman without fear, reaching out to clasp her outstretched hand. "Trent, this is Eveleen. She's a sylph."

"Good to meet you," Trent offered, though it sounded suspiciously like a question.

"Eveleen let me stay here for a while when I first came to

Vancouver," Ciaran explained. "I didn't know anyone," he said instead of the more precise truth, which was that he was simply between lovers at the time.

"What's happened to you?" the sylph asked. Her voice was eerily quiet, but it seemed to reach Trent's ears regardless. "You smell strange. Like a human."

"It's a long story," Ciaran sighed. "But we're trying to fix it. I need to get home; do you think you can help?"

The woman lifted one thin eyebrow. "Home? Your home? That's quite a distance."

"I know," he nodded. "You'd be doing us a great favor."

A tiny smile touched one corner of her lips. "You don't want to travel the human way, little human?"

Ciaran rolled his eyes with a groan. "I'll owe you, all right?"

She chuckled at him and gave a small nod. "You know I'd do anything for you, Scal Balb."

"Who's Scal Balb?" Trent interrupted, looking at Ciaran with a furrowed brow.

"It's just a nickname," Ciaran answered quickly with a sidelong glance at the sylph. "Hard to shake. Don't worry about it."

Trent frowned at him, but let it go for now. He looked between Ciaran and the sylph. "So, not to be impolite, but how is this gargantuan elf woman supposed to get us to Ireland?"

"Not to be impolite," the sylph repeated with an amused smile.

Ciaran chuckled. "You think this is what she really looks like?"

Before Trent could answer, the woman disappeared in a rush of wind, leaving only a vaguely human-shaped vortex of air. A moment later, Trent was in the air, barely stifling his shout of surprise as he was scooped in an invisible grip and lifted over the trees. Ciaran was beside him, laughing as they were carried high above the park and out over the city.

"Fuck this magic bullshit, fuck it," Trent repeated to himself. He dared a look downward and swore again. "What the hell, is that Mac the Moose? How the fuck is that Mac the Moose? How are we in Saskatchewan? Way too fast. Too fucking fast."

Ciaran reached out across the gap between them and took a tight hold of Trent's hand. Trent looked over at him with a tense stare, his grip tightening as they passed beyond the coastline and had nothing but ocean underneath them.

"This is a reliable mode of transport?" Trent called over the roar of the wind, and Ciaran smiled at him.

"Mostly."

"Mostly is just what I want to hear a thousand feet above the Atlantic," Trent snapped back, but Ciaran only squeezed his hand and blew him a kiss.

After what felt like an eternity of salty wind and panic, the sylph dropped them in a tiny coastal town lined with rows of brightly colored houses. A dozen boats were tied to the docks, shifting in the waves the sylph created around them as they landed. Trent took a few steadying breaths, feeling slightly sick to his stomach as he adjusted to standing on solid ground again. Ciaran gave his hand a reassuring pat and called out a thank you as the sylph dissipated before their eyes, presumably returning to her little grove in the middle of Vancouver.

"Next time, let's just forge you a passport," Trent sighed, running a hand over his hair to smooth it back into some semblance of order.

"Well, maybe I'll die here, and you can travel back on your own without worry."

Trent frowned over at him. "Nothing like the power of positive thinking."

Ciaran shrugged and stood up taller to take a long look around them. "Be nice if I had any idea where this was, though."

"Ireland, at least, hopefully."

Ciaran didn't answer him. "Of course she couldn't have taken us the whole way." He paused to cough, then had to reach out and put a hand on Trent's arm to steady himself as he doubled over and tried to catch his breath. When he wiped at his mouth, blood was smeared on the back of his hand.

Trent put a hand on the fairy's back as he straightened. "You need to rest."

"I need to get home," Ciaran countered, more harshly than he meant to. "I'm fine, lad. Don't fuss. Let's figure out where we are and how to get moving." He pulled away from Trent's touch and started down the narrow street without him.

Trent hesitated. Ciaran hadn't called him 'lad' since things had gotten...closer between them. It didn't sound right anymore. He shook his head, convincing himself he was being stupid and sentimental, and followed the fairy away from the docks. He noticed a few people giving Ciaran odd looks as he passed, and he realized with a start what they must be staring at.

"Hey," he called, trotting a few steps to catch up to him. "You have a problem."

"I have a lot of problems, lad."

"Yeah, but I mean, you have a...noticeable problem," Trent said under his breath as he urged the fairy to stop, and he reached up to touch one of Ciaran's pointed ears. He might have been human now, mostly, but that hadn't changed the way he looked. The strangely sharp canines could be considered within the normal range of variance, Trent supposed, but there was no explaining away the tips of the fairy's ears.

"Oh," Ciaran said, his eyebrows lifting in realization. "Right, I suppose that would seem a bit odd, wouldn't it? This being visible all the time takes some getting used to, I will say."

"Come on." They did their best to avoid the people on the street while they explored the small town, and they were easily able to find a small gift shop beside a restaurant that, thankfully, had a small collection of knit caps to choose from. Ciaran decided on the greyish brown, and he pulled the slouchy toque down over his ears and held his hands out at his sides to wait for Trent's approval.

"Cute," Trent muttered, only half sarcastic, and he paid the lady at the counter for their purchase. Ciaran leaned on the countertop to smile at her, happily chatting while Trent made a quick count of his remaining bills, thankful that he had thought to exchange a good chunk of his money for Euros the day before.

The shopkeeper immediately confirmed with her accent that they were, in fact, in Ireland, and she directed them to a place called the Fisherman's Bar, a quaint-looking red building with golden yellow accents and a painting of a puffin on a hanging wooden sign. Inside, Ciaran was able to confirm that the only way out of the little village other than private car was by bus, which only ran to the town of Cahersiveen three times a week. They would have to spend the night. Trent paid for their bus fare, and they sat down to supper at the bar.

"Why can't I eat what I like, again?" Ciaran asked as he prodded his fish and vegetables.

"Because before we left, you ate an entire pack of Oreos because you didn't want them to go to waste, and then you spent the next hour groaning on the couch." Trent looked across the table at him. "Look, I know this is weird for you, but if you're...different now, even if it's only temporary, you're going to have to make some adjustments."

Ciaran snorted and dropped his fork to the plate with a clatter. "It's not enough I can barely walk like this? Everything feels so heavy, and I'm always tired, and the air is so thick, but it's like no matter how much I breathe, I—" He stopped to cough, his shoulders shaking with every heave, until he finally calmed down and let his forehead thunk onto the table beside his plate. "I hate it," he whined, and Trent found himself faintly smiling.

"We'll figure it out," he promised. "But you have to eat something, or you're going to feel even worse. Come on. You want me to pretend your spoon is an airplane?"

"Feisigh leat," Ciaran grunted as he attempted to lift a forkful of fish to his mouth without lifting his head.

"Well that sounded rude."

"I'll show you rude in a minute."

When Ciaran finally finished grumpily spooning peas into his mouth, Trent paid for their meal, and they walked down the sloping street together toward the hostel, Trent taking slow steps so that Ciaran could keep up. The hostel wasn't the most glamorous of places, but it was tidy and cheap, which suited both of them just fine. Their beds were in an open room lined with bunks and single twin beds, all sharing a bathroom at the end of the hall. It was mostly empty, with only a couple of backpacks stuffed under bunks across the room from the beds they chose.

Ciaran immediately climbed into the top bunk and wrapped himself in the fleece blanket, peering down at Trent over the railing. "This time, you have to let me be on top," he said with a sly smile, earning himself a short, sarcastic laugh.

"Just get some sleep."

Ciaran grinned and leaned his elbows on the rail, tugging his hat from his head while Trent unbuttoned his shirt. "The man at the bar said we could get a bus to Brú na Bóinne from Cahersiveen. From there it should be easy. As long as I remember how to get in."

Trent folded his shirt and left it on top of his duffel bag, which he nudged under the bunk with his foot. "Is there a chance of you not remembering?"

"Well I haven't been home in...some time. Doesn't matter. I'll find it." Ciaran turned away from the rail and settled his head on his pillow without another word. Trent stared up at his back for a moment, at least half a dozen questions at the tip of his tongue, but Ciaran started another round of heaving coughs, so he kept them to himself. The fairy had seemed reluctant to make this trip at all. What could he be trying to avoid?

Ciaran woke up hours later in the darkened room, his heart pounding painfully fast, and he sat straight up in his bed with a wild look as he struggled to remember where he was. He touched his chest, the bed rail, the soft blanket. He leaned over the edge to look down at Trent, peacefully sleeping below. He was in Ireland. He was going home. Trent was with him. Why was he going home? His stomach ached, and he felt cold and lost. With a quiet step that sounded clumsy and heavy in his ears, he slipped down from his bunk and forced his way in beside Trent, nudging the other man up against the wall and settling in beside him.

Trent stirred, then grunted a sleepy acceptance of this intrusion, lifting his arm to allow Ciaran to lay his head on his shoulder. It was a tight fit with both of them in the twin bed, but he could feel Ciaran trembling beside him and didn't feel inclined to kick him out. He couldn't imagine what the other man was going through, no matter how he teased.

Just as he was falling back into sleep, Trent felt a hand brush against his stomach, fingers slipping boldly past the waistband of his underwear, and he jumped slightly as those fingers wrapped around him.

"What are you doing?" he whispered in a hiss. He turned his head to face Ciaran and found his lips caught in a demanding kiss, unable to restrain the soft groan that formed in his throat. He pulled away reluctantly and put a hand on the fairy's chest to stop him leaning in again. "We aren't alone in here," he murmured under his breath.

"Then you should be quiet," Ciaran countered, lifting himself onto Trent's lap and bending over him to nip sharply at his collarbone.

Trent shuddered underneath him, and his stomach tightened at Ciaran's touch despite his reservations. He was about to give in, and he reached up to pull the other man to him, but every time Trent tried to touch him, Ciaran pushed his hands away. Ciaran ground his hips against him, panting into the crook of his neck as he pushed at his underwear in a rush.

"Take it easy," Trent murmured, but Ciaran didn't seem to be listening. He pulled and squeezed at the younger man under him but snorted and turned his head away when Trent tried to focus him with a light touch to his cheek. Ciaran left a small tear in Trent's boxer briefs as he tugged them down his thighs, and Trent winced.

"Oh, come on," he whispered. Ciaran nudged his way between Trent's legs and pressed against him with undisguised urgency, causing Trent to pull away in mild panic. "Hey, slow it down, will you?" When Ciaran didn't respond, Trent hissed at him and pushed at his shoulder, but he had to shove the fairy so hard that the back of his head hit the bunk above them before he would stop.

"What the hell is that matter with you?" Trent snapped, keeping his voice low to hide its quaver.

Ciaran stared down at him with a furrowed brow, rubbing at the sore spot on his skull. "What?" he answered in a whisper. "Are we doing this or not?"

"I'm not just here for you to grind up against," Trent countered with a scowl. "I think you need to get some sleep."

The fairy frowned at him, looking as though he wanted to argue, but he only slumped down on the bed with his back to Trent, leaving his lover to lie with one leg over the side of the bunk to fit in the small space left. Ciaran had been so teasing and gentle before. This forcefulness and demanding didn't seem like him—but Trent reminded himself with a twist in his stomach that he hadn't actually known the fairy for very long. He watched Ciaran's back for a few long moments, touching the gold amulet around his neck and trying to convince himself that the man he loved was simply sick, and that he hadn't made a horrible miscalculation.

3

The hotel Julien had chosen was one of the cheapest he'd ever stayed at, and it showed, but at least it meant that they would be able to stay as long as they needed to on the hunter's dwindling savings. The single bed had a threadbare blanket and squeaky springs, and next to it sat a wobbling nightstand. A worn knotted rug to hide a bit of the dirty wooden floor. Noah deserved better while he recovered, but this was the best Julien could give him for now. At least he had managed to save a decent amount of the witch's ingredients, incense, and herbs from the police. Not that Julien had any idea what to do with them. Right now they sat stuffed in a suitcase that he had hidden between the bed and the wall.

Noah had drowsily allowed Julien to put him to bed with only a perfunctory argument. "Just promise you won't sleep on the floor," he grumbled, his eyes already half closed. "You'll get fleas or something."

"Je promets, mon râleur," Julien answered softly as the boy drifted off. He paused a moment to take a deep breath as he looked down at the sleeping witch. The fairy, the only reasonable hope they had of curing Noah, was missing. The creature and its human protector could be anywhere by now. The boy clearly had money—they could have gone anywhere in the world they pleased. But they would have had difficulty going far with the fairy in such a weakened state. At least, Julien hoped it was still in a weakened state. Why go anywhere at all? Did the fairy know something about healing this affliction that Julien didn't? More likely they were still in the city, hiding out somewhere while the creature recovered. And if the fairy was still in the city, Julien could find it. He'd tracked it down before.

He was about to turn and leave Noah to rest while he began his search, but the younger man whimpered and shivered in his sleep, curling his knees up to his chest and tugging the blanket tight around his chin. Julien frowned and reached to touch Noah's forehead with the back of his hand. He still had a fever, and his skin was slightly damp with sweat. He needed a better blanket, needed to sweat the fever out, but there wasn't one to be had. Julien hesitated, weighing his choices, and then he kicked off his boots with a soft sigh. This wouldn't make it easy on the boy if he woke up, but getting him well was more important than any potential embarrassment.

Julien tugged off his pants, then unfastened his sling and carefully slipped his shirt over his head, sliding into the bed beside Noah in his boxers and undershirt. He hesitated with the boy's body so close to him, Noah's body trembling and flinching at the cool air he had let in by lifting the blanket. This wouldn't just be embarrassing for Noah. Julien had been forced to huddle together with his brothers before while camping in northern Quebec, but that had usually involved a lot of elbows and swearing. Lying in bed with a man who had claimed just a few days prior that he wanted to be more than friends was another matter entirely.

He pushed the notion out of his mind. Noah was sick, and he needed warmth. That was all. Julien edged closer to the witch and let his arm drape over him, pulling him back against his chest and nudging his arm under Noah's head to keep his splint out of the way. Noah's skin felt clammy on Julien's bicep, but he quickly nestled himself in the newfound warmth of the hunter's arms. The boy's smaller body fit perfectly against Julien's, and he seemed to settle under the weight of the other man's arm around his waist. Julien brushed aside the thought that it didn't feel nearly as awkward as he had expected. The wine-colored birthmark behind Noah's ear caught the hunter's attention, a subtle, unpleasant reminder of the vast difference between them. Noah's breathing slowed to a steady, sleepy pace, and despite the early hour, the soft scent of incense that lingered in the witch's hair lulled Julien to sleep soon after him.

Julien was roused from a deep sleep by Noah suddenly shaking in his arms, twisting and jerking away from the creaking mattress. Julien reached out to touch his arm in an attempt to steady him. He knew by now what it looked like when Noah had one of his flashbacks; he had seen it enough times in the hospital to become painfully familiar. Noah wriggled under the blanket to face him, and he looked up at the hunter with the distant, empty eyes that Julien recognized. Noah's lips were moving with silent whispers, his chest rising with each quick, shallow breath. The only thing to do was try to keep him calm and let him ride out the vision. He would come out the other side soon, and Julien would tell him to hush and go back to sleep.

Noah's hands slid between them, his fingers curling into the thin fabric of Julien's undershirt. He pressed close against the larger man and reached up to touch his cheek, fingernails scratching softly against his stubbled jaw.

"A rúnsearc, tá mé chaill tú," Noah whispered, his breath hot against the hollow of Julien's neck. The witch slipped his hands under the other man's shirt, pressing his palms against his firm stomach. Julien tensed under the touch and put his free hand on Noah's shoulder to try to keep him at bay as gently as possible, but Noah resisted, tilting his head up to plant a soft bite on Julien's chin. "Is gá dom duit, le do thoil," the witch begged in a desperate, panting voice that needed no translation. His hips rolled against Julien's as he repeated his soft plea in a whisper, sending an involuntary shudder down the hunter's spine. He needed to stop him. He was dreaming, or remembering, or something—whatever it was, it wasn't meant for Julien, and the hunter couldn't let him continue. Didn't want him to continue, he corrected himself.

Noah's tongue drew a slow line along Julien's jaw as his hand dipped lower on his stomach, the tips of his fingers barely slipping beneath the waistband of his boxers and brushing soft, curly blonde hair. Julien's breath caught in his throat, but he squeezed Noah's wrist before he could go on and held it still despite the boy's whimpering complaints. Noah struggled against him for what felt like forever, pleading with him and pressing warm, wanting kisses to any bare skin he could reach. Julien shut his eyes against the sensation and set his jaw until Noah finally went slack against him, his forehead lightly resting on Julien's chest as he faded back into sleep.

As soon as he could, Julien slipped out of Noah's embrace and paced the perimeter of the room, running his hand over his face and silently begging his body to stop overreacting. His heart raced in his chest, threatening to bruise his ribs. This was troubling. It was a memory, he told himself. It was a memory of someone from the fairy's past. Noah wasn't responsible for what he did when he was like that. He wasn't aware. And it certainly didn't mean anything that Julien had had a...response. He'd been alone for some time, longer than he liked to admit—it would be odd if his body *didn't* react that way. Julien was overthinking it because of the conversation they'd had before all of this started. Noah wanted more. Wanted Julien to give him more.

Julien stopped walking and looked down at Noah's sleeping form under the blanket, blissfully unaware of how close they'd come to— nothing, Julien reminded himself. It was just a memory.

He climbed into the bed slightly warily, embarrassment flushing his face as he shifted his erection into a more comfortable position. He settled as quickly as he could, facing away from Noah and doing his best to ignore the witch's warm weight against his back.

Noah squeezed his eyes shut tighter as a thin beam of light hit his face through the flimsy curtain, and he buried his face in the warmth of Julien's back, hugging the larger man's body close against him. A moment later, he panicked, pulling away from the hunter in a scrambling hurry. Images came flooding back to him of his vision from the night before, and he hid his face in his hands as his cheeks grew hot. Of course he would have a flash like that while Julien was in the bed next to him. He strained to remember what had happened, but he never had any memory of anything real during his visions. Had he said anything to Julien, or—he groaned at the thought—done something to him? What if he'd gotten hard, and Julien had noticed? He prayed that he hadn't made a fool of himself.

He jumped slightly as Julien stirred beside him, giving a soft grunt and rolling onto his back to rub at his eyes. Noah felt the urge to crawl under the bed and die as the hunter looked over at him, but Julien only offered him a brief smile and pulled himself out of bed without a word. There was no way Noah could ask. Julien would say something if anything had happened, right? He would make a joke, or tell him it was all right, or something. Right?

Noah looked up as he realized Julien was staring at him. The hunter looked tousled and exhausted, but his face was gentle as he ran a hand through his hair to smooth it.

"How are you feeling?" he asked, snapping Noah out of his gazing.

"Fine," Noah answered automatically, even though he was still groggy, and his stomach ached. "Thanks for taking care of me."

"Are you hungry?" Noah's grumbling stomach answered for him, so Julien crouched down to a plastic bag near the nightstand and retrieved a loaf of bread. They shared a few chunks with the peanut butter Julien had retrieved from his apartment, but neither of them had anything to say about the previous night.

"So if the fairy's gone, what do we do?" Noah asked, doing nothing to ease the dark tension in the room.

"Maybe I can go back to the apartment," Julien suggested. "Maybe they'll have come back."

"That's wishful thinking and you know it," Noah sighed. He tucked his hands under the blanket in his lap to hide their trembling. "Wherever they are, they're trying to fix him just like we're trying to fix me. If we figured it out, they've probably guessed that we mean to find them and finish the spell. They're not going to make it easy."

"They went somewhere," Julien insisted. "I can find them. I just need a lead." He looked over at Noah, his eyes passing briefly over the witch's hidden hands.

"There are a hundred thousand things they might try," Noah objected. "Maybe they went to a friend, or some kind of fairy library, or something else I've never even heard of. Maybe he already knows a spell to fix what I've done, and they're doing it right now." He shook his head. "I did so much reading about fairies after you said that's what you'd found, but it's impossible to know what's true and what's not. There are a dozen different kinds and conflicting stories about all

29

of them. There isn't even a hell of a lot of information out there about the spell I used, other than 'it's bad, don't do it.' I just don't know," he finished dejectedly.

Julien paused as though hesitant to speak again, watching Noah with a furrowed brow. "You have that fairy's spirit inside of you," he said softly. "What you did at the hospital, hiding us like that—you said it was impossible. It wasn't like any magic I've seen a witch do before. You tapped into it, didn't you? That thing's spirit. It's in you now; you could use it."

"Ugh, can you not say it like that?" Noah cringed, rubbing the goosebumps out of his arms with both hands. "Creepy."

"I'm saying if that thing has memories, it has knowledge," Julien went on. "Maybe you could figure out what it knows if you could...I don't know, access it somehow."

Noah frowned. "I don't really want to try to do it on purpose," he muttered. "It's bad enough when it happens on its own. It's...confusing, and weird, and...a little scary. When I see things, I feel like...for a minute, I don't even know who I am."

Julien watched him with a soft expression. "What sorts of things do you see?"

"Battles," Noah answered immediately. "Lots of battles. Terrible, brutal battles. I mean, not even swords sometimes, but—what are those things called, the big Irish clubs with the big round thing on the end—"

"Shillelagh," Julien provided, and Noah nodded.

"That one." He shuddered. "I've seen people on the ground, wounded and begging, and I feel the weight of it in my hands, like I'm holding it over my head. I can hear the sound it makes when it...never mind." He held his own arms tight and shook his head. "Then sometimes...a huge hall, with tapestries, and music, and beer, and people are laughing, there are dogs chewing on bones in the corner. Once there was...a woman. There are lots of women, actually. And..." He swallowed before going on, and he couldn't meet Julien's eye. "And some men, too. I can hear people talking to me, and I can hear me—him—talking, and it's Gaelic, I think, but in my head it isn't and it is. I hear it, and I understand it, but thinking back on it when I'm awake, it's...harder to know what was going on. So I don't know how much help it would be even if I could do it on purpose."

He looked over at Julien apologetically, knowing he wasn't being very helpful, but the hunter only stared at him, looking as though he had another question on his mind.

Whatever it was, Julien apparently thought better of it, because he only got to his feet and said, "In that case, I'll do it the old fashioned way. You stay here and get some rest. I'm going to go hunting."

4

In the morning, Ciaran got himself out of bed and helped himself to the first hot water of the morning with hardly a glance in Trent's direction. If he felt any guilt or remorse about the previous night, he certainly didn't show it. Trent ignored him in return, brushing by him on his way to his turn in the shower, but he couldn't ignore the anxiety building in his stomach. Ciaran was missing a big part of what made him Ciaran, Trent reminded himself. That's why he was acting this way. Soon, they would get to where they were going, he'd get fixed up by whatever fairy magic he had planned, and everything would be back to normal—as normal as things were ever going to get, anyway. Everything would be fine. Maybe Ciaran would even feel guilty about the way he'd acted. Not likely, but it was possible.

Downstairs, Ciaran longed out loud for one of the scones on offer, groaning out a protest when Trent reminded him yet again of his dietary limitations.

"People eat scones, Trent," Ciaran complained. "If people didn't eat them, they wouldn't be here. I'm allowed to eat a scone."

Trent frowned at him. "Can you eat one scone?"

"Yes," he answered promptly, glaring up at Trent like a petulant child as the younger man absently tugged his toque lower over his ears for him.

"Then get a scone," Trent shrugged. "But if you don't eat something substantial, and you bitch later, be prepared for me not to listen."

"You're so sweet," Ciaran muttered, but he satisfied himself with a blueberry scone while Trent ate a plate full of eggs and sipped a cup of coffee.

They finished quickly and met the man who would drive them to Cahersiveen. They climbed into the back of the slightly aged van and waited, but they were apparently the only passengers that morning. As they rode, Ciaran leaned forward to chat with the driver, his brogue seeming to grow thicker with every exchange. Trent was having trouble following the conversation, so he watched the green hills go by outside the window instead.

"What brings you lads all the way out to Portmagee, in any case?" the driver asked, glancing back at them through the rear view mirror.

Ciaran grinned as he slouched back in his seat, and he slipped his fingers through Trent's despite his tense frown. "This one wanted to see the coast," he answered, lifting Trent's hand to his lips and touching a gentle kiss to his knuckles. "It is our honeymoon, after all."

"Our—" Trent began in protest, but Ciaran squeezed his hand and smiled that impish smile at him, crinkling the corners of his eyes, and the objection died on Trent's lips.

"Suppose congratulations are in order, then," the driver quipped, but he was noticeably less chatty for the remainder of the drive.

The trip to Dublin involved too many bus transfers, a fair bit of walking, a train from Killarney, and long stretches of Ciaran asleep on Trent's shoulder in between coughing fits, but eventually they disembarked in Dublin outside a stone building adorned with carved columns and wreaths.

Ciaran wandered the sidewalk, seeming to take in the sights and sounds of the city around them, and Trent watched him curiously as he was pulled along by the hand. He had assumed that Ciaran would know Ireland well, what with being from there, but he supposed things must have changed drastically since the fairy had last seen it. They walked together down the narrow streets, Ciaran occasionally turning and walking backwards to get a better look at something as they passed. They walked by sandwich shops, pubs, and even a friendly green shopfront advertising Chinese take away. Every shop had at least one floor above it, likely hiding a small apartment. Trent thought it didn't actually look all that different from some parts of Vancouver.

Ciaran seemed like he wanted to walk farther, but Trent could see the sag in his shoulders, and the fairy had stopped to cough more and more frequently the farther they went. Trent had caught him trying to hide a smear of blood on his pants after one particularly violent fit.

"We should find somewhere to stay the night," Trent suggested. "You look exhausted."

"Don't fuss," Ciaran sighed. "I'm a big lad."

"Not particularly," Trent chuckled, earning himself a faint scowl. "Anyway, I'm tired. Let's find somewhere to stay."

Ciaran followed reluctantly as they crossed the street to a small hotel on the corner that shared its pink storefront with the bistro next door. Trent counted out some more of his Euros to pay for the room, watching Ciaran lean against the counter out of the corner of his eye. He looked pale, and Trent could see a thin sheen of sweat forming on his forehead. He was sick, no matter what he said. Maybe they couldn't afford to waste another night before they reached his people. But if he pushed himself, he might not make the trip regardless.

He let Ciaran up the stairs first, half afraid that he would fall, but the fairy held onto the handrail to steady himself and only wavered once. The room consisted of little more than a single double bed, a television, and a small desk, but Ciaran happily dropped into the bed without a second thought.

"So where are we going from here?" Trent asked, dropping his duffel bag at the foot of the bed. "I thought you said we could get where we were going from that town this morning, but this looks suspiciously like Dublin."

"Brú na Bóinne," Ciaran said, muffled by his face in the pillow.

"Yeah, but is that a real place?"

"Of course it's a real place," Ciaran scoffed, and he sat up on his elbows to look up at Trent. "I had a look at the map back in Portmagee; seems the nearest place that fits a map is a village called Drogheda. Brú na Bóinne itself is an archaeological site or some such now. I'm sure we can find a ride out there. There'll be a rock, or a...grave mound, or something," he shrugged. "I don't know precisely."

"How long has it been since you were there?"

"Some time," he said again, and Trent snorted as he dropped down on the bed beside him.

"How long is some time? Are we still going by rock timelines, or was it more recent than that?"

Ciaran narrowed his eyes up at him. "I haven't been back...since I left. And that was before."

"Before?"

"Before all...this," he said, waving his hand as if to indicate the city itself. He sighed. "It was a long while ago, all right? What does it matter exactly how long?"

"It matters if you don't even know how to get back there," Trent countered. "You said your memory from that time was a bit...lacking since you got magic-drained or whatever."

"Aye, lacking as in mostly bloody missing. But I'll know it when I see it."

"How?"

"Well I'll feel it, won't I?"

Trent frowned down at him. "Will you?"

Ciaran's expression softened slightly, and he looked up at Trent with a furrowed brow. "I hope so."

Trent tugged the toque from Ciaran's head and bent down to touch a kiss to his hair. "We'll work it out."

"Ach, don't get sentimental," the fairy muttered as he pulled to his feet. "I'm having a wash. Sort yourself out, will you?" He smiled over his shoulder at Trent's irritated expression and disappeared into the attached bathroom.

Trent sighed as soon as he heard the water running. Ciaran could pretend not to be troubled all he wanted, but Trent could see the hesitation in his eyes. He was worried. So was Trent, for that matter. If Ciaran's memories were fading, how long did they have before he remembered anything at all? But there wasn't anything to do about it except keep moving forward. They'd made it this far.

He settled with his back against the headboard and his laptop on his knee, skimming the news on the hotel's questionable Wi-Fi and listening to Ciaran alternate between humming and coughing in the other room. He looked up when the door clicked open and almost let his laptop slip at the sight of Ciaran completely naked in the doorway, his skin slightly pink from the hot water and his hair damp against his forehead. Before he could say anything, the fairy was at the bed, pushing Trent's laptop aside and crawling into his lap.

Trent watched him skeptically, but he didn't protest when Ciaran leaned forward to kiss him. The fairy's fingers worked nimbly at Trent's buttons while his tongue explored his mouth, and he didn't pull away until Trent's shirt was completely open, his hands eagerly finding the warm skin of his chest.

"I was a bit brusque before," Ciaran murmured against the edge of Trent's mouth, pausing to nip at his bottom lip. "Let me make it up to you, a mhuirnín," he purred.

Trent shivered as Ciaran's weight pressed into him, the fairy's fingers trailing slowly down his stomach to toy with his belt buckle.

"I don't know," Trent answered softly, his voice steady through sheer force of will, "you were kind of a dick."

Ciaran touched a light kiss to his chin, his hand sliding down to grip the younger man's traitorous erection through his trousers. "Le do thoil, a rún," he whispered into Trent's neck as he squeezed him. "Ba mhaith liom tú." He pressed a kiss to his chest. "Ná cas mé ar shiúl arís."

"I told you I don't—" Trent inhaled sharply as Ciaran's tongue found his nipple. "I don't know what you're saying."

"I'll translate." He tugged Trent's belt undone in one swift movement and shifted on the bed to pull his trousers down his hips, pausing to kiss and nip at him on his way down. Trent's hand went automatically behind him to grip the headboard as Ciaran's lips closed over the head of his aching cock, his tongue hot against the sensitive skin. Ciaran drew him in deeper, feeling him at the back of his throat and letting out a quiet groan that sent a spark up Trent's spine. Trent swore under his breath, not wanting to watch Ciaran work and push himself over the edge too soon, but finding himself unable to look away. Ciaran ran his tongue over the silky skin, his agonizingly slow pace building until Trent's grip tightened audibly on the wooden headboard. Then he pulled away, leaving a delicate kiss on Trent's hip as a parting gift.

"Is that enough apologizing, a mhuirnín, or shall I go on?" he murmured against Trent's stomach, smiling at the tense trembling he caused. "I want to make sure I'm well and thoroughly forgiven."

"Just shut up," Trent panted, and he sat up to tug Ciaran to him and catch his lips in a deep kiss. Ciaran obeyed, his hand replacing his mouth and continuing its work. He kept just out of reach as Trent's hips bucked up against his, drawing a frustrated moan from the younger man.

When Ciaran could feel the tension in his new lover about to burst, he slowed down, leaving Trent panting and desperate on the mattress, his shirt bunched up around his shoulders from his slow slump down the headboard. With a sly smile that made Trent growl in frustration, Ciaran slipped off of his lap and patted him encouragingly on the hip.

"Come on then; turn over."

"What—turn over?" Trent's brow furrowed as he looked up at the other man, the voice dull in his ear underneath his own pumping heart.

"What, you thought I was joking about letting me be on top?"

"But we're—let me get the—"

"Just turn over," Ciaran said again, nudging Trent by the leg. "Don't worry, lad," he added as he bent to press another kiss to Trent's open mouth. "I'll take good care of you. Now do as you're told."

Trent didn't feel very confident from that assurance, but he slowly lifted up onto his elbows and allowed Ciaran to pull his trousers down completely and toss them away. The fairy kissed a slow line down his back as he peeled off his wrinkled shirt, and he pushed Trent down onto his hands and knees. He could feel Trent's trembling skin under his fingertips, and he smiled to see his gruff and grumpy companion reduced to such a timid state. It was easy to forget how inexperienced he was.

Trent didn't dare look back at his lover; it was embarrassing enough being on hands and knees in front of him without having to see that smug look he knew would be on the fairy's face. He tried in vain to slow his heart, but he was too exposed, too anxious, and too eager. He let out a breath he hadn't realized he was holding as he felt Ciaran's hands slide slowly down his back and settle firmly on his hips. He was prepared for it to hurt. He knew Ciaran wouldn't hurt him on purpose, but there had been no sign of lubrication, and Trent certainly didn't feel relaxed enough to help the situation. He twisted his hands in the sheet and let his forehead touch the mattress, bracing himself for what was to come.

Trent tensed and tightened his grip on the sheets as he felt Ciaran shift behind him, but he let out a sudden, unwelcome groan as the fairy pressed a kiss to the dimple at the small of his back. He wanted to ask Ciaran what he was doing, but his breath left him as soon as the other man's tongue was on him. Ciaran gently urged Trent's knees farther apart, and he complied, though the change in posture caused his painfully hard erection to brush the soft sheet, making him jerk and gasp.

Trent let out a pitifully pleading whimper as he felt Ciaran's tongue press into him, his back arching in response to the wet heat of the other man's mouth. He hid his face in the sheet, desperate to roll his hips against the mattress for any kind of friction but too afraid to move and disrupt the sensation. Ciaran kept a steadying hand on the small of his back, but it did little to calm him as the fairy's tongue delved deeper, drawing helpless, gasping pants from him that fogged his glasses so close to the bed.

Trent jerked at the sudden intrusion of Ciaran's finger, but his discomfort was soon forgotten as the other man pushed deeper inside him, brushing the sensitive spot that Trent himself had rarely dared to touch. He ground back against Ciaran's hand as a second finger entered him, and a third, causing him to bite his lip in a meager attempt to control his increasingly wanton moans.

When Ciaran retreated, Trent shuddered at the loss, finally daring to look over his shoulder. He expected Ciaran to look victorious, but his face was just as flushed as Trent's felt, and his chest rose and fell just as quickly. He caught Trent's eye as he shifted closer to him, a tiny smirk touching the corner of his lip, and both men's breath left them as Ciaran pressed forward. Trent let out a shuddering moan and dropped his head back to the mattress. He struggled to breathe as Ciaran filled him, both aching for more and already overwhelmed.

Ciaran let him have one blessed moment of rest, allowing him to adjust as best he could, and then he began to move. He went slowly at first, brushing that sensitive spot deep inside the younger man, but as Trent panted, Ciaran gripped him firmly by the hips to keep him steady as he sped up. Trent's knuckles went white from his grip on the tangled sheet, his jaw tight as he pushed back to meet each of Ciaran's thrusts. He had expected it to hurt, and he could feel the burning of his stretching skin as the fairy filled him, but he could barely catch his breath for want of more.

Ciaran swore in soft Gaelic behind him, and Trent felt the fairy's breath on his back as Ciaran curled over him. He couldn't help his shaky cry as Ciaran's hand slipped around to stroke him in time with his thrusts. Trent almost asked him to stop. It was too much; he was too full, too close. He could feel himself skirting close to the edge, but Ciaran seemed determined to keep him there, slowing down just enough to let him take a breath before squeezing and stroking him again.

"Please," Trent heard himself say, and the low, rumbling chuckle from the man behind him would have infuriated him if it hadn't been immediately followed by a quickened pace. Trent bucked against Ciaran's touch, desperate for release. Ciaran obliged him, biting at the trembling skin of his back and stroking him until he tensed, and Trent's shaky groan filled the room as he spilled his climax onto the sheet beneath them. Ciaran kept up his pace, his forehead falling against Trent's back, and he pushed into the man under him with eager speed that left Trent helpless to catch his breath.

Finally, Ciaran's fingertips dug painfully into Trent's hips as he growled out his release, and Trent struggled to keep his balance as the full weight of the other man pressed into him. He shivered at Ciaran's slow withdrawal and let his arms finally give out, managing to avoid falling into the quickly cooling fluid staining the sheet.

Ciaran curled up behind him and nuzzled his back, and Trent could hear the smirk on his lips as the fairy whispered, "I dare say you liked that even better, a mhuirnín."

"Shut up," Trent muttered as he pulled away, dropping his glasses on the nightstand as he disappeared into the bathroom to clean himself up. Trent would never be able to tell him how much he had enjoyed that, and it was infuriating to think that the fairy knew regardless. He hated the way his body betrayed him at Ciaran's slightest caress. It was humiliating. But he wouldn't change it. Ciaran followed close behind him despite his objections, and they stayed under the hot shower together until the water ran cold.

5

Trent was woken up well before dawn by the sound of heavy coughs from the connected bathroom. He pulled himself groggily out of bed and pushed the door open to find Ciaran on the floor with his elbows on the toilet bowl. The fairy was noticeably pale even in the fluorescent light, and there were still flecks of blood on his chin despite his obvious effort to clean his face.

Trent clicked his tongue at him and moved to crouch beside him. He reached out to touch his naked back, and the other man's skin felt clammy and cold. "What the hell is wrong with you?" he asked, more harshly than he meant. "Why are you trying to have sex when you're like this?"

"I'm fine," Ciaran croaked, barely holding in another cough.

"You're not fucking fine," Trent scolded. "Why are you pretending nothing's wrong? I can't help if you won't tell me when you feel bad. You think I want you to die and leave me all alone in Ireland?"

"Téigh dtí Diabhail, I said I'm fine!" Ciaran snapped, jerking his shoulder away from Trent's touch.

Trent scowled down at the fairy, then stood and took a step back from him. "Be an asshole, then. Sleep on the bathroom floor if you want to. Just get some fucking sleep, and tomorrow we'll go to God damn fairyland and they can deal with you." He turned and left the room, shutting the door sharply behind him, and he dropped back into the bed with a huff. He kept his back to the bathroom door and gripped his pillow tightly as he heard Ciaran retching again. He wanted to go back in, to tell Ciaran that everything would be all right and to touch his hair, but he wouldn't be where he wasn't wanted.

Ciaran was falling apart. What if he couldn't remember how to get to this place he said they needed to go? What if they did get in, but the other fairies only told them that it was a lost cause? What if he died? Trent hid his face in the pillow, suddenly feeling as though he was out of his depth. He had nothing to go back to, no plans that didn't involve the fairy. Nowhere to go. What would he do if Ciaran died?

Eventually, Trent heard the bathroom door creak open and felt Ciaran's weight shift the mattress, but he didn't turn around.

In the morning, Trent let Ciaran sleep as long as he could, even leaving him alone in the hotel room while he went to change more bills into Euros. They didn't speak on the way to the bus station, but as they stood in line to buy their tickets, Ciaran put a hand on Trent's arm.

"I want to take a detour," he said, his eyes on a small map pinned near the clerk.

"A detour? Are you kidding me? But we're almost there. Drogheda, right, and then Brú na Bóinne. It's just a couple of hours away."

"It won't take long," Ciaran promised, but Trent still stared at him skeptically. "Please," he tried. "I haven't been back in...a very long time."

Trent sighed. "You really think we should be taking our time with this? After the night you had? You know you're kind of dying, right?"

"I know," Ciaran admitted without taking his eyes from the ground. "If I'm going to die, I want to see my home again."

Trent hesitated to answer him, not willing to voice the possibility of Ciaran's death so sincerely. The line shifted ahead of them, and Ciaran spoke to the clerk, reaching back to Trent for money after confirming their new destination. Trent handed off the bills with a frown and followed Ciaran across the station.

He inspected his ticket once they were on the bus and glanced over at Ciaran, who had settled himself against the window.

"I thought that you said you were from Brú na Bóinne," he said softly, almost reluctant to break the silence between them.

"I am."

"Then what's in Dundalk? What do you mean, you want to see your home again?"

Ciaran let out a soft sigh but didn't turn around. "Dundalk—Dún Dealgan—it was mine. My village. My people."

"Your people? What, fairies? It was a fairy village?"

"Something like that."

Trent frowned at Ciaran's reflection in the window. "Is this some side effect of that spell, that you're only capable of giving bullshit half-answers to everything? What the hell could the big fairy secret be that you won't even tell me about it?"

Ciaran finally turned to face him, a tired look in his pale green eyes. "More answers than you want are coming soon, a mhuirnín. I just...want to stay a little longer."

Trent's brow furrowed in confusion. "Stay?"

"Stay Ciaran."

Trent opened his mouth to question this evasive answer, but the fairy looked so somber and exhausted that he kept the question to himself.

The trip to Dundalk only took about three hours, but time seemed to crawl by. Ciaran coughed so regularly that the woman across the aisle began to look at him as if he was infectious, and the handkerchief he kept pressed to his mouth was quickly stained completely red. When he wasn't coughing, he had his head leaned against the window with his eyes shut, fading in and out of sleep. Trent had a brief look around to make sure no one was watching them, and he reached across the armrest to take a gentle hold of his lover's hand. Ciaran peered at him with one half-open eye and a small smile, then drifted back to sleep.

Trent had to nudge Ciaran to wake him when the bus finally stopped, and the two of them exited into the town of Dundalk. Ciaran led the way as though he knew exactly what he was looking for, so Trent followed him through the village's winding streets. The fairy walked slowly but with purpose, more than once pausing to catch his breath or lean against a wall, but he always brushed Trent's hand aside and carried on after a moment. A few times he hesitated, peering down side streets or just looking around as if lost, but he always continued once he had his bearings.

They reached a large building on a hill that looked like a hotel—sprawling, pale stone walls surrounded by hundreds of red flowers. Ciaran walked right by it, leading Trent past the entrance to a dirt path that twisted down through the trees. He only stopped when they reached a break in the trees, the worn path stretching across the trim grass of a golf course.

"They built a golf course," Ciaran mused, mostly to himself. "Of course they built a fucking golf course."

"What exactly are we looking for, here?" Trent asked as they crossed the course.

"It's close," Ciaran muttered in response.

"Very helpful."

They walked down a few more simple paths, taking whichever fork Ciaran decided was the right one, until they came upon a clearing and an arrangement of large rocks that split the path in two. Two rows of rocks formed an alley in the grass, the end of which was covered by a larger, flat stone to create a small, squat cave. Ciaran stepped off the path to approach the rocks, and he ran his hand over them, reverently, one by one. Trent moved forward to stay beside him and paused at the sight of an aging green and white sign, dented and pulling away from its frame.

PREHISTORIC GALLERY GRAVE
ASSOCIATED WITH PROLEEK DOLMEN

Trent didn't know what a dolmen was, but the first part of the sign caught his attention.

"This is a grave?" he asked Ciaran curiously as he took a step back from the stones. "Who's buried here? Someone you knew?"

"Many," Ciaran answered softly, and Trent waited, but he didn't say anything more.

Ciaran moved on without warning, and Trent followed him silently down still more paths, farther and farther away from the town. He wondered about the fairy's ability to get back to the bus station at this rate, but he wasn't about to stop him now. The next time the path split, it circled a large stone structure unlike anything Trent had ever seen. Three bluntly pointed stones stood straight up out of the dirt, each easily a head or two taller than Trent himself, and they formed a triangle that supported a much larger boulder at what looked to be a rather perilous angle. A collection of smaller stones sat on top of the boulder, though Trent couldn't guess how they'd gotten up there. Or how the big one had gotten up there in the first place. He supposed this was a dolmen.

Ciaran walked up to the stones without hesitation, letting his hand brush against the stone as he slowly circled the structure. "Is this really all that's left?" he whispered, so softly that Trent almost didn't hear him.

"What were you expecting to find?"

The fairy shook his head and stopped walking. "I don't know. Something. Anything. I guess this counts as anything," he added with a dry chuckle. He looked out over the town at the bottom of the hill with a faint frown on his lips. "I suppose it's fitting. Here and gone, replaced. And all that's left is the dead."

"Will you tell me what the deal is now?" Trent moved to stand next to him, both of them looking up at the heavy stone. "What is this place?"

"It's fuzzy," Ciaran admitted, and for the first time, Trent thought he was being honest. "This is where I...used to be. It was mine, I...think. I can't remember." He swayed on his feet, and Trent put an arm around his shoulders to steady him. "I think I'd like to sit down, now," Ciaran murmured. Trent obliged, helping him find the grass and sit without falling.

They sat together on the small hill where the dolmen stood, Ciaran leaning heavily against Trent's shoulder. His breathing was labored and slow.

"I can tell it used to be beautiful here," Trent said softly after a while, turning his head to let his cheek touch Ciaran's hair. "I see why you would miss it. And I'm...glad you brought me here." He gave a short sigh. "I shouldn't have yelled at you this morning. I don't know what you're going through. I know that it's hard. But you should know that...whatever it takes, we're going to figure this out, and

45

we're going to make you better. I'm going to be here no matter what."

He waited, expecting gratitude, or sarcasm at the very least, but no answer came. He leaned forward to get a look at the fairy's face and found him fast asleep.

"Oh, I fucking hate you," Trent grumbled, but he touched a soft kiss to Ciaran's head and let him sleep.

Ciaran complained of being hungry when he finally woke up, but for once, he didn't complain about the food. He ate his sandwich while they waited for the bus to Drogheda, too weary to make a fuss. Trent almost wished he would complain if it meant he was feeling better than he looked.

"I'm surprised there's a bus straight to Brú na Bóinne through the village," Ciaran said as they boarded what seemed like their fiftieth bus. "Maybe there's a town there now, like Dundalk. I just hope they haven't destroyed everything."

"I'm sure it'll be fine," Trent assured him, both of them knowing it was baseless. Ciaran leaned against him in the seat and squeezed his hand anyway.

"We'll have to be quick if we want to find the entrance before dark," Ciaran went on. "I'm sure that I'll know it when we get there."

Trent only nodded. Ciaran's spirits seemed to be lifting somewhat the closer they got to their destination—even if he was still coughing up blood—and the last thing Trent wanted was to bring him down again. The fairy actually sat up in his seat as they passed through Drogheda and drew nearer to Brú na Bóinne. He pressed his cheek to the glass as their goal came into sight, but Trent saw his face fall as it came fully into view. It hadn't been destroyed, but it wasn't a village—it was a museum.

Trent got stuck behind a couple with too many bags and almost lost Ciaran in the crowd as he hurried off of the bus.

"Now he moves fast," Trent muttered to himself, squeezing by the couple as soon as he was able and trotting ahead to catch up.

The Brú na Bóinne visitor center was a concrete, utilitarian structure surrounded by heavy metal gates and carefully organized rock gardens. Ciaran only stopped at the entrance to wait for Trent because he needed money to get in. Trent paid the small fee for both of them to enter the exhibit, but they were told immediately that the remaining tours for the day were sold out, and that they would have to return another day if they wanted the full tour of the tombs. Trent looked to Ciaran for guidance, but the fairy had already wandered into the central room of the exhibit, so he only sighed, thanked the woman at the desk, and followed.

A wide, round hall made up the main hall of the museum, centered around a stone circle and a glass case containing small artifacts that were presumably from the site. There were smaller exhibits with recreations, drawings, and tall plaques bearing explanations, histories, and speculations. They passed a fiberglass boulder strapped to fiberglass logs in front of a mural of some prehistoric-looking men using the logs to roll heavy boulders along. Ciaran's lip curled at the artwork as he walked by, but he stopped in front of a diorama of a simple thatched hut.

Trent stood beside him, shifting his duffel bag on his shoulder as he looked down at the scene. "So, what," he began, "is this what your house looked like?"

"No, I did not live in a bloody hut," Ciaran scoffed. He paused. "I'm pretty sure." He waved vaguely back in the direction of the fake boulder. "And we didn't roll things around like that—pointless—we just carried them."

Trent remembered how casually Ciaran had lifted his sofa one-handed and how easily he had broken the hunter's wrist. It didn't particularly surprise him to learn that others like him were equally strong. "I know this is startling for you, but maybe keep your voice down about all this us and we business when you're talking about prehistoric cultures, do you think? People will hear you."

Ciaran folded his arms across his stomach and frowned as he turned to take in the entirety of the exhibit room. "I don't like this," he said softly. "My history, my people—on display like something dead."

Trent moved closer to him, allowing their shoulders to touch. "How are these your people, anyway? You keep talking about it, but these look like people-people to me." He dropped his voice to a low murmur. "I thought you were a fairy. Do we have museums dedicated to ancient fairy civilizations and we just don't know it?"

"I am a fairy—or I was," Ciaran answered defensively. "As far as you understand it."

"What the hell does that mean?"

He shook his head. "Not right now. We need to get to the hill. What did they call it—Newgrange? I don't like it here. We need to go."

"She said the tours are all sold out," Trent reminded him.

"Then we'll go on our own." Ciaran looked up at him with a pleading look in his eyes, and Trent noticed how gaunt his face had become. "We need to go," he said again.

Trent frowned at him. "Okay."

It was easier than expected to get left behind for the night—they simply had to wander far enough away from the visitor center to avoid being spotted by the security guards or the bus drivers who rounded up stragglers as the building closed. They weren't that far from some rural residences, and people trying to stay overnight in the middle of nowhere didn't seem to be a problem that anyone was particularly on the lookout for.

They started out in the direction Ciaran seemed sure of, crossing the river and heading through empty green fields. Ciaran led them away from the road before long, as though he was sensing the way to their destination.

"What exactly are we looking for?" Trent asked, his voice low in the quiet dark. He felt like he should whisper. "Can I help somehow, or are you literally just hoping you get a good feeling when we get close?"

"Sí an Bhrú is the entrance," Ciaran answered, sounding so certain that Trent wondered if he was trying to convince himself. "I know that's where it is. I just…I'm not sure how to open it. Or even if I can, since I'm…like this."

Trent pushed his hands into his pockets as they walked, glancing sidelong at the man next to him. "What do we do if you can't?"

"I'm choosing not to consider that eventuality until it presents itself, if you don't mind," the fairy said with a small, wry smile.

"That's fine by me."

They walked quietly together, cutting through private fields and listening to the flow of the nearby river. It was dark out in the countryside, but the moon did a decent job of lighting their way, so that they were only hindered by Ciaran's slow, weary pace. Eventually, Ciaran quickened his steps, and he tugged on Trent's hand and pointed out a low structure sprawled across the hill, the pale stone circle barely visible in the distance.

"That's it," he said eagerly, and he pulled Trent along with him as he trotted to the hill. Trent warned him not to push himself, and Ciaran paused to let out a few heavy coughs on the way, but he kept up his pace until they stood at the base of the hill, only a low hedge separating them from the stone structure they sought. They clambered over and started up the hill toward the mound. Trent kept an eye out for anyone who might be watching for trespassers, but Ciaran was single-minded. They approached the stone entrance, and Ciaran paused to run his hand over one of the standing stones nearby.

"This is the place," he whispered, and without looking back, he jogged up the metal stairs that led to the squat stone entrance. Trent followed along behind him, ducking unnecessarily as he stepped through the threshold. It was too dark to see once they were inside, but Ciaran reached back for his hand and led him deeper.

They walked the narrow passage until they reached a central chamber, where Ciaran almost ran into a tall stone at the center of the room. He reached out his hand to touch it, and Trent's grip on him tightened as the carvings in the stone reacted to the fairy's touch. Sun and flower shapes, zigzag lines, and strange hash marks glowed the faintest blue as Ciaran passed his hand over them, but they faded just as quickly.

"Well, that's not nothing," Trent muttered. Ciaran didn't seem impressed.

"This should be it," he whispered to himself. "I know this is it." He released Trent to press both hands against the stone, and for a moment they shone brightly. Then there was a low, sparking sound, and the light went out again. Ciaran swore. "How can I—" Trent heard him sigh in the darkness. "It doesn't work."

Trent reached out for him, groping blindly for a moment before taking hold of the fairy's arm. "Come on. We'll find another way."

"There isn't another way!" Ciaran snapped. He took a breath and followed dejectedly as Trent led him back down the passage toward the moonlight. They lingered near the entrance, Ciaran staring down the dark corridor as though it had betrayed him.

"Let's sit down, at least," Trent offered. His patience with Ciaran's stubbornness was reaching its limit, but he held his tongue for the sake of avoiding an argument in the middle of the countryside. "Maybe just being here, you'll think of something. Come on," he urged, and he led Ciaran away to a small covered shelter housing a pair of benches. The fairy paced anxiously rather than resting, but Trent was glad to set down his bag after the long walk.

"Take a break, will you?" Trent called after Ciaran had circled the small enclosure a dozen times. "Getting pissed about it isn't going to help."

"And what is, may I ask?" Ciaran stopped and faced him. "We're here—right bloody here, and the door won't open! They're the only ones that can help me, and if I can't get inside, then I'm—" He was interrupted by a round of coughing so strong that he finally had to sit down. Trent put a hand on his back, but he felt useless. When Ciaran finished, he wiped the blood on his hand onto the thigh of his jeans. "I'm going to die here," he finished in a low, rough voice. "I should have known I was always going to die here."

Trent stayed silent. His instinct was to tell the fairy to stop whining and think, but his stomach churned at the thought of Ciaran losing this battle. He didn't have any encouraging words for him. Trent didn't know anything about magic, or fairies, or lost memories, or anything that could have helped. There was nothing he could do.

Ciaran seemed to give in; he leaned against Trent's shoulder and shut his eyes. "I'm not alone, at least," he murmured softly, and Trent reached for his hand and squeezed it tightly.

Trent stayed up, leaning back awkwardly on the bench while Ciaran slept. The night dragged on, and he waited for some sign or hint from the grassy hillside, but that was too much to expect, he supposed. He heard something moving in the brush nearby and went still to listen. Something rustled the leaves behind them, and Trent wrote it off as an animal until he heard the wet hiss just behind his ear.

He jolted up with a start, causing Ciaran to slip forward on the bench and groan in irritation as he woke up. The fairy opened his mouth to object this rude treatment, but he paused when he saw the wide-eyed look on Trent's face. He followed Trent's gaze to the glass behind him. Pressed against the clear panel was a grey, emaciated woman, her stringy white hair clinging to her scalp. She was completely naked, her ribs and hip bones clearly visible under her tight skin. She shrieked at them, her open mouth showing row after row of pointed teeth.

"Neamh-mairbh," Ciaran breathed, and he moved backward to stand between Trent and the creature. "Tóg ort!" he called as forcefully as his tired voice would allow. "Feicfidh tú teacht ar aon íospartaigh anseo!"

The woman's lips curled back from her teeth as she crept along the glass, each step seeming to jerk her forward on unsteady legs.

"What the hell is that thing?" Trent asked anxiously, his hand gripping Ciaran's arm tightly.

"Neamh-mairbh is a demon, a—a vampire, sort of," Ciaran answered without taking his eyes off of the creature.

"Are you fucking serious? What are you, a bad luck generator?"

Ciaran chanced a look back at him as the woman turned the corner and stepped out from behind the glass. "If I say run, you run." Trent opened his mouth to object, but Ciaran snapped, "No arguments, a mhuirnín!" Ciaran put a hand on Trent's chest to keep him behind him and turned back to face the creature.

As it leapt towards them, Ciaran braced himself, knowing he had no defense. He had no magic, held no sway over this spirit as he was. He was exhausted and weak. But before the woman's claws could reach him, the burning red tip of a spear exploded from her chest as she screamed in rage. Her body was pulled forcibly backward out of the entrance and into the darkness, where her shrieks echoed across the hill before being cut short with a strangled cry. Ciaran hesitated, Trent's grip tight on his arm.

A heavy hoofbeat sounded just outside the shelter, and when the two stepped forward, they were greeted by the sight of a man astride the largest horse Trent had ever seen, his strong face illuminated orange by the tip of his glowing spear.

He narrowed green eyes at Ciaran, sparing a brief glance at Trent, and he urged his horse forward another step before speaking.

"It's good to see you again," he said, his voice a low, calm rumble. "Father."

6

Trent could only watch numbly as the strange rider dismounted his horse and fixed both of them with a hard stare, planting the end of his spear in the ground. He had to have heard that wrong. Father? This man was hugely tall and broad, with a strong jaw and a stern mouth—basically everything Ciaran was not—but as Trent watched him in the flickering light of his spear tip, he began to see hints. His eyes were the same pale green, and he had the same sharp cheekbones spattered with freckles. Trent spotted a gold pendant strung around the man's neck with the same swirling design as the one Trent wore himself. His ears were pointed at the tips, so he was at least the same kind of thing Ciaran was, Trent supposed. But that was insane. Ciaran couldn't have a son, could he? Of course. Why wouldn't a lecherous fairy who was literally as old as rocks have a son? Trent probably should have been surprised he hadn't been tripping over Ciaran's offspring since they met.

The man gave the horse's nose a comforting stroke as he passed in front of it, not seeming concerned with Trent or Ciaran's presence anymore. He drew an ax from its sling on the horse's back and swung it easily over his head, the blade landing in the old woman's neck with a sickening crunch. Trent flinched at each thump as he swung four more times, each time removing a limb from the creature's torso, and the man wiped the ax blade on his worn tunic before returning it to its sling. Snatching his spear from its place in the dirt, he touched each shriveled body part with the tip and started a small bonfire that gave off a nauseating scent. When he was finished, he moved to stand in front of Ciaran and Trent again, forcing both of them to tilt their heads to look up at him, and the three of them stood in uncomfortable silence for a few long moments.

"So, Lugh," Ciaran began, "you look—"

"I thought you were dead," the man cut him off. His brogue was deeper, rougher than Ciaran's.

"Well, about that—"

"Tuirenn's sons paid your blood-price. Tuirenn died of grief at their loss," he added, his eyes narrowed accusingly. "Where have you been?"

Ciaran hesitated and glanced back at Trent. "Here and there," he answered noncommittally, and the man softly growled at him, showing a sharp canine as his lip curled in disgust.

"It isn't as though you've missed me," Ciaran countered before he could be scolded. "You think I would have come back here if I had any other option? Look at me, Lugh."

The man took a step forward and glowered down at Ciaran, seeming to take in his pale face and sunken cheeks, and Ciaran flinched slightly at the heat from the tip of the spear. Lugh paused. "You couldn't get in, could you?" he asked with the faintest of smirks.

Ciaran snorted in irritation. "No, I couldn't get in. But I need help. This is the only place I could think to get it."

Lugh leaned back and jutted his chin in Trent's direction. "And this?"

"He's with me," Ciaran said immediately, reaching back for Trent's hand. Trent was a little reluctant to take it with the larger man staring at him, but he laced his fingers through Ciaran's and was thankful for the reassuring squeeze the fairy gave him.

"You think I'm going to just let you both in? It's bad enough you've come back. Leave it behind."

Ciaran glared at the man—apparently his son—and took a step toward him. "I am of the blood of this island, boy; I stood at Cath Maighe Tuireadh Theas when you weren't even a thought. You will take me home to Tír na nÓg, and you will do it gladly."

Lugh stared at him a moment, then gave a quiet snort. "It isn't me who'll have to face máthair." He slipped his spear head first into a pouch that sloshed thickly with some sort of liquid that doused its fire, and fastened it beside his ax on his simple quilted saddle. Lugh tilted his head toward the stone-circled mound and gave his horse a slap on the flank, sending it trotting off into the dark. "Come on."

They walked across the grass back to the stone entrance, Trent watching Ciaran for some sort of explanation. When none seemed to be forthcoming, he went ahead and asked.

"So this is actually your son, or is him calling you his father some weird fairy culture thing I don't know about?"

Ciaran let out a soft sigh. "Yes. Lugh is my son."

"And you named him Lou?"

Ciaran huffed. "Lugh," he corrected, stressing the slight rasp at the end of the word. "Never mind. Sure, his name is Lou."

"You never thought to mention you had a son?"

"Well it's not as if I was going to need to take him every other weekend, is it?" Ciaran gestured at Lugh's broad back as they walked. "Look at him." He leaned forward to catch the much taller man's eye, though Lugh only graced him with a brief sidelong glance. "What did they feed you, eh? Were you this big when I left? You were—"

"Not yet King," Lugh finished for him, pausing at the stone entrance and turning to face his father.

Ciaran's brow furrowed as he watched Lugh's face. "What, really? It's you?"

Lugh's lips pressed into a thin line. "Not anymore," he said with some disdain.

"Wait, what?" Trent interrupted. "You have a son, and he grew up and became King, so that means you were—"

"Don't get ahead of yourself," Ciaran cut him off. "It's not from lineage." He looked his son up and down with a measure of pride. "Lugh must have proved himself worthy of the title. How'd you do that, hm? What happened to—what was his name—that pretty half-blood?"

Lugh gave Ciaran a look that suggested he wasn't going to have very much patience for questions. "I proved myself by killing Balor,

King of the Fomorians," he said simply, "and I left when our people chose cowardice over battle."

"You've just been wandering about in the world on your own? Ever since the split?" Ciaran pressed.

"Runs in the family, apparently," Lugh muttered. He gestured down the dark stone corridor. "Now come."

"Cheery," Trent muttered as they followed their guide down the passage back to the central chamber, but he held Ciaran's hand tightly despite his sarcasm.

The corridor seemed to have a different feeling now that Lugh was with them—before it was dark and silent, but now the cave seemed alive, like the electricity in the air after a storm. When they reached the room at the end of the passage, the carvings on the central stone reacted immediately to Lugh's presence, the etchings in the stone glowing a dim blue as he approached and fading as he passed them. Even when Ciaran had tried, there had barely been any light— whatever magic that was in Ciaran before, it was definitely missing now. The whole room seemed to spark just from Lugh's passing. Thin blue lines began to form at one end of the stone, washing over the simple structure as they drew nearer as though following Lugh's gaze.

Now that they were on the verge of entering—Trent couldn't even remember the proper name Ciaran had called it—everything seemed too real and impossible all at once. Ciaran having a son would have been enough of a shock, but a son who was apparently King of the Fairies, but wasn't any longer for some vaguely warrior-like reason, was stretching credulity. Ciaran had had a full life here, it seemed; what was it that he had been trying so hard to avoid?

"So this is really it?" Trent asked, keeping a bit of distance between himself and the shining carvings. "This rock is going to open up to some secret base where all the fairies live?"

"Fairies?" Lugh sneered. "Is that what he called us?"

He reached out his hand and touched one of the carved suns, exploding blue light from the stone and filling the room around them. Just beyond the stone, a gateway opened, like a rip in the air itself, revealing a tall, stone staircase that descended into a deep cave. Water flowed under and around the stairs, glowing a soft, rich blue, the underground river fed by waterfalls that fell from distant cliffs. At the far end of the stairs, barely visible in the depth of the cave, Trent could make out the skyline of a city full of tall spires and crystalline rooftops rising above the falling water.

"This is Tír na nÓg," Lugh said, gesturing out over the steep staircase and looking back at Trent's awestruck face. "This is the home of the Tuath Dé."

"He makes it sound much more impressive than it actually is," Ciaran muttered, but he seemed just as hesitant to cross the threshold as Trent was. Lugh led the way, clearly much less concerned with the prospect, and Ciaran gripped Trent's hand as he took the first step onto the worn stone stairs. As soon as they were across, the rift behind them snapped shut with an audible pop, and Trent looked warily over his shoulder at the endless blackness that was now at his back. The stairs formed a snaking path in the opposite direction, but he wasn't eager to find out what sort of naked woman monsters lurked in that inky blackness, so he just followed Ciaran down the steps toward the distant city.

"Your pet human will not be welcome," Lugh noted over his shoulder as they went.

"He isn't a pet," Ciaran answered testily. "He's…done a lot for me, and he's here to help."

Trent wasn't entirely sure he found that explanation satisfying, but he could wait to address it until they weren't a hundred feet above a strange river that glowed—despite being in a cave—on a twisting staircase with no handrails. All along the steps, mushrooms of every kind grew right out of the side of the stone, some flat against the stairs and others twisting upwards, their flaring tops shining the same dim blue as the water. Their way was lit, but just softly enough to be unnerving.

He watched Ciaran's back with a frown as they climbed. "He said you're not a fairy," he said quietly, glancing forward to Lugh to see if he was listening.

"I told you that fairy was your word," Ciaran responded in a soft voice, though he seemed to feel at least a little bit guilty.

"So what's a Tuath Dé?"

"Tuath Dé is…what we are," he shrugged. "The stories of fairies you might have heard, they…come from us, in a way. It…will be easier to explain later," he said with a pointed look at his son's back.

Trent frowned. He could tell Ciaran didn't want to discuss it. He wouldn't be able to avoid it forever—this was too much for Trent to let pass without explanation. Was this what he had meant by wanting to stay Ciaran a little longer? How much of what the fairy—or whatever he was—had told him was a lie? He felt sick to his stomach. He had barely had time to think about the fact that this man, for whom he had given up literally everything he had, was an immortal, magic-using fairy with toxic skin. Now he was something more than that, some sort of…Trent didn't even know. A proto-fairy? Something that fairy stories came from? What did that even mean?

"Then, easier question," Trent tried. "What's a máthair, and why are you going to have to face it?" He heard Lugh give an amused snort ahead of them and glared expectantly at the back of Ciaran's head.

Ciaran hummed for a moment as though reluctant to answer. "Máthair isn't a 'what.' It…just means mother."

Trent stopped walking, causing Ciaran to jerk to a halt in front of him as he reached the end of his arm. Trent twisted his hand out of the other man's despite the steepness of the staircase. For some reason, the fact that Ciaran had a son hadn't quite translated in Trent's mind into Lugh also having a mother. Ciaran looked back at him with a grimace, but Trent at least attempted to take a breath before answering.

"So, this woman—"

"His wife," Lugh pointed out. He had stopped and turned to watch them with an amused wrinkle at the corners of his eyes that Trent found irritatingly familiar. Trent stared at him, but the bulky man—fairy—whatever—only folded his arms and waited, so he looked back to Ciaran.

"You have a wife," Trent said bluntly.

"Well, if you want to be technical—" Ciaran began, but Trent held up a hand and cut him off.

"You have a *wife*," he said again. "You didn't think that was important to mention at any point?"

"It isn't what you're imagining," Ciaran objected.

"I'm imagining that you're married," Trent answered with undiluted venom in his voice. "Or does 'wife' mean something else in fairyland?"

"Do you want to talk about this right here?" Ciaran held out his hand and tilted his head toward the city. "Come on. I'll explain everything, I promise." He paused and leaned to cough into his shoulder. "Please."

Trent scowled at him, not entirely certain that his cough was genuine, but after a quick glance over Ciaran's shoulder at Lugh, Trent gave in and took his lover by the hand. "You will explain everything," Trent promised softly as he drew close, and Ciaran nodded before continuing to lead him down the winding path.

They walked for what felt like ages in the tense silence that followed, until they finally approached the tall gate that led into the luminescent city. Above them stretched tall towers built out of strange bluish-black stone, each connected to the next by robust balconies and decorated with the same spiral designs Trent had seen at the entrance to the mound. Who knows how many tourists passed by that entrance every day, walked the corridor and saw the stone Lugh had touched, never knowing that an entire city was below the ground?

Before they reached the gate, Ciaran stopped and stood to one side, as though reluctant to enter the city itself. He waved at Lugh to wait and looked him up and down.

"Right," he said, "let's have your cloak."

"No," Lugh answered immediately, and Ciaran clicked his tongue at him.

"I'm not about to walk right in," he protested. "No one will think anything of you having a pair of servants."

Trent stared at Ciaran with an accusatory look. "And why can't we just walk in? This is your home, isn't it?"

Ciaran made a noncommittal sound. "Yes," he said, and Trent knew the 'but' was coming before the other man could say it. "But it's complicated."

"If he shows his face, he'll be arrested," Lugh clarified.

"Arrested?" Trent frowned, but Ciaran raised his hands in defense.

"Listen, it's only because we folk have such long memories, right?"

"What did you do?" Trent asked with an impatient sigh.

"I didn't do anything to anybody," he protested, and he jerked his thumb at Lugh. "It'll be this one what made the trouble. I may have...let everyone think I got murdered and skipped town never to be heard from again."

"Meaning I was bound by honor to seek recompense for your death," Lugh growled. "I will not be maligned for following our customs. It will be on your head if there is punishment to be had for the death of Tuirenn's sons," he added with a threatening prod at Ciaran's chest that made the smaller man stumble backwards a step.

Ciaran swatted his son's hand away and glared up at him. "Which is precisely why you'll let me borrow your cloak, so that I can get to see Dian Cecht without being forced into slavery, mo mhac grámhara," he said with more force in his voice than Trent thought was still possible.

Whatever Ciaran had called him, Lugh seemed to take offense, because he almost visibly bristled, but then he grit his teeth and tore the cloak from his own shoulders, tossing it over Ciaran's head with a growl.

"Find your own way," he said as his father scrambled to pull the large cloak away from his face, and he walked through the gate without them.

Ciaran muttered something in Gaelic that Trent was sure wasn't complimentary, and he fixed the cloak around his shoulders and pulled the hood up to hide his face. It was too large; he had to twist the fabric in his hands to keep the end of the rough cloth from dragging along the ground.

"Beautiful," Trent muttered, "but what about me? Not that that isn't big enough to fit both of us under, but I think it might draw attention."

Ciaran snorted out a small laugh and hid his cough in his hand. "Aye, he did grow up like an oak, didn't he? That's his mother's blood, no doubt." He looked up, remembering himself just in time to see the uncomfortable look on the younger man's face at the mention of Lugh's mother. "Listen, a mhuirnín, about her—"

"Shouldn't we be more concerned with taking you to whoever Dian Cecht is?" Trent interrupted, clearly in no mood to discuss the issue.

Ciaran gave a short sigh. "Aye. That's my father."

"Your father. The same father who you said murdered one of your brothers?"

"That's the one. He's the best healer the Tuath De have ever known. If anyone can heal this illness, he can."

"Wonderful. And getting me there?"

Ciaran considered a moment, then he put a hand on Trent's arm to move it and unzipped the other man's duffel bag. He retrieved a spare belt and tested its length. "Give us your hands," he said, but Trent scowled down at him and retreated.

"Are you fucking with me?"

Ciaran huffed. "There aren't many humans in Tír na nÓg, and the ones there are certainly aren't welcome guests." He shook the belt at Trent encouragingly. "This is how we get you by unnoticed."

Trent's lip curled, and he hesitated with his eyes on the offending belt, but then he zipped up his duffel bag and held out his hands with his wrists together. "If we get caught anyway, I'm going to beat you to death with this belt," he grumbled.

A sly grin touched Ciaran's lips as he tightened the belt around Trent's wrists. He leaned in close to the other man and nipped at his earlobe. "Just don't get too excited at being tied up," he murmured against Trent's cheek, and he fastened the buckle tightly.

"Fuck off," Trent snapped even as he blushed, his hands bouncing as Ciaran tugged experimentally on the end of the belt.

"Now now, that's no way to speak to master," he teased.

"You'd better hope you go ahead and die before I get out of these."

Ciaran smiled at him and pulled the hood down lower over his face, then moved toward the gate, pulling Trent reluctantly along behind him.

Trent had been told from the very beginning that Ciaran was going to take him to the homeland of the fairies, but whatever he had expected that to be like, the sight of the broad avenue in front of him was still a surprise. Homes and shop fronts lined the thoroughfare, lit at regular intervals by hanging lanterns that seemed to glow behind their glass without anything inside them to cause the light.

As they passed through the arched gate, Trent could feel a hundred eyes on him. The boulevard leading through the center of the city wasn't crowded, but every person they approached stopped what they were doing to watch them go by, stopping conversations mid-sentence to turn and stare. Even from the windows of the homes above them, Trent felt like he was being watched. He was sure he heard a few sets of shutters slam open as they got close.

"Ciaran," he whispered uncertainly, "am I about to be murdered?"

"Just look servile," he murmured in response, pulling Trent forward by his wrists. He ducked into a narrow side street and slowed his pace. He kept moving, but Trent could hear the rasping in his breath and he struggled to keep air in his lungs.

They made their way through cobblestone streets for at least an hour, and a few times Trent almost asked if Ciaran was sure where they were going, but he didn't want to draw any more attention to them than was necessary. The city was like a medieval reenactment. The men wore tunics and cloaks showing varying degrees of affluence, and the wealthier a man looked, the more decorative was the hilt on the gleaming silver sword at his hip. The women all wore floor-length dresses, some simple and some intricately embroidered. People chatted amongst themselves, trading goods, making small talk—it was a living, breathing city. Not at all the dank and mystical cave Trent had pictured when Ciaran had first mentioned grave mounds and secret entrances.

As Ciaran led him from an alleyway out onto a main street, Trent stopped dead in his tracks and made Ciaran jerk to a halt as an ornate carriage passed in front of them. Strapped to the trace, where one might reasonably expect to find a horse, was a beetle as tall as Trent himself, its thick shell iridescent in the light and its bristly legs ticking heavily on the stones as it passed them by. Long, delicate horns grew from its head like antlers, almost stretching the whole length of its body, and thin leather reins were fastened securely to each one, the ends held lightly in the driver's hand.

"What the fuck is that?" Trent hissed in a whisper before he could stop himself, and Ciaran followed his gaze for a moment before looking back at him.

"A ciaróg," he answered simply. "Eyes down."

Trent snuck another glance at the passing beetle before doing as he was told. The bug-drawn carriage really threw off whatever medieval vibe the city had had a few seconds before. Now it was just weird.

Which was a little comforting, actually.

Eventually they approached a large, sprawling house surrounded by a wall, the stone dark and slick as obsidian in the blue light of the lanterns. A long path led from the front gate to the foreboding building, the surrounding space covered in neatly fenced-off gardens full of herbs of every shape and color. Trent wasn't prepared to waste time thinking about how they grew out of the stone in the face of everything else he'd seen that day. He followed Ciaran down the path to the door, but the fairy hesitated at the threshold.

"A few words about my father," Ciaran said softly, and he turned to peer up at Trent from underneath his hood. "You recall I mentioned he killed one of my brothers." Trent nodded, so he continued. "He killed him out of envy. My father fashioned a...sort of a prosthetic arm for one of our past kings, and my brother built him a better one. My father doesn't like being second best. So just...if he asks your opinion on anything, just tell him it's grand, right?"

"You're sure this person is our best option?" Trent asked. He glanced at the door uncertainly.

"Second best," Ciaran answered with a wry smile, "but he killed the best one. Welcome to Tír na nÓg, a mhuirnín." He stood up as straight as he could and pulled the hanging rope by the door, sounding a soft ringing inside the house. When a young woman answered the door, Ciaran pulled back his hood to greet her. Trent listened pointlessly as the two had a brief exchange in Gaelic that ended with the woman gasping with her hands at her mouth and disappearing down a corridor in a flurry of skirt.

"So they do know you here," Trent mused, and Ciaran tugged spitefully on his bonds.

A moment later, a man in a trim, dark tunic appeared in the doorway. His hair was silver white, as was the beard on his jaw, but he still looked strong and healthy. Trent could see the resemblance between father and son much more easily than he could between Ciaran and Lugh—Ciaran's father seemed to be a normal size, at least. Familiar green eyes widened as he approached and then narrowed as he stared down at Ciaran's pale face.

The older man said something in gruff Gaelic that Trent couldn't understand, but when Ciaran answered him, the man's bright eyes snapped up to Trent's face.

"Bring it inside, then," he said, and Trent followed warily as Ciaran stepped through the doorway.

7

Julien walked the city all day and well into the evening, following the scent of anything magic that crossed his path. It wasn't difficult finding supernatural creatures in a city as large as Vancouver—the trick was pinning down the right monster. His compass had led him to Stanley Park, where he was fairly certain he'd spotted a selkie, to Gastown, where he had run into a vampire who seemed more interested in flirting with him than being intimidated, and now he had found himself in South Cambie, where a shapeshifter was trying to throw him off by heading into Queen Elizabeth Park. Shapeshifters were dangerous; he was willing to let even a vampire off the hook in his current state of emergency, but a shapeshifter was always a violent killer. The creature tried to hide in plain sight by changing its face, but Julien could see through him. He saw him for what he was under the illusion—a grey-skinned, white-eyed thing with fangs like a snake. He could pick it out of a crowd every time it changed.

By the time he made it back to the hotel, he was covered from chest to knee in silvery blood, which he had unsuccessfully tried to clean. A few people had given him strange looks on his way back, but luckily, the blood didn't actually look very much like blood. Most people probably assumed it was paint, which allowed him to pick up some food on the way. He had left Noah alone in the hotel and had periodically—frequently, if he was honest—checked his phone during his search to make sure he hadn't missed any messages, but he'd been out of contact all day. He'd started to call more than once, but he didn't want to risk disturbing the witch's rest.

Noah recognized the blood immediately, of course, and fussed when Julien stepped into the room.

"I'm fine," Julien assured him, though killing the creature with only one good hand had taken more of a toll on him than he was willing to admit. "How are you feeling? All right?"

"Better," Noah answered, but Julien suspected he was lying. The boy had dark circles under his eyes, and he looked slightly feverish. He let it pass and offered Noah the simple bowl of noodles he had brought for him.

"I'm sorry I couldn't find anything," Julien sighed. He dropped down onto the foot of the bed and reached down to search his bag for a clean shirt. "But I'm not going to stop looking. I'll change, and then I'll go back out. There has to be something I'm missing."

Noah fidgeted with the blanket pooled in his lap and prodded at his noodles. Julien was working very hard to help him—Noah could see the exhaustion on the other man's face no matter what he said. He'd run himself ragged searching the city blindly.

"The only thing I can think," Julien began as he pulled off his damp shirt, "is to try to find something that's a better tracker than I am. There must be something in the city that can hunt magic. A targeted search. Something we can use, or tame somehow."

"That's a tall order," Noah said, trying and failing to keep his eyes away from Julien's bare chest. He had a few new bruises forming. The witch chewed at his bottom lip and let out a short sigh at the empty hole he found.

Julien looked over immediately at Noah's sigh. "What is it?"

"Just my piercings," Noah shrugged. "The hospital made me take them out." He reached up to touch the smooth skin of his bottom lip. "It feels weird not having them. I hope the holes don't close up."

Julien made a soft sound as though he'd remembered something, and he crouched by his bag to retrieve a small ring box. With a quiet creak, he pried it open, and he stood to offer it to Noah. "I got them from your apartment," he said as the boy reached out for the thin silver rings. "I thought you'd want them back."

Noah's face felt hot as he looked up at the hunter. Julien had been thinking of him—not in a dramatic, saving his life and on the run from the cops sort of way, but in a small, quiet way that made Noah's heart thump. Don't get excited, he told himself. It doesn't mean anything.

"Thank you," he said instead of something stupid, looking down at the silver circles in his palm rather than at Julien's face.

"Pas de quoi. You look strange without them."

Noah chuckled. "Strange?"

"Well, not strange strange. Just your face. I mean, your face looks strange. Without them."

The witch stared up at him. "My face looks strange? Thanks a fucking lot, Julien."

"No, I mean—" Julien hesitated, and Noah almost felt bad for him. The hunter was never at a loss for words. "You look fine without them, you know," he went on, "but they're cute on you."

Both men paused, the words seeming to take a moment to register with both of them. Had Julien just called him cute? Noah was imagining it, surely. Julien wasn't someone who would call a bunny "cute," let alone another man. Noah clutched the rings in his hand and pulled himself out of bed, quickly snatching up a spare shirt, muttering something about needing a shower, and shutting himself in the tiny bathroom.

Julien let out a quiet curse and put a hand to his forehead. He had hoped his gesture would be comforting, not awkward. He'd only made things worse. Noah was sick, and he needed Julien's help, not to be exposed to his profound lack of social skills. It was even more difficult now that Julien had begun to notice things the he was positive hadn't been happening before—the way Noah avoided his eyes sometimes, or the way he had watched when Julien changed and pretended he hadn't been. Julien tried to put it out of his mind, reminding himself that Noah had confessed feelings for him that the hunter absolutely could not return and that it wouldn't be fair to lead him on. Better to let him deal with it in his own way.

That didn't change the fact that every time Noah spoke, Julien could feel the ghost of the witch's lips on the hollow of his neck.

Julien shook his head and finished changing into unbloodied clothes, tugging his jeans up with a grunt of frustration. Loneliness, that was all this was. A three-year dry spell had made him touchy, and Noah was someone who needed him. These were two entirely separate issues, and one could not help the other.

Was this what it was going to be like if they ever got to have their promised talk? Julien didn't even know what Noah would want to talk about. He would expect some kind of answer, surely. But how could Julien answer him? How could he refuse him, after everything he had put the boy through? But he would have to refuse him. Even if Julien had been willing to try—to go on dates or make an effort—it would never be right to enter into a relationship with someone you had no romantic feelings for. And aside from everything else, Julien wasn't even gay.

He heard the water shut off in the next room, and Noah reappeared with all of his piercings in place, rubbing a rough towel over his damp hair.

"So," he started before Julien could speak, "I really feel pretty good, and I know I kind of hogged the bed last night, so I can sleep on the floor tonight so you can get some rest."

"No," Julien answered, already bending to pick up his small bag of supplies. "I'm going back out. This can't wait any longer."

"Are you serious? You were gone all day; it's already dark out!"

"It can't wait, Noah," Julien answered firmly, and for a moment they only looked at each other.

"Then I'm coming, too."

"Absolutely not. You need to rest."

"I'm not made of glass, Julien." The witch squared his shoulders as best he could and tried to stand up straight despite the turmoil in his stomach. "We don't have to just run everywhere, right? I'll keep up. And if you actually find anything, I can help. I know way more about monsters than you do, after all."

"I know about monsters," Julien countered, but Noah had already tossed his towel back into the bathroom and was heading for the door.

"I can't just sit around while you run your ass off chasing ghosts."

"You can, and you will."

Noah turned on him with a harsh scowl. "I wasn't asking your permission," he snapped, but he seemed to regret his outburst as soon as the words were out of his mouth. He swallowed and tried again. "I'm going to help."

"I got you into this," Julien sighed, attempting to move between Noah and the door. "It's my responsibility to fix it."

"I made my own decision." Noah looked up at him with a frown. "You want to find a monster that can track things, right? Something similar to the fairy would probably be best. There aren't that many Irish spirits in Vancouver that I know about, but maybe we can find a sluagh, or a banshee, or something." He had already opened the hotel room door and taken a step into the hall, forcing Julien to hurry after him. "Let's try Mountain View Cemetery."

Julien smiled faintly despite himself. "Who put you in charge, anyway?"

"Somebody has to be the brains of this operation. And the pretty face. But I still need muscle to back me up, so you should probably come along too."

Julien followed Noah down to the street. He would need to keep a careful eye on him while they were out, but it was good to hear Noah sounding more like his old self. Noah walked slowly, occasionally seeming to pause and take a breath to steady himself, but they made it to the bus station without incident, and Julien pretended not to notice the smaller man's soft weight against his shoulder as they traveled.

The cemetery was closed to the public after dark, but as there were no high fences or walls to keep them out, they found a bit of darkness outside the range of the nearby streetlight and slipped over the chain link fence. Julien dug a small flashlight out of his bag once they were away from the street and lit up the grassy lanes and faded tombstones around them.

"Don't suppose you know any tricks for luring out something like a sluagh or a banshee, do you?" Julien asked softly as he scanned the stones around them with his light.

"Well, banshees tend to turn up when someone is about to die, so I might be more useful than you thought," Noah quipped, a faint smile on his lips that Julien met with a stern frown.

"Don't joke like that," he whispered. He started to speak again, but his flashlight sputtered in his hand, and he smacked it against his thigh to try to bring it back to life. It cranked back up for a few moments before dying completely, and Julien let out a curse. "Ce vettes piles," he muttered, giving the flashlight one last useless shake.

"Don't worry about it." Noah lifted his hand, and in a moment, a ball of orange fire formed in his palm, illuminating the area around them. "Come on. Let's have a look around at least."

Julien glanced at Noah's hand, noting the slight tremor in his fingers. "Are you all right to do that? Don't tire yourself out."

"It's fine. I won't push myself. Promise."

Julien followed Noah down one of the lanes, watching him with a wary eye. The magic made him anxious; he still wasn't accustomed to being around someone who could hold fire in his hand and not trying to kill them. Still, his main concern was the boy's shaking hand. This was Noah, he reminded himself. Noah may have been a witch, but he would never be a threat.

The hunter paused, the full weight of his thought making him stop mid-stride. Noah would never be a threat to him. Julien had known very few people that he could implicitly trust—not even all of his brothers were counted in that category—but, somehow, this witch had become one of them. He had been so wrong to shout at him, before. Noah would never put him at risk. He would never hurt anyone, and never had—until Julien asked him to. He felt an unpleasant tug in his stomach as Noah noticed he had stopped moving and turned to face him.

"What's up?" Noah asked, his face reflecting the orange light of the fire in his hand. "Did you see something?"

"No," Julien answered after a moment. "It was nothing. Let's keep moving."

They explored the cemetery for a while, Noah occasionally pausing to peer down at an interesting gravestone and Julien regularly checking his compass. Suddenly Noah hesitated, and he absently pressed his non-burning hand against Julien's chest to stop him.

"Do you feel that?" he whispered, and Julien glanced down at his compass.

"Something's close," he answered.

Noah stood still, his eyes slipping shut as he listened to the still air around them. The sound of passing traffic was distant and quiet, allowing Noah to focus. A harsh, raspy squawking sound jolted him out of his concentration and made both men jump. Noah raised his hand in an effort to see farther, but there was nothing around them. The noise sounded again, even closer to them, and Noah looked up to the top of a tall grave marker nearby, where an owl sat perched at the top of a slender obelisk. The animal peered down at them with wide, golden eyes, its round face outlined by a ring of white feathers.

"Tabarnak, it's just a bird," Julien sighed, but Noah held out a hand to quiet him and took a step closer to the marker.

"I hear you," Noah said softly in response to the owl's quiet chirps. "Can you help us?"

After a moment's pause, the owl spread its wings and alighted on the grass in front of them, its form melting seamlessly into a petite woman in a simple leather robe. Her grown was lined in soft white fur and decorated with tiny beadwork in a range of warm colors. The black hair framing her kind, tanned face spilled like a waterfall down over her shoulders and pooled on the ground around her. She smiled gently at the men before her, and Noah couldn't help noticing the slightly stunned look on his companion's face. The woman was beautiful, but did Julien really need to stare like that? Noah furrowed his brow and tried to focus on the task at hand.

The woman tilted her head at him and asked, "Suvin?" in a soft, distant voice. Noah could sense the meaning of her question without understanding the words, and he could feel Julien's eyes on him as he answered.

"We're looking for someone. A fairy; a gean cánach."

Her lips pursed ever so slightly. "Suksaq?"

"Because I'm sick. I need him to get well again."

Julien watched with growing anxiety as Noah conversed with the spirit, but he was resolved to keep his place as long as it didn't seem to be a threat. This was what they were there for, after all, though he noted that he seemed to be spending an awful lot of time not killing magical things lately.

The spirit's words became clearer the longer Noah listened and the closer he moved to her as they spoke.

"I am called Nipailuktak," she said. "I can see the other inside of you."

"The other? You mean the fairy."

"What hides inside you is from the otherworld, as I am. From the beyond. The under. It is ilitkusik." Her brow furrowed with concern as she looked at him. "You are right when you say you are sick. It will kill you to have this thing inside of you. You cannot keep it."

"Believe me, I don't want to keep it," Noah answered with an empty chuckle. "Can you help me?"

She shook her head. "Only the one inside you can help."

"Great," he said, his cheeks puffing out in a sigh. "I don't suppose you've seen him around."

A knowing smile touched her lips. "Actually, yes."

Noah perked up instantly and stepped closer to the spirit, which didn't seem to concern her. "Can you show me where he went?"

"Yes." She lifted her arms, and in an instant she was an owl again, her spread wings lifting her into the sky and away to the northwest. Noah chased after her without waiting to see if Julien was following, but he was soon out of breath, wheezing and coughing as he stumbled and was forced to rest against a nearby tree. The flame in his palm flickered and died, the tightness in his chest almost unbearable. The owl waited for them momentarily, but didn't seem to mind them falling behind.

Julien was suddenly beside him with a supporting hand under his arm. "Envoye," he said, and Noah found himself lifted onto the hunter's broad back with no room for argument. He wrapped his arms around Julien's shoulders to steady himself while the hunter held him under his thighs, awkwardly balanced by his splinted wrist. When the hunter began to jog, Noah held on tightly to keep from slipping. He was still having trouble breathing, and he felt sick and miserable from the simple effort of walking around the cemetery, but Julien's back was warm against his cheek, and he could feel the hunter's heartbeat. Julien was doing all of this for him. Even with a broken wrist, even after being out all day, searching, fighting, and getting knocked around—Julien was doing everything he could to help him.

Noah hid his face in Julien's back and tried to fight the tears that were beginning to burn his eyes, but he couldn't help letting them fall. Stupid thing to cry about. Julien was his friend. Of course he was helping. He shouldn't read into it any more than that. Noah tried to hide his quiet sniffle and hoped the hunter didn't notice the wet spot on the back of his shirt.

Julien followed the owl through the streets and across the city for almost an hour. If he got any strange looks from passers-by for carrying another man piggyback down the sidewalk, he didn't notice. He kept his eyes on the bird flitting between trees and streetlights above him, conscious of the delicate cargo he carried on his back. By the time they stopped, he was out of breath, the muscles in his legs trembling from exertion, and he gasped for air as he let Noah down at the entrance to Vanier Park.

"Inside is the one who carried your other half away," the woman in front of them said, gesturing behind her into the park as Noah approached. "She will not want to help you, but if you show her what you carry, she may listen. I cannot do more than this."

"Thank you," Noah said earnestly, one hand on Julien's back as the hunter doubled over to catch his breath.

"Amiunniin," the woman answered. "Goodbye, anatkugnak." The owl took flight again and vanished into the night sky, leaving Noah to tend to Julien as he slowly straightened.

"Osti, I need to quit smoking," Julien panted, taking one last deep breath before looking around. "Is this Vanier Park? Outside of Vanier Park? This is as close as she could get us? She could have just told us instead of making me run halfway across the city."

Noah smiled at the hunter's complaining and turned toward the entrance to the park. "Let's go find whatever's in here."

Noah and Julien walked through Vanier Park, both of them equally exhausted now. Noah could barely form a spark in his hand, so the two men walked in the darkness, hoping for some sort of sign.

Julien snorted in frustration. "How are we supposed to find whatever that owl woman wanted us to find with nothing to go on but 'it's in there somewhere?'"

"Someone that carried my other half away," Noah mused, half to himself. "Whatever it is, she called it a 'she.' So we're probably looking for something human-shaped, at least. But then, the owl was a she, too, apparently," he added, not without a slightly morose sidelong glance at Julien.

74

"That's the other thing. Where did she carry your 'other half' away to? For what?"

"Somewhere he thought he could get better, probably. Somewhere—" Noah swayed on his feet, and Julien paused to look back at him as he stopped speaking.

Julien barely reached him before he hit the ground, but he managed to keep him relatively upright with one arm around his waist. The boy was trembling uncontrollably in his arms, but he still pushed against the hunter's grip and leaned away from him to search the dark line of trees ahead of them.

"Something lives nearby," the witch whispered, his voice sounding strange and harsh. He fought Julien's grip even while he stumbled and struggled to breathe, and the larger man caught the glisten of blood on his upper lip. "Cabhrú liom, le do thoil!" he called, and Julien held him tighter. This was not the time for him to have one of his episodes.

"Noah," he tried, knowing it was probably useless. "Noah, listen to me; let's go back now. I'll come back myself and—"

"Aon!" Noah cried, and he pried Julien's arm from around him and fell to his knees.

"Noah, whatever this thing is can't help you if you're dead!"

"A fháil amach anseo!" the witch begged in a voice only half his own. Something stirred in the leaves ahead of them, and he fought to pull to his feet. "Inis dom áit a bhfuil mé!"

Julien stumbled as a sudden gust of wind knocked him forward, but Noah stood still, though his shoulders slumped heavily.

"I gcás ina tá mé? Inis dom!" Noah cried with more ferocity than the hunter would have thought possible. Julien stepped forward to hold him steady, keeping a firm arm around the boy's shoulders.

"Noah, you'll hurt yourself," he whispered against the witch's ear. "Stop now."

The wind blew from behind them, pushing them forward, and Julien scrambled to keep Noah in his arms as the boy went slack, wincing as he was forced to put weight on his broken wrist. Noah was dead weight now, completely unresponsive to Julien's tapping on his cheek. A sharp, cold breeze drew the hunter's eyes up, and he set his jaw at the sight of the woman in front of him. He had had quite enough of randomly appearing women tonight, especially ones that looked as large as this one did. She stared down at Julien with a sneer on her thin lips, the wind blowing her blonde hair away from her sharp face.

"So this is the one who stole Scal Balb's magic," she said in an airy voice. "What are you doing here, human?"

"We came to find the fairy," Julien answered, shifting Noah in his arms to hold him tighter. "The owl spirit said you could help, so can you, or what?" The hunter was taking in what he could in the darkness, trying to add up the details of the spirit in front of him. Some sort of spirit of air—a sylph, or something similar. The broad shoulders and scowling face seemed to suggest a sylph, but he wasn't going to risk offending it by calling it the wrong name just now.

"I know where he has gone," the spirit answered, "and I know you wish him ill. I also know you, seventh son," she added with a pointed nod. "The woods have cried out in loss for the creatures you have killed in the months you've been here. And now you hunt Scal Balb. I should kill you where you stand."

Julien couldn't fight this spirit. Not now. Not with Noah unconscious in his arms, and not when he needed its help. "I didn't come to fight," he said through grit teeth. "Not today. Something's happened to my friend—we need the fairy to put it right. For both of them," he pointed out. The spirit eyed him skeptically, so he tried again. "Noah is innocent," he pressed. "You can deal with me as you like later, if that's what you want, but help him now. Please," he added as a reluctant afterthought.

The woman approached him, and he almost retreated, but she only reached out and put a light hand on Noah's damp forehead. "No one is innocent," she said. "This is black magic. Blacker still will be required to undo what's been done."

"What does that mean? Can none of you people speak plainly?"

She glanced down at him. "It means you don't know what you're in for, seventh son." She hesitated a moment. "Take him home. Let him rest." She tilted her head at him and pointed over his shoulder to a small grove of trees nearby. "Come tomorrow, at dusk, to that little glen. I will tell you more then. If you can be respectful, I may provide you the answers you seek."

Julien opened his mouth to thank her, but she was already gone, vanished into the breeze. He lifted Noah over his shoulder with some difficulty and carried him back through the park to the street. He hailed a taxi, made a joke to the driver about his friend not being able to hold his liquor, and let Noah lean against him during the drive back to their hotel. He cringed to pay the driver so much as they exited the car, but the prospect of carrying the witch any further than he had to had been unthinkable. It was bad enough holding him as he climbed the stairs to their room. The hunter's legs already felt like Jell-o.

Julien kicked the door shut with his heel and laid Noah down on the bed, stripping him of his shoes and tucking the blanket up around his chin. He gently cleaned the blood from the witch's lips and nose and stood looking down at him with a small sigh. He meant to make a place for himself on the floor, but after being on the move for almost twenty-four hours, even the squeaky mattress next to the man who made his stomach tighten seemed inviting. After only a moment's consideration, Julien undressed and slipped into the bed beside Noah, though he kept his distance from the warm body next to him and tried not to remember the previous night.

8

Noah's head hurt. He opened his eyes and immediately regretted it, flinching away from the light and hiding his face in the warm skin under his cheek. He had already settled back into the mattress when it occurred to him that there was actually warm skin under his cheek. Noah peeked up at Julien's sleeping face, feeling the hunter's muscular arm surrounding him like a barrier. He wanted to move, to pull away and act as though it had never happened. At the same time, he wanted to stay with his cheek in that soft little crook in Julien's shoulder forever. If Julien woke up and found them like this, he would be uncomfortable, Noah knew. But he smelled so nice. Even though they both must have just fallen into bed the night before, and Julien smelled of sweat and trees and old graves, Noah could have stayed under the hunter's arm for days, listening to his heartbeat. He reached up and tentatively let his hand lay on Julien's chest, his fingertips brushing the soft blonde hair near his collarbone.

It wasn't right to stay. Noah pulled himself up slowly, scooting up the bed to lean against the headboard. Julien wouldn't have wanted him there.

He frowned down at the hunter's sleeping face with an uncomfortable feeling in his gut. No matter how kind Julien had been to him over the last few days, it was still difficult to overlook the anger in the man's voice when he'd shouted at Noah about using magic in front of people, or how he had coerced him into using the dangerous spell. Noah had said he had made his own decision, but he knew the sting in his heart that came from being manipulated. Julien had used him. He might feel bad about it now, but the fact remained that the hunter had used Noah's feelings against him to twist the witch into doing what he wanted. Julien had apologized and seemed to mean it, so Noah wouldn't hold a grudge, but he had promised himself that he wouldn't be used again. He wouldn't be manipulated or convinced, no matter how softly Julien spoke to him or how often he assured him that they would have their talk. Noah just hoped he could keep his promise to himself.

He craned his neck to get a look at the alarm clock on the nightstand. The numbers said it was the middle of the day already, but he felt like he'd hardly had any sleep. He rubbed at the back of his neck and gave a short sigh through his nose. They had been in the park last night, and he felt something in the air, something magic nearby—but then nothing. He had no idea what had happened after that, or how they got back to the room. Julien must have had to carry him back after he passed out. Noah let out a tiny groan. He wasn't exactly being helpful. His chest still felt congested, and every muscle in his body ached, but he was determined to be of more use the next time they went out. Assuming Julien would even let him try again.

Noah inched away from the hunter, trying to edge his way out of the bed without waking him, but Julien shifted, turning onto his side with a mild grunt and draping his arm across Noah's lap as though seeking his lost warmth. His head rested heavily on Noah's hip, making the witch freeze in place. Noah suddenly didn't know what to do with his arms. A rush of panic went through him, and he willed his body to behave itself despite the hunter's proximity to his more private parts. Julien was sleeping. Any closeness—or brushing, Noah mentally added with a shiver as Julien settled his arm—was entirely unintentional.

Don't be a creep. Noah took a slow breath. He didn't want to move and risk waking Julien up, but he definitely needed something to take his mind off of his precarious situation. He took a quick glance around the room for inspiration and spotted his notebook propped against the nightstand, his pen abandoned on the floor beside it. Noah reached out a hand and felt the familiar tug of magic in his veins as he willed the notebook and pen within reach, not wanting to disturb the hunter sleeping against him.

It had been too long since he'd written to Sabin. Noah had met the younger boy six or seven years ago, back when he was only thirteen, and Noah had caught him doing magic in public. He had tried to warn him what a bad idea that was, but Sabin had only scoffed at him and told him to mind his own business. The boy had clearly been cold and miserable, and a Vancouver winter was no time to be alone on the street, so Noah had offered to take him home and feed him. As it turned out, Sabin did actually have a foster family but was a recurring runaway. From that first show of kindness, Sabin had stuck to Noah like glue, and Noah had enjoyed having someone to whom he could pass on some tricks. No one in Sabin's foster family had had the aptitude, it seemed.

A couple of years ago, however, Sabin had been suddenly and mysteriously whisked away to America, to some secret facility for magic-users—at least, that was Noah's understanding. He wasn't sure exactly where Sabin had gone, and his letters were half blocked out with black marks, but the boy had assured Noah that he was safe and reasonably happy where he was. Wherever Sabin was, he was able to exchange letters and the occasional email, so they had kept in touch regardless of the distance.

Noah flipped to a blank page in his notebook, skimming past notes on fairies, Gaelic, and various herbs, and he balanced it on the knee furthest from Julien's head. He tried to steady his hand, but his fingers still trembled, and his penmanship—which wasn't great to begin with—suffered for it. He hoped Sabin would still be able to read it.

He tried to fill him in on everything that had happened over the last couple of weeks, but he quickly became aware of how worrisome most of it would be. He focused on the high points—getting to see a barghest and take samples, patching up Julien's injuries. Sabin was well aware of Noah's feelings for the hunter, and was probably tired of hearing about his mentor's inner turmoil by now, frankly. Noah glossed over it and moved on to being on the run from the police, which he knew the boy would find exciting.

He looked down at the page with a small frown, considering for a moment before returning pen to paper. He chose to say that he had been injured in their last meeting with the fairy, rather than telling the whole truth. It would worry Sabin to death to know how close Noah was coming to—well, death. Instead, he promised him that he would be fine, since he had his big, scary hunter to take care of him, and that they were right on the fairy's tail. It was a tricky matter, but Noah was confident in Julien's ability to outsmart the fairy.

Noah asked after Sabin's well-being in his secret government facility. The last time he had heard from the boy, there had been some drama or other about newcomers and the personality clashes that always followed that sort of thing. Noah promised to include a couple of barghest teeth with his letter so that Sabin might experiment with them—supposedly they were good for divination spells, sensing danger, and that sort of thing. It was imprecise magic, but Sabin would have more time to figure it out than he would.

He hesitated as he reached the bottom of his second page. He glanced down at Julien's peaceful face, and his brow furrowed as he looked back to his paper.

I might not be able to write for a while. I'll let you know where I am as soon as things settle down. Be good.

Love from,

Noah

He flipped the notebook shut and leaned to put it back on the nightstand, then sat quietly and watched Julien sleep. Noah still didn't want to wake him up, but his leg was going to sleep, and he'd been able to feel a cough building up in his throat for the last ten minutes. When he finally had to let it out, he tried to hide the noise in the crook of his arm, but his sudden shift made the hunter stir in his lap. Julien took a moment to realize where he was, and then he sat up quite suddenly, putting a polite distance between them.

"Désolé," he grumbled as he turned to let his feet touch the floor.

"Good morning, sunshine," Noah offered in an attempt to diffuse the awkwardness. When had it become awkward between them? They had always gotten along well despite Julien's workaholic nature, but now something was different, and Noah had the uncomfortable feeling that it was his fault. Julien looked over his shoulder to give the witch a small, lazy smile, and Noah felt his stomach do a quick flip. He had gotten used to seeing Julien look tired—coming back from a long day out hunting, or keeping watch over Noah in the hospital for the last few days—but it was somehow much more intimate and embarrassing to see the hunter actually wake up in bed. He looked disheveled and warm, and Noah could watch the muscles in his back as he rolled his shoulders to stretch them. He longed to touch them, and a little voice at the back of his head whispered to him to just do it. Just take him, kiss him, a rúnsearc—Noah subtly pinched his own arm in an effort to focus. He would not be kissing anyone, especially not at the prodding of some intrusive fairy spirit.

"So, what happened last night, anyway?" he asked as Julien pulled to his feet and twisted his arm this way and that to inspect the abused splint on his wrist. "I don't remember anything really after we got to the park."

"There was something there," Julien answered. "A spirit. You called to it—yelled at it, more like. In Gaelic. It seemed like it wanted to kill me, but it said if we came back at dusk tonight, it would help us. Might help us," he admitted after a moment. "Either way, I plan to get some answers tonight." Julien tilted his head slightly and looked down at the witch with a furrowed brow. "Do you feel all right?"

"Yeah," Noah assured him. "As fine as I can be. What are we going to do until dusk?" He pushed aside the invasive thought that sprang to mind—though he could picture perfectly exactly what he and Julien could do to pass the time.

"You should rest. I'm going to go back out and keep looking for leads. If this thing doesn't pan out, or isn't as helpful as we hope, I don't want to have wasted a day."

"Are you kidding?" Noah scooted over to the edge of the bed and carefully stood, trying not to show how lightheaded it made him. "You need to rest every now and then, too. That shapeshifter almost got the better of you yesterday, and you still only have one good arm. What will you do if you screw your wrist up even more? If it doesn't heal properly?"

Julien scoffed and tried to wave away the boy's worry.

"I'm serious," Noah pressed, and he took a step closer to the hunter and reached out to grip his hand. "You've been pushing yourself too hard. If this spirit in the park can't help us, then fine, we look for something else, but—until then, please just stay. Please don't hurt yourself anymore because of me."

Noah was aware of how pathetic he sounded, but it was worth the sacrifice to see Julien's face soften. The hunter gave a soft sigh through his nose and nodded.

"Fine."

It was more awkward than it should have been to spend the day with Julien. The hunter seemed to be keeping his distance—at least, as well as he could in the tiny hotel room. Julien had never paid much attention to Noah's presence before. He had always been so caught up in his work that he barely seemed to notice the witch was there, and he certainly had never seemed bothered or tried to shy away when Noah had been near him. But ever since they'd started sharing this small space, Julien had been acting as though he was afraid to let Noah near him. It had begun when they were in the hospital, after Julien had promised him that they would have a 'talk' about Noah's confessed feelings, but it had only gotten worse over the last day or so. Noah didn't know if he'd done something to make it more awkward, or if Julien had suddenly realized what it was he had agreed to talk about, but spending the day resting quietly in the room together wasn't going as peacefully as Noah had hoped.

Julien had insisted that Noah remain in bed, for one thing, which was the only piece of furniture in the room that was made for sitting on. The hunter seemed content on the floor with his chunky laptop on his knee, but Noah couldn't get any sleep with Julien in the room. His whole body felt sore, and he kept trying to hide his hacking coughs in his sleeves, but he couldn't help keeping Julien in the corner of his eye. He was able to watch him more blatantly once when Julien got a call. Noah peeked at him from his seat on the bed as he paced the room and spoke rapid French into his cell phone. Noah could only make out a few words. One of his brothers, maybe. Noah had always wanted to ask about them, but Julien got very quiet whenever Noah tried to ask him about his personal life. He got the impression it wasn't a particularly pleasant history.

Julien hung up the call with what sounded like an irritated swear and dropped his phone on the bedside table. When he spotted Noah staring at him, he sighed through his nose and ran a hand through his hair.

"It's nothing," he said, which was a blatant lie. "Just my brother checking in. He wants me to move on—says there's something big brewing back home. I told him I still had business here, and we had to have an argument about daring to disobey the will of Edouard Fournier le Grand," he finished with a sarcastic wave of his hand.

Noah attempted a smile. "So...your brother's name is Edouard?"

Julien paused, as though realizing he'd given away secret information. "One of them," he admitted after a moment. He sighed and counted off on his fingers. "Edouard, Joseph, Arnaud, Laurent, Hugo, Antony, and me."

"Wow. Seven seems like more when you actually list them like that. Your poor mother."

"I'm sure we weren't easy. Father was usually busy with his own brothers," he shrugged.

"It's weird to think of you as the baby," Noah chuckled, his gaze moving over the hunter's thick shoulders and scarred biceps. Everything about Julien seemed weary and experienced; he couldn't imagine what older versions of him might be like.

"I wish my brothers didn't," he muttered, seeming to forget himself for a moment as he dropped down onto the bed beside Noah.

"I'm sure they're just worried about you," Noah offered, but Julien scoffed out a short laugh.

"You don't know them," he said.

Noah hesitated. He didn't want to make Julien any more uncomfortable than he already was, but acting like things were strained between them was a guaranteed way to make sure it stayed weird, wasn't it? He told himself he was just trying to act natural as he reached out to put a comforting hand on Julien's shoulder. It was a friendly gesture, one that he hoped the hunter wouldn't misinterpret. Noah's thoughts about the firm muscle of Julien's shoulder and the voice whispering in the back of his head about the various ways Noah could offer the other man comfort were his own problem, not Julien's.

Julien turned to him, his eyes glancing down at the hand on his shoulder before looking back up into the witch's face. He seemed to linger a moment before he remembered that they were being awkward, and then he stood and moved out of Noah's reach. Noah let his hand drop back to his lap, trying not to frown. He didn't like this. Things were strange now, and it was all his fault. Was this really because of him letting slip that he wanted to be more than friends? Julien had promised they'd talk about it when this was over, but was the very thought of it really making him this uncomfortable? Was he dreading it so much?

For a few moments, they only stared at each other.

"Look," they said at the same time, and they both paused.

"Me first," Julien cut in. He wiped his palm on his pants leg, the fingers of the hand in the sling fidgeting anxiously. "I know what I said," he began softly, "about us having our...talk."

"Julien, you don't have to—"

"No," he interrupted. "Let me finish. Please." He waited for Noah to nod and took a breath before continuing. "I said that it had to wait until we found this fairy. And I'm not giving up," he assured him, "but we have so little to go on. If it does take some time, and you get...worse, I don't..." Julien seemed to be having trouble getting the words out. "We don't know how this will affect you if we take much longer. So I want to talk with you. With you, not...the thing that's in there with you. If you want to have a talk...I want to have it now."

Noah's heart leapt into his throat and threatened to thump right out of his mouth, so he tried to swallow it down. He wasn't ready for this. He hid his hands under the blanket pooled in his lap so that Julien wouldn't notice their trembling wasn't only from his illness. "Well," he tried to say as calmly as he could, "if that's...if you really want to, then...we should talk."

Now that they had decided to talk, neither of them seemed to know what to say. Julien shifted his weight for a moment, as though afraid to advance or retreat.

"When you said you wanted more," the hunter started quietly, but then he stopped, and Noah thought he saw the faintest hint of redness in the other man's face. "When you said you wanted more. What...more? What does that mean?" he clarified. If the conversation had been different, Noah might have laughed at the stoic hunter stumbling over his words, but his stomach was in too many knots to make jokes.

"Julien," Noah sighed, "I don't want to make you uncomfortable. I know you're all about your work, and I know how you feel about magic, and I don't—I mean, I assume that if you were attracted to men at all it would have come up by now."

"I want to know what you want," Julien asked again. He swallowed. "I want to know...why you said that."

Noah didn't want to answer. Julien seemed so anxious; he wasn't going to like the answer Noah gave. But if he was anxious...he at least cared about letting Noah down easy, didn't he? The witch tried to ignore the tiny flutter in his stomach that wanted him to believe Julien was nervous for a different reason—that he actually wanted to hear what Noah wanted to say. He took a deep, slow breath.

"I said it because...because I love you, Julien." He lowered his eyes to protect himself from seeing whatever look of disgust he was sure he would find on the hunter's face. He wanted to ramble, to explain himself, to say that it hadn't happened overnight—that he'd been enjoying the hunter's company for months, and that he'd never had any ideas that anything could happen between them, but he'd let the secret out in his anger even though he had never meant for it to be a burden to anyone but himself. He kept his mouth tightly shut, refusing to say any of those things. He waited in the tense, endless silence until Julien spoke again.

"I...thought you would say that," the hunter said in almost a whisper. Noah finally looked up when he heard Julien take a step forward, and he felt like he wanted to retreat when the other man sat beside him on the bed. Julien didn't look disgusted. Pensive, and nervous, with a furrowed brow and an anxious, tight frown—but not disgusted. Noah thought he should say something, tell Julien to forget it, make a joke, anything. But the hunter stared at him with such intensity in his hazel eyes that Noah felt rooted to the spot.

Neither of them said anything. Noah's hands fidgeted with the blanket, but he couldn't seem to pull himself from Julien's gaze. He needed the other man to say something. Every moment of quiet that passed between them was agony, but Noah didn't want to rush him, no matter how badly he wanted to shake Julien by the shoulders and shout—So?!

The witch's patience had almost run out, and he opened his mouth to speak, but then Julien suddenly closed the distance between them, his good hand gripping Noah tightly by the back of his neck as he pressed their lips together. Their noses bumped awkwardly—and a little painfully—but Noah's chest still tightened, and his breath left him. He was too stunned to move, even to reach out and touch the chest or face he'd so often imagined caressing. Something felt wrong. It was a tense, stiff kiss that was impossible to settle into. Julien had made the move, but it was only lips against lips and nothing more—like he wasn't really kissing him at all. The realization turned Noah's stomach, and he pushed the hunter away from him forcefully. His hand moved up automatically, his knuckles wiping away the memory of the touch.

"Why...why did you do that?!" he snapped before he could stop himself, though Julien only watched him with a bewildered stare. "What is wrong with you?"

Julien stuttered for a moment before answering. "This is what you want, isn't it?" he asked incredulously. "You just said that you—"

"I tell you I'm in love with you, and you think what I want is your...your pity kiss?" Noah hugged his stomach to try to quell the sick churning in it. "God, gross, Julien," he shuddered.

"That isn't what I—" Julien sighed in frustration and pushed away from the bed, circling the room with an anxious pace. "I don't—pity you," he said when he finally stopped. "I just want to give you what you want."

Noah felt his throat constricting around his words, but he did his best to get them out without trembling. "I don't want you to kiss me," he said. "I want you to...to like me."

"I do like you," Julien objected, but Noah only shook his head. The witch held himself tightly, his fingernails digging painfully into his sides through his shirt. It was too familiar. The empty kiss, the empty words, the one-sidedness. He'd been down this road before. He'd had the same hollow feeling in his chest when Travis had kissed him. He'd ignored it then, tried to tell himself he was imagining it, but he wouldn't do it again. He wouldn't fool himself this time.

"I don't want...sex from you, Julien," he managed to say. "Not because you think it's what I want. You really think either of us would enjoy that?" Julien frowned but didn't answer. "I just..." Noah sighed. "I just want you to be honest. I thought that's what this talk was for—not so that you could hear what you already knew and try to...whatever it is you thought you were doing."

"I thought I was—" Julien stopped himself and stared down at Noah as he sighed through his nose. "Okay," he said instead, only moderately more calm. "You want me to be honest?" He didn't wait for an answer. "I trust you. You've been a good friend to me, and that...means a lot. I care about you, and I want to help you. Because you've helped me, because you're in this state because of me, because of the way I treated you. And because...even if none of this had happened, I still wouldn't want to leave Vancouver because it would mean leaving you behind."

Noah could only stare up at him open-mouthed, too stunned to speak. It was disarming to hear Julien speak so frankly about something that wasn't tactics or hunting strategies. Noah was forced to break the silence by a round of coughing, but at least hiding his face in the crook of his arm gave him time to process an answer. He had expected an "I think of you as a friend" response, had steeled himself for it ever since the first time he realized how deep his feelings for the other man went, but this was...more than that. When Noah lifted his head, Julien had moved closer to him again and was watching him with concern.

"I didn't think the kiss was that bad," the hunter said with a soft smile, and Noah felt a warm tightness in his stomach. He couldn't help his quiet chuckle.

"It was pretty bad," he said as he caught his breath, but the hunter only smiled.

"Désolé," Julien answered. "I'm out of practice." He lowered his eyes and shrugged one shoulder apologetically. "I don't know how to handle things like this. Fighting monsters, pfft, c'est facile. Not being an ass to you is proving much harder for me."

Noah couldn't take the sad look on the hunter's face. He wanted to tell him it was fine, but it wasn't. He couldn't let himself be walked over anymore. "Just don't...do anything you don't want to, just because you think it's what I want. I'm glad you—I'm glad you care about me," he said, hoping Julien couldn't tell how tight his throat felt. "But if that's all it is—I mean, if you just care about me as a friend—I'm okay with that. Really," he promised when Julien gave him a skeptical look. "I'd rather that than have you try to force something that isn't there and ruin everything. So let's just…go with that for now, okay?"

Julien nodded, though he still seemed unsure. "I can do that."

9

Ciaran's father's house was just as dreary on the inside as the dark stone had made it seem. The same blue light as outside shone through sconces on the empty walls, giving the interior a gloomy atmosphere. There was a real fire in the fireplace in the room Ciaran's father led them to, which made it seem a bit more welcoming, but even the warmth of the orange flames couldn't offset the chill that the man's icy stare caused in Trent's spine.

He stood awkwardly while Ciaran unbuckled the belt around his wrists, only taking his seat when Ciaran tugged him down beside him by his hand.

"Áthair," Ciaran began, "this is Trent Fa. He helped me above ground when I was injured. He's helping me still, but I came here for your expertise." He glanced over at Trent. "Trent, my father—Dian Cecht, foremost physician of the Tuath Dé."

Under any other circumstance, Trent would have wanted to make fun of Ciaran for speaking so formally. For now, he decided against it, but he wasn't given the opportunity to speak before the older man answered.

"And what is it that's done this to you?" the man rumbled, and Trent was grateful that he at least was willing to speak a language he could understand. "I can smell your sickness. There is an emptiness in you that will pull you into itself until none remains."

"Hopeful prognosis, áthair," Ciaran sighed, but his sarcasm was cut off by a thick, heavy cough the left splotches of red on Lugh's cloak when he pulled his hand away.

Dian Cecht's brow furrowed, and he got to his feet and snatched up the cloak to peer at it in the flickering light of the fireplace. "Red," he murmured. His gaze flicked back to his son. "What did this?" he asked again.

"It was a spell," Ciaran answered in a croaking voice. "Dúnmharú anam."

The older man dropped the cloak as though he was afraid whatever Ciaran had was catching. "I'm surprised you're alive at all."

"I don't think the spell was complete. The witch who cast it lost consciousness."

Dian Cecht reached up to stroke his white beard as he pondered. "A single possibility," he said, and then he sighed through his nose. "There is only one solution. The witch who cast the spell must be brought here, the magic undone. The witch has stolen your magic from you, and it must be taken back if you hope to live. If what you say is true, you may take comfort in the fact that his suffering likely equals your own."

"Not exceptionally comforting, actually," Ciaran muttered. Trent could feel the fairy's weight press into his shoulder; he was trying to rest against him without his father noticing.

"There is also, of course, the small matter of you having disappeared for the last thousand years," Dian Cecht added dryly as he took his seat across from them again. "Weren't you dead?"

"Working at it," Ciaran said with an empty chuckle. "Do you really want to hear my reasons, áthair? Are you going to turn me in?"

The man paused as though this actually seemed like an enticing possibility, but then he sighed through his nose and shook his head. "It's no business of mine. But if someone comes asking for you, I'm not putting myself in the middle of your bullshit."

Trent actually snorted despite himself, and Ciaran turned to frown disapprovingly at him.

"What?" Trent shrugged. Ciaran only narrowed his eyes.

"Your brothers will want to be informed of your fortunate survival, of course," Dian Cecht spoke up. "I'd be surprised if word hasn't already reached them through the servants."

As though on cue, a side door into the large room burst open, and a man rushed in, followed immediately by a second who scolded him for running through the house. There was no mistaking them. Both men shared Ciaran's sharp cheekbones spotted with freckles, his dark, wild hair, and his bright mint green eyes. One of them looked slightly better put-together than the other, and slightly paler, but they were clearly brothers.

"Tá sé fíor? Tá sé anseo?" the first man asked with a wicked grin on his face, which only brightened when he spotted Ciaran on the settee. He rushed over and scooped Ciaran up out of his seat, lifting him from the floor in a hug. "Mo laethanta, deartháir, tá tú beo!" He let him down and kept his hands on his shoulders, staring into his face with a broad smile.

"Tá mé beo," Ciaran agreed, chuckling, and he gripped his brother's forearms and returned his smile.

"Saghas," the brother laughed as he took in Ciaran's weary face. "Cad atá mícheart leat?"

Ciaran held up a hand and pulled away from his brother's grip. He tilted his head down towards Trent, who was sitting and staring at them, completely uncomprehending. "This is Trent," he said in purposeful English. "Trent, this is my brother, Cu." He gestured to the other man lingering more politely behind them. "And my brother Cethen."

Cu gave a dark chuckle and leaned in toward Ciaran as though he needed to speak softly to avoid being understood. "Do leannán is déanaí? Tá sé ina ceann deas."

"Don't be rude," the last brother cut in as he stepped forward. His hair was neater than either of his brothers', and he seemed to have a gentler face, somehow, despite how closely he mirrored his siblings. He offered his hand to Trent, who took it as he got to his feet. "It's a pleasure. Thank you for bringing our brother home."

Trent only nodded, not sure how to reply. The whole situation was a bit overwhelming. He kept glancing back to Ciaran's father, who sat in stony silence while he watched them. Trent listened while Ciaran recounted the same story he'd told his father, both of his brothers frowning with concern and slowly sinking into chairs.

"Let's just go get this witch, then," Cu said when Ciaran had finished. He was already on his feet again. "And have it done."

"Do you even know where he is?" Cethen asked. Dian Cecht rose and helped himself to a glass of dark liquid from a decanter on a side table, silently listening to the exchange.

"Vancouver, in Canada," Ciaran answered.

Cu snorted out a laugh, temporarily distracted. "Canada? What were you doing all the way in the new world?"

"Not being here," Ciaran said, and his brother's expression softened.

Cethen sat forward in his seat. "Do you have any reason to think the witch would have left?"

Ciaran shook his head.

"Well then let's go get him," Cu said again.

"Planning to walk, are you?" Dian Cecht finally spoke up from behind them, startling all three brothers. "And how do you propose to bring this witch back, once you find it? Bound hand and foot on your back?"

Before any of them could produce an answer, they were interrupted by the sound of a sharp voice from the entrance corridor. A moment later, a woman was in the room, with a servant offering profuse apologies behind her. The woman had ghostly white skin and shimmering blue-black hair decorated with silver pins, and she wore an inky black gown that showed her slender shoulders. She was beautiful, but in a slightly frightening way, and she stared across the room at them with deep orange eyes. As soon as she spotted Ciaran, she strode over to him with a stern frown, the delicate silver woven in her hair tinkling with every movement. Ciaran didn't shrink under her glare, despite her being easily a head taller than him, even when her nose drew close to his.

"Nice to see you, my treasure," he offered with a slight smile, and she cut him off by putting one long-nailed finger to his lips.

"Save your endearments. What are you thinking, showing up here after all this time?" She answered him automatically in English, not seeming to care which language she scolded him in.

93

"It isn't as though I had much of a choice," Ciaran argued, and the woman hissed impatiently as she leaned back from him.

"You carry the stench of the Milesians above," she said. "You should have stayed with them. As if anyone here has missed you," she added with a click of her tongue that made one corner of Ciaran's lips twitch up into a faint smile.

Trent's stomach felt like lead. There was only one person this could be, and it was the one person Trent had hoped he could go this entire adventure without meeting. He could deal with a murderous father, aggressively affectionate brothers, and even beetles that pulled carriages, but his fairy boyfriend's wife standing right in front of him was skirting the limit of what he could handle. Especially when he saw the faint wrinkles appear at the corners of Ciaran's eyes as the woman spoke to him. Trent sank back down onto the settee, feeling slightly sick. Only he was supposed to be able to put that smile on the fairy's face. What was he doing here?

Ciaran spotted Lugh leaning against the doorway with his arms folded across his chest, watching the scene with a frown.

"I suppose I have you to thank for this reunion," he said, and his son shrugged one shoulder.

"I wasn't going to face her fury when she found out about you anyway."

Ciaran seemed to remember Trent's existence, which the younger man wasn't certain he was thankful for. "Trent," he started softly, clearly realizing he was treading on tender ground, "this is the Lady Ethniu."

"Oh, Cian," the woman sighed, turning to face Trent and crossing her arms. "What poor unfortunate have you dragged down here?"

Dian Cecht cleared his throat pointedly and moved to the center of the room. "If you've all quite finished your family reunion in my sitting room," he said gruffly, "might we get back to solving the problem of my dying son?"

Ethniu's eyebrows lifted in surprise, and she looked down at Ciaran with renewed interest. "Dying?" she echoed.

"Short version is we need a witch brought back from Canada," Cu offered. "Or Cian is going to die."

The woman's gaze instantly moved to Lugh. "You'll fetch it," she said with no indication that it might have been a request.

Lugh straightened and answered his mother with a frown. "And why will I do that?"

"Because you have the Enbarr of Manandán," she answered simply. "Your horse can have you across the sea and back in a day."

"That's what gives me the ability to do it," Lugh snorted. "Not the inclination."

"My will is enough for your inclination," Ethniu said icily, and a shudder went down Trent's spine at the woman's stern expression. How could Ciaran smile so gently at this person? Trent didn't consider himself easily intimidated, but Ethniu seemed on the verge of dropping her civilized veneer and using those long, sharp fingernails to tear into the throat of the first person to cross her.

Lugh looked like he wanted to argue, but after a few moments of consideration, he gave a short sigh of frustration. "How am I even to find this witch? Surely even in Canada there must be more than one."

"He's with a hunter," Trent spoke up, reminding everyone of his presence. "A man named Julien Fournier. Tall, white, blondish, Quebecois. The witch is a younger, punky guy with dark hair. I don't know his name, though."

Lugh stared down at Trent as though irritated that there had been an answer to his question at all. "In Vancouver, Canada," he clarified, and Trent nodded. Lugh let out one more huff and shook his head. "This is the very last that I want to have to do with all this nonsense," he grumbled. He turned to leave, paused, then stalked into the room and snatched his cloak from Ciaran's shoulders before making his exit.

"Don't bring the hunter back," Ciaran called out behind him, but his only answer was a heavily slamming door.

"Well," Ethniu said brightly, "I'm glad we got that sorted. Cian, will you be coming home?"

Trent kept his eyes on the floor. He didn't want to think about Ciaran's home being with that woman. With his wife. He waited for the inevitable news that they would be staying at Ciaran's family home, and that Trent would be forced to sit quietly like an outsider while Ciaran reminisced with his wife and called her pet names like 'my treasure.'

But Ciaran said, "No. I'll stay here for now, if áthair will allow it. If word gets out that I'm here, which seems likely, the first place they'll look will be with you." He took hold of Ethniu's hands and looked up into her face, causing a sharp, needling pain in Trent's chest. "Will you send word, if they come? Give me time to get out?"

The woman's hard face softened, just slightly, but then she seemed to remember herself, and she tutted at him. "Don't be ridiculous," she said. "As though I want any of your scandal being traced back to me." She pulled her hands from his on the pretense of putting a strand of hair back into place. "But we will discuss this further," she added before turning to give Dian Cecht a cursory curtsy. "By your leave, my Lord," she offered politely, and she excused herself, leaving the room with the sound of heeled shoes clicking softly on stone.

Cu stepped forward to take her place and clapped his brother on the shoulder. "You need a long sleep," he chuckled. "I'll put him near me, áthair, shall I?" He waited for the older man to nod before giving Ciaran's back a pat. "Now come along, deartháir, and bring your pretty one."

Trent scowled at the label, but he shifted his duffel bag back onto his shoulder and followed the three brothers from the room. The rest of the house was creaking and aged, but the hallway at the top of the stairs at least seemed lived in. They walked up a set of stairs and down a few long corridors before they reached a closed wooden door, which Cethen pushed open for them with a heavy creak. This room seemed warmer than the rest of the house—there was at least a rug on the floor and soft furs on the bed. Cu and Cethen stayed in the doorway as Trent and Ciaran stepped inside.

"Get some rest, and just ring for one of the servants if you need anything," Cethen said.

Cu chuckled. "And we'll discuss you disappearing without so much as a fare thee well later on." He winked playfully at Trent and pulled the door closed behind him, leaving the two of them alone in the suddenly quiet room.

Ciaran visibly wilted, and he dropped onto the bed with a round of heavy coughs. Trent set his bag down and sat beside him, waiting until he lifted his head again. He must have been putting on a show for his family, though Trent couldn't guess why. Ciaran looked over at him and offered a tired smile.

"You have questions," he murmured, his voice sounding rough.

"They can wait," Trent answered against his better judgment, but Ciaran shook his head.

"No. Let's have it all out. Shall I start with why I ran away, or my relationship with my wife, or maybe my name? You must have noticed them calling me Cian."

"What they call you is pretty much on the bottom of my list," Trent said.

"Well, it's an easy answer. I didn't want anyone to know where I was. So I changed it when I left."

Trent paused, narrowing his eyes at the man beside him. "You changed your name to keep anyone from finding you...so you changed it from Cian to Ciaran?"

The fairy shrugged. "Well I didn't want to forget to answer to it, did I?"

"You're an idiot."

"Generally agreed," Ciaran smiled. "But I'll answer the question you don't want to ask. About Ethniu." Trent scowled down at the floor without answering. He didn't really want to ask about her. He didn't want to know how close she and Ciaran were. He definitely didn't want to hear Ciaran say her name so softly.

"I warned you," Trent said in a voice weaker than he liked. "I told you that I was jealous. I asked you if women would be a problem. That might have been a good time to mention that you were married to one."

Ciaran stopped him with a hand on his leg. "It was political," he said. "That's all. She's the daughter of a Fomorian king, and she was a gift to the Tuath Dé to ensure peace between our people. I was the oldest son of the most influential peripheral royalty at the time, so we were...matched. That's all."

Trent resisted the urge to pull away from him. "You can't just say 'it was political, that's all,' when I've met your son. You had a child together."

"You think that wasn't expected?" Ciaran scoffed, and he let out a soft, empty laugh. "A mhuirnín, things aren't as simple as you want them to be. Ethniu and I..." He shook his head. "I never loved her. And she never loved me. I'm fond of her, but...we had a responsibility, so we fulfilled it. And that's why I ran away," he said. He looked exhausted, and Trent almost told him to forget about it and lie down, but Ciaran went on. "I wanted to live. I wanted to be somewhere where I wouldn't have to go to banquets and be polite to people that hated me and have every part of my life dictated by other people. I didn't want to go to battle again. I'd seen enough," he finished with a weary sigh, his shoulders slouching as he exhaled.

"Why didn't you tell me any of this stuff? You know, maybe when I was considering leaving my entire life behind to go traveling around with you? Why didn't you trust me?"

"I'd hoped it would never come up," he answered simply. "Not much point in trying to escape your old life and then running about talking about it all the time, is there? I'd put it behind me."

"Well it's not very fucking behind you now, is it? It's right in front of both of us."

Ciaran sighed and stood without answering. He undressed himself and crawled under the down-filled blankets and furs across from Trent, tugging them up until his mouth was half covered. "I can ask Cu to take you back to the surface," he offered. "Before you get any deeper into this. You didn't ask for this—I know that. If it had just been us against the world, I could have—" He stopped and pressed his lips together before continuing. "You could go, is what I'm saying. And there isn't a soul in the world who could blame you if you weren't there when I came back. If I came back," he added softly.

Trent frowned down at him. Deep inside, part of him wanted to run. Part of him wanted to say that this was too much, that Ciaran hadn't told him the truth, that he didn't want to deal with any of it. He wanted to say yes, please let your brother take me back up the creepy mushroom path out of fairyland, away from your secret wife and son and back to where the world makes sense. But Ciaran looked so somber, so weary—Trent could still hear the fairy's groggy voice as he had leaned against his shoulder on the bench outside the mound. At least he wasn't alone. Trent's stomach twisted uncomfortably as he remembered the fairy's gentle touch on his cheek, and the bright, teasing smile that seemed all but lost now. Even if Trent had anywhere to go back to, he couldn't leave now.

Trent sighed and pushed his glasses up his nose with one knuckle.

"That wasn't the deal," he said finally. "Until the stars burn out," he added with a frown. "That's what you said, isn't it?"

Ciaran chuckled under his breath and lowered his eyes for a moment before peeking back up at him. "That is what I said," he agreed.

Trent kicked off his shoes and folded his glasses on the small table nearby. He left his clothes in a pile by his bag and slipped into the bed beside Ciaran. The fairy's hands felt cold even under the heavy blankets, so Trent held them tightly to his chest and let his forehead rest against the other man's.

"But your father can fix you, right?" Trent whispered, and Ciaran shifted just enough to press a warm kiss to his lips.

"If anyone can," he murmured sleepily before settling under Trent's chin. Ciaran was asleep in no time at all, and Trent lay quietly and listened to his love's labored breathing. He tried to tell himself that none of this meant that Ciaran didn't trust him, but he wasn't sure how convinced he was as he shut his eyes.

10

By the time dusk finally approached, Julien was desperate to get out of the hotel room. He had managed to briefly escape to fetch some food for the two of them, but ever since he had made the insanely idiotic decision to talk about feelings with Noah, the air in the room had been suffocating.

Julien didn't know what had come over him. He had suspected what Noah would say before the witch had said it, but to hear the words and see the pained look on his friend's face—it had made his chest ache. Noah had been just as certain that Julien would reject him as the hunter himself had been, but when the moment had finally come, Julien hadn't wanted to. He had wanted to—well, to do what he did, but the whole thing had backfired. His hesitation and his nerves had ruined it. Julien had all but confessed undying devotion— at least, it seemed to him that he had—but it had come too late or shouldn't have happened at all. He wasn't sure anymore.

Now Noah thought he had been pretending, or just doing whatever he thought Noah wanted, or that he was trying to force things. Noah wanted to keep things as they were. But all Julien could think about was Noah's skin-warmed silver lip rings pressing into the corners of his mouth and the soft sound the witch had made as his breath caught in his throat.

Every time he looked at Noah, Julien remembered the boy's hot fingertips on his stomach, the way he had whimpered and ached to be touched—even if Noah hadn't been himself then, Julien's imagination had begun to run wild. Between helping him settle during his flashes, which seemed to be coming more frequently now, Julien had forced the thoughts out of his mind and tried to focus on his laptop screen. He had almost run out of cigarettes, which was poor timing. This decision to...move forward had been a sudden one, and one that had his mind running a thousand miles a minute. He couldn't rush. He couldn't push. All he could do was carry on, like Noah wanted, and hope that he would have the opportunity to prove himself before the boy's illness got any worse.

So when the time came to leave the hotel room and return to the sylph in Vanier Park, Julien eagerly strapped his bag across his chest and stood at the door to wait. He let Noah take his time moving onto the street, just as he would have yesterday, and he let the witch lean on his shoulder on the bus, just as he would have yesterday, but today it was torturous. It turned his stomach to think that he had made Noah feel pitied. Julien wanted to protect him, keep him safe, repay everything he'd done, it was true—but Noah had carried on, insisted on continuing to help when other, lesser men might have given up. That wasn't worthy of pity.

There were still people in Vanier Park even though it was close to dusk, and Julien had difficulty remembering which exact copse of trees the spirit had pointed out to him the night before. He frequently walked ahead to check his compass while Noah waited and leaned against a nearby tree or just sat down in the grass wherever he was. Finally, Noah stopped him, and he tugged the hunter by his sleeve toward a drooping willow far away from any paths. Julien followed, knowing better than to question Noah's senses. They pushed through the low-hanging branches into a tiny hidden grove, but there was nothing there.

"Wait," Noah said simply, and he sat down on the ground and coughed into the crook of his arm. Even the simple exertion of getting here had taken a toll on him. Julien vowed not to let him push himself any harder. Noah would stay in the hotel and rest the next time Julien needed to go out, even if the hunter needed to strap him down. But that didn't help now. Julien let out a quiet sigh and sat beside Noah in the grass to wait.

The air grew slightly chilled around them as the sun dipped below the skyline of the city, and Julien could feel Noah shivering beside him. He slipped off his coat and draped it over the smaller man, and he put out an arm to let the witch settle against his shoulder. Before he had too much time to focus on the warm press of Noah's body against his, a sharp rustle of branches startled both of them, and a whirlwind of leaves appeared in the center of the little grove, quickly forming themselves into the shape of the woman Julien had seen the previous night.

"You did come," she said with an air of amusement as Julien got to his feet in a rush and helped Noah up beside him.

"You said you had answers," Julien said.

"So I do," she answered. "But you are too late. The answers aren't mine to give."

"Too late?" Julien snapped. He took a step toward the spirit, conscious of the iron blade tucked into the front pocket of his bag. "You told us to come at dusk! How can we be too late?"

The spirit's eyes moved to Noah, pale and sweating behind the hunter. "One comes for him who I dare not defy."

Julien's chest tightened. "Comes for him?" he echoed. "Who's coming for him? Why?"

The spirit shook her head. "Whatever answers you seek, seventh son, the Lonnbeimnech will decide if you deserve them."

"And just what the hell is that?"

At the back of Julien's neck, he suddenly felt a hot snort of breath, and he turned on the spot, automatically pulling Noah behind him and drawing the knife from its pocket in his bag. A massive mottled grey horse with pitch black eyes stood in front of him, idly treading one heavy hoof in the grass, but it was the rider who drew his attention. The man looked down at them with a stoic frown, his thick grey cloak wrapped tightly up to his chin. He was broad, with hard, pale green eyes and dark hair cropped short enough to show his pointed ears. Julien's gaze moved immediately to the various weapons hung from the stranger's simple saddle, especially the enormous pole with its head wrapped in some sort of leather pouch.

The rider looked right past Julien, his eyes narrowing just slightly as his steely gaze focused on Noah.

"Is é seo an cailleach?" he asked in a calm, deep voice, and the spirit answered him with a nod and a bow. The rider let out a soft grunt of acknowledgment and tipped his chin toward Noah. "You'll come with me."

"The hell he will," Julien growled, conscious of Noah's fingers tightly gripping his sleeve. "We came here for answers, creature. Where is the fairy?"

The stranger's eyebrow ticked upwards. "I came for the witch, and only the witch," he answered.

"I'm not letting you take him anywhere. Not without me."

The man glanced down at the knife in Julien's hand. "You shouldn't draw a weapon you don't intend to use, an duine."

"I never do," Julien answered sharply. He was very aware of how awkward the blade felt in his left hand, since his right was still in a sling, and of the size of the creature he was threatening, but he didn't have an option. He couldn't let this thing take Noah. The rider let out a quiet snort and lowered himself from his saddle in one fluid motion, leaving one calming hand on the side of his horse's neck. He was just as intimidating on foot—an easy six inches taller than Julien, with an air of quiet calm despite the hunter's threats.

"If you've a challenge, an duine, let's hear it," he said.

"Julien," Noah whispered, his grip tightening on the hunter's sleeve. "Don't do anything stupid. For once."

"Stupid would be letting this creature take you away and probably kill you," Julien muttered in response. He gently urged Noah farther behind him and dropped his bag to the ground. He fixed his grip on his blade as he locked eyes with the stranger in front of him.

"You won't take him without going through me," he said.

The rider gave a quiet grunt, almost seeming amused, and he slipped his cloak from his shoulders and casually folded it over his horse's back. His clothing was simple, but old-fashioned—rough brown trousers and a dark green tunic cinched at the waist with a leather belt, the short sleeves of the shirt showing tanned, firm muscle. His boots sounded heavy in the grass as he took a single step to reach the scabbard hanging from his saddle. The sword scraped softly on the leather as he pulled it free, the silver blade reflecting the faint evening light that made it through the trees.

Julien might not have had the same sense for magic that Noah did, but he knew a magic weapon when he saw one. This was getting better and better. But he couldn't back down now. The only other choice would have been to grab Noah and run, and Julien didn't like his chances against that horse. Aside from the fact that running was a completely stupid idea, he wasn't about to make a break for it in front of Noah now that he'd issued the challenge.

The rider took a few steps away from his mount and held the longsword easily in one hand, then gestured to Julien to begin with a frustratingly careless motion.

Without hesitation, Julien rushed at him, knowing that all it would take was a few choice cuts to wear the creature down. This was clearly a fairy of the same kind as the one they'd been searching for. If Julien could weaken it with the iron, maybe they could force some answers out of it.

Unfortunately, the stranger barely seemed to be making an effort to counter Julien's strikes. The hunter's iron blade clanged harmlessly against the silver sword at the fairy's slightest movement, and the rider himself showed no sign of concern. The fairy wasn't even attempting to fight back; he only deflected Julien's blows with almost condescending ease. It was embarrassing.

Only when Julien pushed forward with reckless fervor did the fairy take a step to the side to avoid him, and the stranger easily caught Julien's ankle with the tip of his blade, sending him tumbling forward into the grass. Julien twisted enough to avoid landing on his already broken wrist, but he still had the breath knocked out of him as he hit the ground. He heard Noah shout at them as the stranger turned Julien over with his boot, but when the cold silver edge of the sword touched Julien's throat, it was as if an electric shock went through him, pinning him motionless to the ground.

"You know you're outmatched, an duine," the rider said in a low voice, and Julien answered a quiet "Yes" before he even meant to speak.

"And if I let you up and try to take this witch, will you attack me again?"

Julien stared up at him with narrowed eyes. "Until you kill me."

A very faint smile quirked one corner of the fairy's lips. He took a step back, pulling his sword from Julien's neck without leaving a scratch. He only watched as Noah rushed to Julien's side, helping him sit up and hastily checking him for injuries. As the fairy slid his sword back into its scabbard, Noah stared at his broad back.

"What the hell was that?" Noah asked. He kept glancing back to Julien's throat to look for marks, but Julien just brushed his hands away. He didn't want Noah fussing over him after that shameful display of incompetence.

"Fragarach," the man answered simply with a quick look over his shoulder. "Magic sword," he added. "To keep you from telling lies. You shouldn't feel too bad, an duine," he said as he looked to Julien. "I suspect I've had a fair bit more practice in battle than you have."

Noah squeezed Julien's shoulder tightly to keep him from saying something snide, and instead asked, "Who are you?"

The stranger turned back to them as he idly stroked his horse's white mane. "I am called Lugh Lámhfhada, son of Cian mac Cainte, who is the one you seek. He sent me here to bring you to Tír na nÓg."

Julien pulled himself to his feet, but he didn't raise his knife. "I'm still not just going to let you take him."

Lugh gave a small one-shouldered shrug. "My father said not to bring you," he said, "but my father is a prat, and I like your attitude. So come along if you insist."

Julien looked down at Noah, still kneeling in the grass, and bent down to listen as he heard the witch whispering to himself. Noah reached up suddenly and gripped Julien's arm tight, looking up at the hunter with the blank, distant eyes he recognized too well. Julien crouched by him to listen to his murmuring, but it was in Gaelic, as usual. Lugh tilted his head in mild interest but said nothing.

"Is féidir linn muinín dó," Noah said urgently as he squeezed Julien's arm. "Ní mór dúinn dul leis." Noah repeated this last sentence a few more times, shaking Julien's arm for effect, until he drooped, and Julien had to move quickly to keep him from falling to the ground.

"I don't suppose you caught any of that," Julien muttered as he held Noah close to him, patiently waiting for the boy to come to his senses.

"Not that you'll believe me," Lugh said dryly, "but he said you need to come with me."

"Of course he did. That's your father fucking up his brain, after all."

"You want a way to make him well? Let me take him to Tír na nÓg."

Julien looked down at Noah, resting wearily against his chest, and he sighed. They had no better lead than this. They had to risk it, or Noah would die while Julien searched. Whatever was waiting for them, Julien would protect the witch in his arms until his last breath.

When Noah opened his eyes, he was still leaned against Julien with the hunter's furrowed brow looking down at him.

"What'd I miss?" he asked with a small half smile, and Julien released him slowly and helped him to stand up. He was getting a little too accustomed to waking up to Julien's face.

"You said we need to go with this...person," Julien answered, causing Lugh to lift his eyebrows in mild offense. "So if you want to, we'll go."

"I think...I think I know him," Noah said, putting a hand to his temple. "I think he's telling the truth. This was what we wanted, right? A way to find the fairy. So let's let him take us to him."

Julien took one last slow breath. "All right."

Lugh nodded his approval and slipped his cloak from his horse's back, fastening it around his shoulders again. "Give him to me," he said, and he snorted out a sigh as Julien's hand kept firm on Noah's arm. "I said that you could come, an duine; I'm not a thief. Give him here."

Noah gave Julien a faint, reassuring smile and stepped over to Lugh, who lifted the witch by his waist without hesitation and settled him easily on the tall horse. He couldn't help the soft sound of surprise that escaped him at the strength of Lugh's arms. He had lifted him like he was nothing. Noah swayed slightly, steadying himself with both hands on the animal's thick neck, but as Lugh hefted himself up into the saddle and put a protective arm around Noah's waist, he froze. He felt an embarrassing heat in his face as the fairy held him securely against his firm, muscular chest. They were really going to ride this way? Noah was in a very bad position emotionally to be thrown around and held tightly by someone as tall, dark, and handsome as Lugh, even if the stranger was carrying him off to some unknown place. A pang of guilt touched his stomach at the scowl on Julien's face as he approached, though he wasn't sure why. Julien just didn't like putting his trust in a fairy, that was all.

Lugh offered the hunter his hand and helped him up behind him much less carefully than he had Noah. Julien had no choice but to hold on to the back of the fairy's cloak.

"We're riding a horse to wherever we're going?" Julien asked skeptically, drawing a snort from the animal underneath him.

"Most humans never get to see the Enbarr of Manandán, let alone ride him," Lugh said. "So be a little respectful, and hold on." Lugh spared a grateful nod at the sylph lingering at the edge of the grove and then urged the horse on with a sharp shout. Julien scrambled to take a firmer grip of Lugh's cloak as the horse surged forward, barely keeping himself from tumbling off the animal's rear end.

Noah turned around as best he could to make sure Julien was still there, but Lugh's grip tightened on him as he shifted, so he quickly faced front. The horse thudded heavily across the park and onto the street, its hooves clattering hard against the pavement, and Noah was thankful for Lugh's firm arm around him. They seemed to be moving too fast, and the cars in the street seemed to shift out of their way without moving. Before Noah could count to ten, they were approaching Vancouver Harbor.

"Isn't this a little conspicuous?" Noah asked, but he regretted it as he tilted his head to look up at Lugh. The fairy was staring straight ahead with a stern frown, and when he glanced down at Noah's question, their faces were far too close together for the witch's comfort, especially when he could smell the warm scent of soft leather on the other man's skin.

"The Enbarr is only seen by those he wishes to see him," Lugh answered, and Noah could feel the low rumbling in his chest as he spoke.

"Fair enough," Noah blurted out, and he turned back to watch where they were going. He told himself to ignore Lugh's hand holding onto his waist, the way he pressed into him every time the horse moved, and the bouncing—the bouncing was the worst. Noah forced himself to focus on the reality of his situation—he was traveling with the son of the fairy whose soul was locked up in his head, going to who knows where and hoping that it meant that he was going to get cured instead of dead. That was reality. Strong, handsome men who held you while you rode horses were not a useful part of this equation—especially when the man to whom Noah had awkwardly confessed his love just a few hours earlier was bumping along uncomfortably just behind them.

The ride was long enough to become tiring, which Noah was thankful for, because if he had spent the entire journey in the state of nervous frustration he had started it in, he probably would have flung himself from the horse in desperation. Lugh showed no signs of slowing down, and the horse didn't seem to be wearing out despite carrying three people, so they carried on, passing through small towns and empty countryside. They frequently rode alongside the freeway, which was a bit surreal.

As they rode along, Noah was suddenly startled by Julien's sharp voice behind him.

"He needs to rest," the hunter snapped over Lugh's shoulder. Noah realized with a little churn of embarrassment in his stomach that he must have fallen asleep against the fairy's chest.

"He's still ill," Julien went on. "He can't just do this all night."

"I'm fine," Noah protested, though now that the idea of stopping had been mentioned, he began to notice the soreness of the muscles in his thighs.

"That's Montreal," Julien said, pointing ahead of them at the approaching skyline. "We've gone almost five thousand kilometers. Let him rest."

Lugh glanced down at Noah as though weighing the idea, and he let the horse slow to a canter as he leaned around to look at the witch's face.

"Can you go on?" he asked, and his expression was so serious that Noah felt a slight brush creep back into his face.

He looked back at Julien as best he could around Lugh's broad shoulders, and he saw the concern on the other man's face, but he shook his head and held in a cough.

"I'm fine," he said. "Let's just get there."

Lugh didn't bother answering; he only gave the horse a light kick, and Noah fell back and held tightly to the fairy's arm as the horse burst into a gallop again. They passed through Montreal without incident, but as they approached the coast, Noah began to grow uneasy. This was clearly a magic horse, since it had run five thousand kilometers in one night and hadn't died, but they were about to run out of land, and Lugh didn't show any sign of stopping. Noah edged backward closer against Lugh's chest as they approached the water, and he could hear Julien shouting behind him, but the horse carried blithely on, galloping out over the water as though it were a grassy meadow.

Noah waited for them to run out of steam and slowly sink into the water like a Looney Tunes cartoon, but it didn't happen. The horse was quite happy to run along the surface of the water, leaving soft sprays of mist with each touch of its hooves. When it was clear they weren't all going to drown, Noah leaned forward as much as he dared, watching the horse's legs as they skimmed the waves. They rode until there wasn't any land to be seen around them, which was more than a little unnerving, the horse climbing tall waves like hills and letting loose when the water was smooth. It was ridiculous and frightening and exciting, and as the sun rose over the dark sea, Noah found himself wishing that it was Julien's arm around him instead of the fairy's.

The longer they rode, the more sore Noah's rear end got, but he was determined to finish the journey without any more interruptions. He dozed off against Lugh a few more times, feeling less embarrassed about it every time since the fairy didn't seem to mind, and eventually he opened his eyes to land in the distance.

"Oh my god, is that actually it? Please say yes; my ass is so sore."

"Éire," Lugh said simply. He spurred the horse on when they reached the shore, and Noah cringed at the heavier thumping of the horse's hooves as it ran on solid ground.

When Lugh finally slowed the animal to a stop, they were near what looked like a tourist attraction—a low, broad hill surrounded by stone, with a couple of tour buses parked nearby and lots of people with cameras milling about. Noah heard Julien drop down from the back of the horse with a pained groan, and he felt the loss of Lugh's warmth as the fairy dismounted. He started to move to get down himself, but then Lugh's hands were on him again, lifting him from the horse and setting him on the ground as easily as if he were a child. When Noah's legs immediately gave out from under him, Lugh caught him with one arm and passed him off to Julien in favor of tending to his horse.

"Are you all right?" Julien asked him softly, and Noah nodded with a small smile. If he was honest, even with everything that had happened between them, the ride had been worth the ache just to see that gentle concern on the hunter's face.

"Come along," Lugh interrupted, and he gave the horse's nose a quick stroke and sent it on its way with a swat to the rump. He started up the small hill toward the crowd of people, then seemed to remember himself and turned back to his two companions. He muttered something to himself as he passed his hand over their faces in turn, and when he snapped his fingers, Noah thought he could hear a small crackle in the air. He knew without asking that it was invisibility magic. It was the same as he'd done in the hospital, except this time he was actually fully conscious. Julien looked more than a little uncomfortable at having magic cast on him without notice, but Noah squeezed his arm and urged him on as Lugh continued up the hill ahead of them.

They passed through the people around them unnoticed, but the closer they drew to the stone entrance, the tighter Noah's chest felt. His heart pounded painfully in his chest, and he could hear the blood coursing through his body. The heavy stone laid at the opening to the underground passage made him wary, and he tried to skirt it, but when he avoided a passing oblivious tourist, he was forced to lay his hand on it to keep upright. Instantly, he was seeing through another's eyes, and the ambling crowd around him vanished, the buses and fences disappearing and leaving only empty fields and forest lit by a bright full moon. He exhaled and saw his breath leave him in a puff of steam, the cold air chilling his bare arms.

Still bleeding. My hand kept tight against the wound in my

BECAUSE YOU NEEDED ME

stomach, my own blood the only warmth on my skin. They tried to kill me. And I wanted to die. No more. No more war, no more politics, no more a prisoner in my own house. No more lies. No more a husband to a distant wife and father to an absent son. I slide down to the ground, panting out steam as I lean against the stone. I may die here. Let them find me when the sun rises, finally free from their reach. Or else let me see the sun myself, and never set foot in this cursed place again.

Noah jolted out of the vision as quickly as he'd entered it, looking up from his slumped position on the ground to see Julien crouched in front of him. Noah's hand clutched at his stomach, putting pressure on a wound that wasn't his, and the morning air was suddenly hot and stifling in his lungs.

"Es-tu correct?" Julien asked, gently touching the witch's shoulder to steady him as he wavered. Noah tried to quell the nausea that washed over him, but he had to cover his mouth with both hands to calm the bile threatening to rise in his throat. He didn't want to be here. He wanted to be anywhere but here. He looked up at Julien's worried face and took a slow, calming breath. These weren't his feelings. Not his fear.

"Let's just...let's go, okay?"

Julien nodded and helped him to his feet. Lugh stood idly nearby, looking supremely bored by the whole scene. He led them down the stone passage without a word and through to the central chamber. None of the people around them seemed to notice as the fairy touched the standing stone and opened a portal in the air just a few feet from some of them. Julien visibly tensed beside him, clearly uncomfortable with the very idea of taking a step through the passage. Lugh looked back over his shoulder from the other side, at the top of the long stone staircase leading into the dark.

"You want your 'fairy,' don't you?" he asked, making the hunter frown at him. "Come."

Noah wanted to hold Julien's hand, but he wasn't sure the hunter would respond well to such an intrusion when he was already on edge. So he simply stayed close, and they stepped through together, following Lugh down toward the distant glimmering outline of a city.

11

Ciaran woke up early, though the constant dim glow of the lanterns through the windows made it impossible to tell the time. He'd grown so accustomed to living above ground, to seeing the sun rise and set and adjusting his schedule accordingly, that to be back under the earth, where the days and nights blended together, made him feel sick and weary. He laid in bed and watched Trent sleep for as long as he could. Trent felt lied to, he knew. But Ciaran had honestly never intended for him to know any of this. The few times in his history he had told the whole truth to his lovers, it had always turned out the same. They became overwhelmed, distant—as if it mattered what his people were really called, as if it changed him at all. It was easier to be Ciaran the Cheeky Fairy than Cian mac Cainte, called Scal Balb, the silent phantom of the Tuatha Dé Danann, champion of the first great battle of Maighe Tuireadh. It wasn't a life he'd enjoyed when it was his, and now that the memories were faded and half missing, it seemed even worse to be forced back into the role he knew he'd abandoned so long ago.

He sat up slowly in bed so as not to disturb Trent, and he slipped free of the furs and dressed himself in the spare clothes Trent had brought for him. They didn't fit well, but they smelled of Trent, so he was happy to have them. Many memories had left him over the last few days, but he still knew this smell. He pulled open the bedroom door as quietly as he could and moved out into the corridor, where he immediately bumped into Cu.

"By heaven, look at you," his brother laughed. "What are you dressed as?"

"Someone too bloody tired to be fussed about what he's dressed as," Ciaran muttered in response.

"Come with me. Your wife is downstairs asking for you, and you don't want to show up in front of her in that human mess."

Ciaran almost flinched at the words 'your wife,' but he only sighed and let Cu lead him down the long corridor to his own expensive chambers. A servant girl stirred in the bed as they entered, not seeming overly concerned with covering any more of her nude body than the blankets already happened to hide. Ciaran had only a vague sense of memories of living with his brothers before he was married, but the sight didn't surprise him, so it must not have been an unusual occurrence. Cu threw open the doors to his wardrobe and hummed, stroking his chin as he inspected the contents.

"You always wore black well, didn't you?" he mused. "Here." He reached up into the wardrobe and retrieved a warm black tunic with simple silver embroidery at the cuffs and collar, and he pushed it onto Ciaran without leaving room for argument. He found a simple pair of black trousers and tossed them over his shoulder for his brother to catch.

"Come along then," he said when Ciaran hesitated. "Give me those things; I'll be sure they make it back to your pretty one."

Ciaran sighed. He pulled Trent's shirt up over his head and replaced it with Cu's borrowed tunic, which fit him almost perfectly.

"What's this then?" Cu asked, reaching out to slip a finger under the silver chain around Ciaran's neck. He slipped the jade circle free of his brother's tunic and leaned closer to inspect it. "Lost your token, have you?"

Ciaran pulled away and tucked the pendant back under his shirt with a frown. "It was a gift."

"A gift, eh?" Cu chuckled. "Or an exchange? And you've brought this human home with you. Curious," he teased.

"I don't know what's curious about it," Ciaran grumped.

"It's just curious. You disappear for ages, let everyone think you're dead, and then you come back here—actually at death's door—with this man with you who seems adorably out of his depth. And you've given him your amulet. Was that witch the only one who's put a spell on you, I wonder?" Cu smiled knowingly at his brother, but Ciaran only snorted.

"It's nought to do with you," Ciaran frowned, ignoring Cu's sly smirk. He changed into the offered trousers and even slid on the tall, dark boots his brother presented to him, shifting his weight to test the soft leather. He caught a glimpse of himself in the polished glass across the room and felt a lead weight in his chest. That wasn't Ciaran the Fairy looking back at him. That was Cian mac Cainte, looking stoic and proud. The only thing he was missing was the weight of his shillelagh on his hip. He was glad to feel its absence.

"Go on now," Cu urged him, nudging him toward the door by his shoulder. "Ethniu will bring the whole house down if you keep her waiting."

Ciaran left his brother to his business as the bedroom door was shut behind him, and he took a moment to steel himself before making his way downstairs. Ethniu sat straight-backed in the seat nearest the fireplace, her hands folded neatly in her lap, and her long, dangling earrings caught the light of the fire as she turned her head.

"Cian," she said simply, a very faint frown on her painted lips.

He moved to sit across from her and leaned his elbows on his knees, looking down at his laced fingers rather than at her face. They sat in silence for a long while, but eventually the woman let out a soft sigh.

"You didn't say anything," she murmured in a voice softer than usual. "I know that we were never in love, but I thought that I was your friend. You let me think you were dead. You let me mourn you. Why didn't you say anything?"

Ciaran sighed through his nose and finally looked up at her. "I'm sorry," he said. "I don't...I can hardly remember. This spell that was cast on me, this...sickness. I've...lost a lot. I know that I didn't want to be here anymore. I was—I think I was trapped here. I felt that way." He shook his head. "I know you, but I can't remember being

114

with you. Not really. If I meant to tell you where I was, and something happened, or if I cut all ties and ran…either way, I'm sorry that you grieved for me."

Ethniu's brow softened, and she reached out to take one of Ciaran's hands in hers. "Whatever's been done to you can be undone. That must take priority. Lugh has gone to fetch this witch; when he returns, Dian Cecht will lift the black magic upon you. And if your wish is to return to the surface with your human, then at least this time I'll know to wish you well."

Ciaran let out a quiet chuckle. "I don't think I deserved a friend like you."

"Doubtless you didn't, my treasure," she answered with a little smirk. She glanced toward the door and politely released his hand, straightening in her chair. "But we have company," she said in English, and Ciaran looked over his shoulder to the empty doorway. "Come inside, dear; don't linger in hallways. It's impolite."

Ciaran tensed as Trent leaned his head into the room. He entered as he was called, but he didn't seem to want to come too close.

"I suppose you're surprised to find that Cian left behind a wife when he came to your world," she went on.

"It hadn't come up, no."

"I don't imagine so, what with the lengths he apparently went to to avoid me," she said in a slightly irritated tone. She shot Ciaran a frown, but he could only offer a weak smile in return. "But you're here now, aren't you? And we haven't been properly introduced. I am Ethniu, daughter of Balor, the last king of the Fomorians. You may call me Ethniu," she added, "in light of our…mutual acquaintances."

"Trent Fa," he answered simply, not having any titles of his own to add on to the end.

"Lovely. Do I have you to thank for the state in which you've returned my husband to me, or did he bring this distress upon himself?"

"He didn't do anything, Ethniu," Ciaran cut in. "Don't tease him."

"Oh, don't look so sour, treasure. I'm only trying to talk with your latest love."

Ciaran winced, but when he looked up at Trent, he didn't look angry. He looked resigned, and that made Ciaran's stomachache worse. He moved over on the settee and let Trent take a seat beside him.

"I do have one question," Trent said, and Ethniu lifted her eyebrows at him expectantly. "You're a woman."

"Very astute, dear."

"But Ciaran said he was a...a gan-whatever. Women are supposed to be poisoned by him, and they die without him, right?"

"Ah, so he did tell you that part. The gean cánach; yes. My darling husband is this creature, and the only one of his kind. You would be right about his poisoning me, were I a human woman. But, as I'm sure you've gathered, I am not. The Fomorians are—were—a people more ancient even than the Tuath Dé." She glanced back at Ciaran with a sly smile. "Regardless, lucky for Cian's lovers that his tastes seem to have changed since last I saw him."

Ciaran scoffed in an attempt to diffuse the tension he could feel growing in the young man beside him, but before he could say anything, the bell rang at the front door, and all three of them turned their heads. They heard a servant open the door, and then the conspicuous heavy tread of Lugh's boots in the corridor.

"I've brought your witch, áthair," he called from the front hall. As he entered the room, Noah and Julien followed close behind, and Ciaran got to his feet immediately at the sight of them.

"I told you not to bring that hunter here," Ciaran snapped, his eyes on Julien and a scowl on his lips.

"Oops," Lugh offered dryly.

Ciaran gave a soft growl, but he didn't feel very threatening. He hadn't eaten since early the day before, and his lungs still felt weak and straining. Even just standing was an effort.

Julien stood his ground beside Noah, keeping a protective hand on the witch's shoulder. "As much as I would like to finish what we started," he said through a tight jaw, "it's become more complicated than just killing you."

Ciaran's gaze moved to Noah, and he stepped around the settee to get closer to him. "You," he said in a low, deadly voice. "You have something of mine."

"Believe me, I want to give it back," Noah answered with as much humor as he could muster.

Ciaran drew near to him and reached out to take the witch by the front of his shirt, but as soon as he touched him, a burning flash hit his eyes and he felt the weight of a thousand years of memories crushing down on his shoulders. Everything was a blur—a battlefield, a bedroom, a stretching field of wheat—heat, and hate, and blood. He suddenly found himself on the ground, shoved by Julien's forceful hand, and Trent was at his side, keeping his head from hitting the floor.

"That's quite enough," a stern voice spoke up from the door, and Dian Cecht stepped into the room to stand between the two emerging sides. "I will not have brawls in this house."

Ciaran sat up with a slight wince. "That hunter is the cause of all this," he growled.

Dian Cecht folded his hands behind his back and turned to calmly examine the two new humans in his study. He gave a soft grunt and glanced over at Lugh.

"You had to cause more trouble, didn't you?" Lugh only shrugged.

Dian Cecht took a step closer to Julien and gave him a brief look up and down. "My grandson may have brought you here, but you are not welcome in Tír na nÓg. If you wish to stay, it will be where we can keep a close watch on you. Seventh son," he added in a darker, purposeful tone. He looked past Julien's shoulder at the servant lingering near the door and gave him a brief nod.

"I'm not leaving Noah," Julien insisted, jerking his arm away from the servant's touch.

"Julien," Noah whispered. "This is what we wanted, right? I'll be fine. Just go with them for now. We don't need extra trouble."

"Come along and behave, an duine," Lugh said, and he tilted his head toward the door to urge Julien out with him. The hunter spared Noah one last frowning look and followed Lugh out.

"Airmed should be here shortly," Dian Cecht said, eyeing the distance between Ciaran and Noah. "She will attend to the witch and ensure he survives until we can gather what we need for the spell." He turned to face Noah as Ciaran pulled unsteadily to his feet. "You are needed here, cailleach, but you are not a guest. Do not mistake our aid for hospitality."

"At this point, I'll settle for being kept alive," Noah answered.

Ciaran watched him with narrowed eyes but said nothing. It was infuriating being so close to him, to know that his own stolen memories and magic were hidden away inside of him, just out of reach. He looked over at his father.

"How long do you need before we can do this?"

Dian Cecht stroked his beard thoughtfully. "No more than three days. It will take time to prepare the ingredients, but I will consult your sister." He paused at a ringing from the bell at the door, and he glanced down the hall to wait for the servant to bring their guest.

A woman with dark hair and freckles on her face appeared in the doorway, and she rushed to Ciaran immediately, bypassing her father in favor of taking her brother's face in her hands.

"Cian, go raibh maith dana," she said, her voice wavering just slightly. "I thought I would never see you again." She pulled him down to kiss his cheeks, and Ciaran smiled as he returned her embrace. Airmed was the youngest of them, and he had sometimes felt sorry for her for having so many brothers, but she had always handled their teasing with patience and a gentle smile. Her pale green eyes were bright with restrained tears as she looked up at him, and she took one quick, stabilizing breath.

"I can't believe father didn't send word to me until this morning. Look at the state of you. Why are you on your feet?" She tutted at him and practically pushed him backwards onto the settee. "You'll need a nice hot tea." She turned to the servant who had escorted her in and quickly listed off half a dozen ingredients to include in the tea, then suddenly seemed to remember she was surrounded by people as she was testing Ciaran's temperature with her wrist to his forehead.

"Oh. Lady Ethniu, hello," she said with a faint flush of embarrassment on her face. She gave a quick curtsy and then started at the sight of Trent. "Oh my." She switched to a pleasantly accented English. "And you're the human Cian brought with him? Goodness, what a face; where did you come from? Look at your eyes!"

One of Trent's eyebrows ticked up, and Ciaran could tell the next words out of his mouth would not be polite, so he answered before Trent could.

"Trent is Chinese, Airmed," Ciaran cut in. "It's far from here. You wouldn't have seen anyone from there before," he added with a pleading look at Trent, hoping his lover wasn't about to snap at his tender sister.

"Oh, I didn't mean—" She put a hand to her cheek and then took a step closer to Trent as she touched her heart in apology. "I only meant—it's a lovely face," she finished awkwardly.

"Uh-huh." Trent stared down at her with a tight-lipped frown, and she looked back at Ciaran as though she wanted him to save her. Across the room, Noah attempted to bite back his snort of laughter and only half succeeded.

"Airmed, child," Ciaran said, "since you came all the way here, maybe you could see to the one you're here to keep alive for me?"

"Oh. Oh of course. Yes." She edged by Trent with a shy smile and stepped across the room to Noah, already digging in a small pouch on her belt. "Hello," she offered quietly. "Oh, look at you. You aren't well at all, are you? Father, he needs a place to rest straight away."

Dian Cecht gave a short sight through his nose. "Take him to the guest wing, then," he nodded. "But make sure one of your brothers is watching him before you leave. I won't have him wandering about the estate."

"Yes, father." Airmed turned Noah by his shoulder and pushed him gently out of the room, and the pair of them disappeared down the hall.

Ciaran sighed, and Trent took his place beside him. He was clearly trying not to look too concerned in front of the others. "Three days," Ciaran muttered. "I can wait three days."

"Oh, don't act so sorry for yourself, treasure," Ethniu said with a mild chuckle. "With little Airmed looking after you, you're likely to spend the next three days taking naps and hot herbal baths. We'll have you sorted before you know it."

She seemed much more confident than Ciaran felt.

12

Noah didn't feel particularly good about his situation as he followed the fairy woman down the stone hallway. Being told that he wasn't really a guest and that he would essentially be kept alive until they needed him wasn't exactly comforting. He wished Julien could have stayed with him, but he at least hoped he could count on Lugh to keep the hunter from being murdered.

The woman took a detour to knock on a door along their way, and Noah stared up at the man who answered. He was lightly tanned, with sharp cheekbones and a dusting of dark stubble on his jaw. His grey tunic was rumpled and lopsided as though he had put it on in a hurry, and his brown hair was mussed. His gaze moved from Airmed to Noah with what the witch thought was an almost predatory look, pinning him in place.

"Cu, you're on guard duty," Airmed said, leaving no room for argument. "Come along."

"What, now?"

She gestured back at Noah without looking at him. "This is Cian's witch," she clarified, and Cu's eyebrows lifted as he gave Noah a little look up and down.

"Well," he said with a dark chuckle, "lead on then."

Airmed turned without waiting, and she led them both back down the hall. They turned a few corners and passed a few heavy-looking doors until she reached the end of a corridor, and she pushed open the last door and poked her head inside.

"Yes, this will do nicely," she said to herself, and she waved Noah along behind her as she stepped into the room. She shut the door behind them and gestured at him. "Strip down, then, and let's get a good look at you."

"Strip—what? Why? You know what's wrong with me."

She put her hands on her waist and raised her eyebrows. "I know what my father told me you did to Cian, not your symptoms. Anything might be a clue as to how to treat you. I won't miss something and have you take a turn for the worse. Now go on," she urged.

Noah frowned, and he glanced warily at Cu, who only waited by the door with an amused smile on his face and his arms folded across his chest. Undressing in front of someone who was clearly a fairy version of a doctor was one thing, but stripping naked in front of a man who was watching him the way Cu was—that was something else entirely. Airmed gestured at him to hurry up, and with a short sigh, he pulled his shirt up over his head and let it fall to the floor. He wasn't usually embarrassed by nudity, but it made him uncomfortable to be put on display. He kicked off his worn sneakers and unbuttoned his jeans. He hadn't really meant to lock eyes with Cu as he slid them down his hips, but he caught the fairy's hungry look anyway.

Noah stood on the cool stone floor in his underwear, suddenly wishing he'd been able to afford any new pairs recently—maybe one that didn't have a stretched-out elastic waistband. He tried to avoid looking at Cu and embarrassing himself further.

"Go on," Airmed sighed. "It's only a body."

"What, all of it?" Noah objected, only barely resisting the urge to cover himself. "Why?"

"I won't miss something because you feel timid," she said again, and she gestured encouragingly at him.

"Shall I cover my eyes?" Cu asked in a low voice that ran a shiver down Noah's spine. Why was this fairy adventure suddenly full of ridiculously attractive men? He already felt like an idiot for swooning over Lugh the way he had, and now Cu was standing in front of him with that sly smile and waiting for him to take his underwear off. All of the crap he'd been through with Julien over the last week had kept him constantly on edge, and their kiss definitely hadn't done anything to help. Even though it had been a pretty terrible kiss, Noah still hadn't been able to help that initial rush, the way his heart had stumbled in his chest as the hunter's lips had pressed against his.

Noah felt a stirring in his gut and hastily switched mental gears. This was definitely not the time for thinking about things like that. Not while that smirking fairy was watching him.

Noah glared at him defiantly and pushed his underwear down in one quick movement, determined not to blush. He succeeded, but he suspected it was only because he stopped looking at the other man the instant he straightened again.

Airmed moved forward and began to inspect him, lifting his arms, tilting his head every way it would go, testing and prodding at his every joint. Noah bit his lip and refused to look as she crouched down near him, though he could still feel her hands on his legs as she studied him. He kept his eyes on the far wall and stood as calmly as he could manage, but he jumped slightly when she stood and put her ear against his chest, her hand on his stomach to keep him still.

"Take some deep breaths," she said, and the witch did as he was told. Women had never really done anything for him, but after the week he'd had and the many months he'd spent alone before that, even Airmed's warm touch on his stomach was making him nervous.

She stood up and looked him in the face again with a pensive frown on her lips. "There's fluid in your lungs, and you have a slight fever. Have you been vomiting?"

"A few times," he admitted, and she nodded.

"I thought so. Stay here; I'll mix you some things." She turned and left the room in a soft flurry of skirt, leaving Noah standing naked in the middle of the room with Cu lingering at the door and staring at him.

"What's your name, witch?" the fairy asked as he took a slinking step forward. Noah tensed when he drew close and watched him out of the corner of his eye as the other man circled him.

"Noah," he answered. He started as he felt the man's hand on his back, pressed against the space where Noah's hamsa tattoo sat between his shoulder blades. It was a delicate, ornate hand shape, filled in with a pattern of tiny flower petals, stars, and crescent moons. The fairy's hand slid slowly down his back until his fingertips brushed the curling mandala shapes tattooed onto the witch's hip.

"What are these?" Cu asked instead of addressing the answer to his question. He was so close that Noah could feel the heat from his body, but he didn't dare move.

"They're...just tattoos. The...the hand one is a hamsa, it's...supposed to protect against evil."

"And this?" Cu purred against Noah's ear as his hand settled on the smaller man's tattooed hip.

"It's a mandala," he answered automatically in an attempt to steel himself against the warmth of the touch. "It's a religious thing," he added hastily. "Anyway, could you not?"

Cu gave a soft chuckle as he removed his hand. "Pardon. I've always been an admirer of works of art."

Noah frowned at the fairy's meaningful smile, refusing to acknowledge the sudden thump in his chest. He felt like a teenager, overreacting to the slightest flirtation. It had been way too long. He was starting to get stupid.

"Can I get dressed now?" Noah asked as he shuffled slightly farther away from the other man.

"Oh, I don't think so. Airmed will undoubtedly want to rub you down with some oil or another. Better you just get into bed," he said with a sage nod. "I can help you, if you feel weak."

"I'm good," the witch said before Cu had even finished speaking. He did actually feel weak, of course—he'd been feeling weaker and weaker every day—but he wasn't going to let the fairy touch him again if he could help it. He moved over to the bed, glad to be able to pull the soft down-filled blanket around his hips. For a moment, he felt safer, but then Cu sat down at the edge of the bed beside him, stretching casually back to lean on his hands.

"So what do you have against my brother?" he asked plainly, and Noah sighed.

"I don't have anything against him."

"Then you really ought to consider being more judicious about throwing around those spells of yours."

"It wasn't an accident," Noah objected defensively. "I'm not an idiot."

"Then why try to kill him?"

"What do you care?" Noah sighed, pausing to cough into the crook of his arm. "Why are you talking to me at all? Don't you want to just kill me for what I did?"

"Well, I did," Cu chuckled, "but honestly, I wasn't expecting you."

Noah's brow furrowed as he watched the fairy's face. "What does that mean?"

"It means that in Tír na nÓg, if you call someone a witch, it's a wrinkled old druid or some crone in a mud hut somewhere. Even our word, cailleach, just means a hag. It certainly isn't a young, handsome man."

"Good to know," Noah muttered, and he looked away from Cu's soft green eyes. "So what, you don't want to kill me now?"

"I wouldn't mind giving you just a little death," the fairy answered.

Noah let out a small laugh despite himself. "Really, that's the best you could come up with?" He ignored the faint jump in his stomach. "Is that what counts as flirting down here?" he asked, hoping he could joke his way out of the uncomfortable emptiness he felt. He had spent so long being ignored by Julien, and then being awkward around him, that just to have someone smile and flirt with him seemed like something out of a dream.

"I'm nothing if not forward," Cu smiled. "So tell me why. Why try to kill my brother? You're a witch; you're not some sort of magic hunter like that other one they mentioned, are you?"

"Of course not," Noah said immediately, but it felt a little like a lie. How many creatures had he helped Julien hunt down and kill over the last few months, just because Julien had decided they were dangerous? Granted, most of them were dangerous—but so was a lion, and nobody was hunting them down for extermination.

He sighed. "I've been…helping him. A little. He asked for my help with this. Your brother was giving him a lot of trouble."

"I imagine so," Cu laughed. "Cian isn't someone I'd want to start a fight with, and I know all his tricks." He tilted his head and leaned slightly closer to Noah. "But why help? Why seek out and kill your own kind?"

"My own—oh, no," Noah said. "It's not like that. Julien doesn't kill witches. The things he hunts are monsters—lamias, shapeshifters, werewolves—"

"Magic things," Cu clarified for him.

"Yeah, but it's not—"

"You're the exception, then?" the fairy asked. "The one good magic creature in a sea of evil?"

Noah remembered the way Julien had shouted at him, warned him about using his magic in front of people. No matter what the hunter had said about trusting him, about being his friend, Noah had known in that moment that if he stepped too far out of line, Julien's code of ethics would have forced him to take action. Noah didn't know what he would have done, but it wouldn't have been pleasant. The thought of having to run from Julien turned his stomach.

"I guess I thought I was," he answered after a moment.

"I know that face," Cu said in a low voice. "I've seen it on poor Cethen's face a hundred times."

"What face?" Noah said defensively, instinctively curling his fingers into the blanket. "I'm not making a face."

The fairy smiled at him. "Oh, no. That's the unrequited love face. This hunter's caught you by the heart, hasn't he?"

Noah couldn't answer. He'd avoided framing it in his mind that way—unrequited love. He'd had a crush on Julien, he'd told himself, or he'd cared about him like a friend and wanted to help him. Even when he'd admitted to himself that it was love, he'd always thought of it as a stupid, pointless thing—a feeling that didn't matter and could never mean anything. Now that Julien had answered his confession with a simple "I care about you," the whole thing seemed even more futile.

"Not to worry," Cu went on in Noah's silence, "we've all done stupid things for people that don't appreciate them, hm?"

Noah could feel his resolve crumbling. He didn't want to be in this place—partly because of the fairy's memories inside him and partly because he was just tired of the whole situation. He had shown his hand with Julien and gotten a pity kiss for his trouble, which hadn't done anything but make him even more frustrated. He had been forced to abandon his apartment, his job, and he'd even left his last letter to Sabin in the hotel room. Now he was terminally ill and dependent on the family of the person he'd tried to kill to make him well again—all for Julien's sake. He felt like an idiot.

"I was just trying to help," he said before he even realized he'd opened his mouth to speak. "I just wanted to make him happy, and I tried to do what he wanted and help him, and he just never noticed, and I know he thinks I'm dangerous and he just won't say it, and then when I finally told him he just felt sorry for me, and now everything's fucked up and he's so fucking straight and I'm sitting here talking to the brother of somebody I tried to kill for him, and that's not me, I don't want to hurt anybody, I just wanted him to notice—"

"Woah, woah," Cu interrupted, and when he held out his hands to get Noah to take a breath, the witch slumped forward with his forehead against the fairy's shoulder, dripping hot tears onto his shirt. Cu hesitated for a moment, uncertain, and then he laid a gentle hand on the boy's back and let him slowly learn to breathe again. He quietly shushed him until he stopped trembling, waiting patiently while the witch huffed a final sigh against his chest and sat up.

"I'm sorry," Noah murmured miserably as he wiped at his cheeks with the back of his hand. "It's been a rough week."

"I couldn't tell," Cu chuckled. "Well, in a moment my sister will come back and make you uncomfortable again, so you have that to look forward to." Noah smiled down at the blanket, and Cu reached out to touch a knuckle under the witch's chin. "We'll get the magic sorted out, and we'll get you and my brother back to normal. As for that hunter," he added, Noah looking up at him with a wary frown, "you don't ever let him tell you that your magic is anything but a gift. Magic is beautiful, and rare, and all too overlooked in the world above. Magic built this city, and magic made my people what we are. It's made you what you are—I've only just met you, and I can see that you're handsome, and strong, and kind. If he can't see that, then that's his own failing, not yours."

Noah didn't answer, but he felt a slow warmth in his stomach that he'd almost forgotten. He'd spent so long chasing after Julien, justifying himself, that just to hear someone tell him that he was worthwhile made him want to cry all over again. He held it in and simply nodded.

"In the meantime, if you get lonely, apparently I'm guarding you, so let me know about that little death situation."

Noah felt his face go hot, but before he could answer, the door opened again, and Airmed entered with her arms full of bottles and vials of various sizes. Cu gave Noah an I-told-you-so smile and moved out of the way to allow his sister to unceremoniously toss the blankets away from Noah's naked body.

13

Lugh didn't need to keep a hand on Julien to keep him in line as they walked the path from the house, and they both knew it. Julien wasn't going to risk doing anything that might make them retaliate against Noah, and he was sure Lugh didn't think of him as any kind of a threat. They both followed the servant down a winding path that led from the back of the enormous house through the back garden, the light from the house growing dimmer the farther they went.

At the far back end of the garden sat a stone entrance to what looked like a cellar. The servant pulled the heavy doors open and led the way down the dark staircase into the ground. Julien followed despite the wariness in his gut, and Lugh brought up the rear. The blue lanterns were farther apart down here, keeping the stone corridor dark and damp. When they reached a short row of small cells barred with silver, the servant unlocked the one deepest in the cellar with a key from the heavy ring on his belt, and Lugh unceremoniously lifted Julien's bag from the hunter's shoulder and dropped it to the ground at his feet.

"Any other weapons?" Lugh asked flatly as he stared down at him, clearly not even entertaining the possibility that Julien would lie to him.

With an indignant sigh, Julien began to disarm himself, leaving his iron knife, a few other small blades, vials of various liquids, and one of his small handguns in a pile on top of his bag. It took him a while with one arm still in its sling, but Lugh was patient, and Julien finally looked up at Lugh with a small huff as though asking if he was satisfied.

"Be thankful you're getting to stay at all," Lugh said. He pushed Julien into the cell with one firm hand and shut the barred door behind him, allowing the servant to lock it again. "My father would have been within his rights to kill you. He still may."

"What are they going to do with Noah?"

"Make sure he stays alive until they can perform the reversal spell, probably," Lugh shrugged. "Once that's done, they'll decide what to do with you. You really should have stayed behind."

"You mean they'll decide what to do with us," Julien clarified. He stepped forward to grip the silver gate with his good hand.

Lugh gave a quiet scoff. "If the witch survives, I suppose, yes."

Julien's heart sank into his stomach. Had he brought Noah right to a certain death? "Why wouldn't he survive? What are they going to do to him?"

"He has my father's magic in him," Lugh answered. "Getting it out again isn't going to be easy on him. It's been days already, and a Tuath Dé's spirit is strong. The longer it takes, the tighter the hold it will have on your little witch."

Julien fought not to sway on his feet. He'd known there would be risk involved in whatever they tried, but to hear that Noah's chances diminished every moment, and Julien had just allowed himself to be locked in a cage—what had he done?

"Worry about yourself," Lugh advised, and he glanced down at the servant and tilted his head to indicate that they were leaving. "The witch is dead no matter what." They left Julien alone in the dank corridor with only the echo of the cellar door shutting heavily behind them, and the hunter sank to the ground with his heart as heavy as lead in his chest.

He only allowed himself a moment of despair before he set his jaw and pulled himself back to his feet, checking every inch of the silver bars for weaknesses. The other three walls of his cell were made of heavy stone, but he still inspected each mortared line, digging his fingernails between the stones in search of anywhere he might be able to breach. He took the small pocketknife he'd left hidden in his boot and scraped at the stone in a few places, testing every spot that seemed likely in the slightest. There was always an answer. There was always a way out.

By the time he heard the door open at the end of the corridor, his hands were filthy—he had abandoned his sling on the stone floor in favor of being able to use both hands to search, despite the pain it gave his wrist to use it. As soon as the door banged open, Julien folded his knife and tucked it back into his boot. He leaned forward to peer through the silver bars but took a half step back when his visitor stepped into the light of the lantern outside his cell. The woman was slender and petite, with wide green eyes and dark hair swept up into a messy knot at the back of her head, showing the tips of her pointed ears. Her dress was simple but elegant, the soft purple fabric brushing the stone as she took one last step toward him. She peered up at Julien curiously, a basket of vials and small boxes held in her hands.

"So you're the vicious hunter," she said with a light, gentle brogue, and she set down her basket just out of his reach. "The one who came with the witch?"

"Where is he?" Julien asked instead of answering. "What have they done to him?"

"They," she said, touching a hand to her chest to indicate she was really talking about herself, "checked him for injuries, applied some healing oils, and put him to bed. He asked if I would check on you down here."

Julien stalled, temporarily stunned into silence. "Oh," he said eventually.

"He's fine," she added with a reassuring smile. "And you don't seem so vicious." She took a step toward him and leaned forward to peer down her nose at his hands. "Though you do seem a bit dirty. Is that a splint?"

Julien glanced down at his wrapped wrist. Noah had re-bandaged it for him, reapplied his oils, and tucked his herbs into the gauze, but his hand was still pretty useless, especially after he had spent the last hour or so abusing it by trying to scratch through stone. He nodded with a small shrug.

"It's broken," he said, and she clicked her tongue at him and held out her hand.

"Give us a look." Julien hesitated a moment, and she wiggled her fingers at him encouragingly, so he stepped forward and slipped his arm through the bars for her inspection. She immediately began to undo all of Noah's work, brushing aside his carefully chosen herbs and only pausing to sniff at the oil-soaked bandages before letting them drift to the floor at her feet.

"Did he do this? Your witch," she clarified, and Julien felt a tug of guilt in his stomach at the second person to refer to Noah as <u>his</u> witch. He nodded, and the woman gave a soft sound of approval. "He isn't bad," she said, "but this will still take weeks to heal. We can do better than that, I think." She took Julien's hand gently in both of hers and ran her palms slowly over his skin, humming a quiet, mournful tune in her throat that made Julien's whole arm go warm. She squeezed his wrist and seemed to press it effortlessly into place.

"Joint to joint, sinew to sinew," she said with a somewhat sad smile. Heat radiated upwards from her touch, into his shoulder and just barely brushing his chest, and then she stopped, turning his hand in hers once more before releasing him.

Julien tested the joint, rolling his hand and twisting the wrist a few times, but the pain was gone. He looked down at her, impressed, and she smiled.

"My name is Airmed, by the way."

"Julien," he answered. "Julien Fournier."

Airmed paused in digging through her basket and looked up at him. "I haven't heard a name that makes that sound in some time. Are you a Gaul?"

Julien frowned at her. "A what?"

"A Gaul," she said again, and she picked a vial from her collection and stood to face him again. "A similar people to the Milesians who settled here, but men from the mainland. I spoke to them sometimes, in the days when we still went above ground. Their language made the same sound as your name. Julien Fournier," she repeated, exaggerating his French accent.

"I'm from Montréal," Julien shrugged. He watched her curiously as she turned the vial in her hand, her pale eyes on his.

She urged him closer and reached out to put a hand to his forehead, testing him for fever. "You're overtired," she said, "but not ill. Drink this." She passed him the vial through the bars, but he hesitated and stared down warily at the dark liquid.

"What is it?"

"Just a tonic. It will revive you, help you rest."

"More magic," Julien muttered. She ticked an eyebrow at him.

"You didn't complain about the magic that fixed your broken wrist, Gaul," she scolded, and Julien felt a small smile touch his lips despite himself. He spared her one more glance before uncorking the vial and downing the contents in one swallow. It tasted bitter, and the heat of it sank to the bottom of his stomach like a weight, but he felt it working immediately. His head was clearer, and his muscles stopped aching. Airmed held her hand out for the vial, and he gave it back to her with a look of surprise.

"I told you," she said with a smile. She dropped the empty vial back into her basket and looked back at him. "So, Julien Fournier of Montréal," she began in a mockery of his accent, "why have you come to Tír na nÓg? I know why my nephew brought your witch here, but why did you come? Trying one last time to kill my brother, right when we've got him back?"

"Your brother?" Julien echoed, and she nodded.

"That is who you followed here, of course."

Julien hesitated. He didn't particularly feel like baring his soul to this woman, but she stared at him with such openness that he would have felt guilty to lie to her.

"I came to protect him," he said, deciding on the simplest of answers. "The witch—Noah. I got him into all of this. I should be the one to keep him safe."

"Interesting," she hummed. She picked up her basket and held it in front of her while she gave Julien one last look up and down. "And a seventh son, besides," she mused, almost to herself. "Hm. Well, Julien Fournier, if you can behave yourself, I'll be back later this evening with some food for you." She turned and started back down the corridor without waiting for an answer, the sound of her footsteps disappearing as the cellar door dropped shut behind her.

Julien let out a sigh and leaned against the bars of his cage, letting his forehead touch the cool metal. At least they would keep Noah alive and healthy until they could do whatever it is they planned on doing to reverse the spell. He had some time. He had no way of knowing how much, but any time at all was enough. He still wished to God he had any cigarettes left. He waited a moment to listen for anyone else in the hall, and then he took his knife from his boot and returned to his work.

As promised, Airmed returned a few hours later, and this time her basket was covered with a cloth. She set it down near the door to Julien's cell and sat down on the stone beside the bars, spreading her dark skirt out around her gracefully tucked knees. She looked up at Julien when he hesitated at the far end of the cell.

"Come on; you must be hungry," she urged him. She lifted the cloth from the basket, and the smell of warm bread and tea wafted across to him and made his stomach growl audibly. "I promise only half of it is poisoned," she teased as he relented and took a seat at the other side of the bars. She passed him breads with soft, sweet fillings and filled a tin cup with some tea for him, which he drank eagerly. She sat with him and ate her share of the meal, letting him have his fill in silence.

"Your witch is fine," she said after a while, and Julien paused to look at her through the bars. "He had something to eat, and a hot bath, and I left him asleep. My brother is keeping an eye on him—not that brother," she added at the sight of Julien's scowl. She shrugged one shoulder and offered him an innocent, sidelong smile. "I thought you'd like to know."

"Thank you," Julien answered without lifting his eyes from his empty cup. He still had time.

"How did you get involved with a witch?" she asked, her mouth still half full of bread. "I understood you were some sort of magic hunter. Isn't a witch a magic creature?"

"Noah isn't a creature," he countered immediately, but she only watched him with a placid, patient smile. He shifted his weight to better settle himself on the hard stone floor. "He helped me," Julien admitted after a moment. "He did...research for me, and he helped me hunt down things that put people in danger. He became my partner without my realizing it."

"And how long have you two been together?"

"A few months," Julien shrugged. He turned his empty cup in his hands. "Since I arrived in Vancouver."

"Well it's very sweet of you to do all of this for his sake," she said. "It must be hard for you to be away from him."

The hunter sighed through his nose. "It is," he murmured under his breath, but then he paused and looked up at her with a puzzled frown. "Wait, did you think—when you asked if we—we aren't *together*," he clarified, though he could feel the unwelcome heat in his face as he said it.

She lifted her eyebrows at him. "Oh? But you came here knowing what might happen to you. Tír na nÓg is a dangerous place. Not a journey to be made lightly, and yet you came, determined to protect him, and it's obvious you've spent every minute in that cell looking for a way to get out. Don't argue," she cut him off when he opened his mouth to object. "I can see your hands. You aren't concerned for yourself at all, are you?" she asked with a warm smile.

Julien couldn't meet her eyes. His stomach churned uncomfortably. He knew that she was right, of course—he'd known there couldn't be any more avoiding the truth when he had heard Noah say out loud, "I love you." He was unsure of himself, and that was an unfamiliar feeling that he hadn't taken to well, but he couldn't pretend anymore that he didn't have feelings for the witch. Unexpected feelings that bordered on romance, maybe—Julien had so little experience with romance of any kind that he wasn't certain he would recognize the feeling anyway. He wanted Noah safe, and happy, and protected, and he wanted to be the one to keep him that way. He'd thought that was what romance was, and he thought he'd made his feelings clear, but Noah had acted so put off at his kiss that he wasn't sure he hadn't ruined the whole thing.

"It's complicated," he said rather than explain himself.

Light laughter bubbled out of her, and she set down her half-eaten bread and nudged closer to the bars with a little shuffle. "Nothing is so complicated or so simple as being in love, Julien Fournier."

The hunter tensed, his grip tightening on his cup.

"Then you want to be together, but you aren't? What's stopping you?"

Julien shook his head. He didn't want to tell this woman everything. He could barely tell Noah how he felt, so a complete stranger was—he paused. She was a stranger. And a fairy, besides. What did he care what she thought of him? But if she had any insight at all, any advice—Julien felt like an idiot, but if it meant avoiding making a fool of himself in front of Noah again, he would gladly make a fool of himself in front of this woman who seemed so eager to listen.

He took a slow, steeling breath. He could just pretend he was talking to himself. He was just trying to work things out. She was only a sounding board. "Well firstly, he's a man," he began, "and that's...untried territory for me."

"Oh," she breathed, putting a delicate hand to her mouth.

"Right. And he's a witch, and I'm...a seventh son," he sighed. "Hunting magic things is what I do. It's my lineage and my life. Professionally, I wouldn't consider Noah a danger, but personally...I can't help feeling I shouldn't get too close."

"But you are close?" Airmed asked in a whisper.

"Closer than I realized," he answered softly. "He told me that he wanted to be more than friends, and I...I used him. I convinced him to cast that spell on your brother, even though we both knew it was dangerous. He did it for me. I knew I was using him, but I just..." He scoffed and shook his head. "I assumed everything would be fine. It never occurred to me that any of this would happen. That Noah would actually get hurt, that we'd end up chasing this fairy down and that I'd put him in danger all over again. I was too focused on my work, on making the kill, and I—I don't know if he knows how much I regret it."

"Well, have you told him how much you regret it, perhaps?"

"Of course I have," Julien insisted. "I told him that I was sorry, that I would make it right, protect him—"

"But did you tell him how you *feel?*" she pressed.

"That is how I feel," the hunter defended himself.

She sighed. "Well, and then? He said he wanted to be more than friends, and you told him you were sorry?"

"I said that we would...talk. There are a dozen reasons we shouldn't pursue anything, of course, like I said," he started, anxiously fidgeting with the cup in his hands until he set it down with a huff. "I've never even been attracted to men, and he's a witch, and he's so much younger than I am. He's so...careless, and he laughs so easily, and I've always been...single-minded. He would get bored with me. And he was happily settled in Vancouver, and I travel all over; I couldn't ask him to uproot his life for me. Even if that's what ended up happening anyway," he finished solemnly.

Airmed had moved closer to him as he spoke, so that now her chin was almost resting on one of the silver cross bars separating them. "But you had your talk?" she asked. Julien nodded. "And what happened? What did you talk about?"

Julien peeked up at her and wet his lips before speaking. "He told me that he loved me." The hunter's heart skipped at the simple memory of Noah's face, resigned but smiling as he had spoken what he must have thought was the obvious truth.

"And you said?" Airmed put her hands on the bars.

"I...told him that I trusted him."

Airmed stared at him, her shoulders deflating. "That you trusted him. He says, Julien Fournier, I'm in love with you, and you told him that you trusted him."

The hunter frowned defensively at her. "I don't trust anyone," he said, as though that should have explained everything.

She slumped against the bars with a soft laugh. "Men are hopeless," she sighed.

"But we—" He felt his face burn with embarrassment, but we went on. "I'm not good with words. I tried to...show him." She perked up again, her lips pursing just slightly as she listened. "I...kissed him, but I guess it—it didn't go as planned. He pushed me away, and I said I just wanted to give him what he wanted—"

Airmed visibly cringed, and Julien stopped talking to frown at her.

"What?"

"You said that? You said those words. That you wanted to give him what he wanted?"

"Yes?" Julien answered, though he felt less than confident about his response.

She reached through the bars and swatted at him with both hands. "Oh, I should have left you here to starve to death, you absolute brute.

You must have crushed him!"

Julien leaned back and lifted his hands to block her blows. "What? Why? I do want to—"

"But you can't just kiss someone who's in love with you and then make them think you didn't want to!"

"I didn't—how did I do that? Why would I do it if I didn't want to?"

"Let me help you." She leaned back and held up one hand to count on her fingers. "He tells you he has feelings for you. You respond by convincing him to cast a spell that might kill him. You feel bad about it, and you tell him you're sorry," she sighed, puffing out her cheeks. "You say you'll have a talk with him about your feelings, and he says that he's in love with you. So you say, I trust you, and you kiss him, but you tell him that it's only because you thought that's what he wanted. Can you honestly not tell how any of that might be taken poorly?"

Julien frowned down at his hands rather than look at Airmed's despairing face. Put like that, he couldn't deny how badly he'd handled the whole situation. As awful and unsure as he felt, Noah must have felt ten times worse.

"Answer me this," she said as she folded her hands back into her lap. "What is it that you want from him?"

Julien hesitated. He knew what he wanted. He knew how impossible it had been to get the witch out of his mind, in every way imaginable—he wanted to sit with him in his cheap apartment and eat takeaway noodles, and he wanted to see him smile and watch him grind up strange herbs in his mortar and pestle while he sat cross-legged on the floor. He wanted to feel the press of the boy's body against his again, but because Noah wanted to touch him, and not because the fairy spirit in his head was having a dirty memory. He wanted to kiss him and not be pushed away. He wanted to be sure in himself, but failing that—he wanted to try.

"I want...him," Julien admitted under his breath. He didn't have to look to know there was a smile on Airmed's face.

"Then you ought to try telling him that you're in love with him," she said softly. The thought wasn't so startling now.

"Maybe I should," Julien whispered, mostly to himself.

"I'll tell you what," she added in a brighter voice as she tapped on the bars, "tomorrow I'll see if I can sneak him in. If he's with me, I don't think anyone will question it so long as we're discreet. You two can talk."

The hunter let out a low chuckle and looked back up at her. "You're being very kind to the two men who tried to kill your brother."

She waved a hand at him. "I love my brother, but he's had people trying to kill him for thousands of years, I'm sure. Besides, I can't resist a good love story. Now, in the meantime, how about some practice?" She turned to rest her back against the bars and settled in. "Tell me some stories. About your witch. Tell me everything that made you fall in love with him, and then maybe it will be easier to tell him that you have."

Julien actually gave a soft laugh. "Well, I met him one night after I'd had a run-in with a lamia."

14

Ciaran had tried to pace anxiously after he and Trent had finally gone back to their room, but he kept coughing and stopping to lean against the mantle above the fireplace.

"Will you sit down already?" Trent sighed from his chair. "Drink your tea."

"He's here; he's right here," Ciaran growled. "That witch has my—he has *me*, and he's right here, and I have to wait?"

"What do you want to do? Stick your arm down his throat and pull your soul out, maybe?"

"And that hunter," Ciaran went on, apparently not listening. "They're just going to let him stay? Why would Lugh bring him here? He's the cause of all this," he snapped. "I ought to strangle him in his sleep."

Trent frowned as Ciaran worked himself into another fit of coughs. "Just drink your tea and contemplate cold-blooded murder later, hm?"

Ciaran grumpily took a drink from his cup and immediately made a face, since the brew had long ago gone cold. "This is bullshit," he muttered.

"This is what we came here for," Trent reminded him. "A hundred things could have gone wrong before we got to this stage, but now we're here, he's here, and they're going to do whatever fairy bullshit they need to do to fix you. Isn't that enough?"

"Three days," Ciaran muttered. "Anything can happen in three days."

Trent sighed and leaned back in his chair. Ciaran was understandably agitated, but it wasn't doing his health any good to stay so worked up, and it was pissing Trent off, besides. "Look, I let you walk me through town pretending to be your slave, so you can relax in a fairy castle and take hot baths for three days. You'll survive."

Ciaran let out a soft snort, and he paused in his pacing to peer across the room at Trent. "You were only pretending to be my slave?"

"Shut up."

The fairy slipped over to him and leaned down to rest his hands on the arms of Trent's chair. He bent close to the younger man's face with a teasing smile. "You can't fool me," he murmured softly. "I saw the way you jumped when I tightened that belt. If you wanted me to tie you down, you know you only had to ask, a mhuirnín."

"Oh fuck off," Trent mumbled, and he pushed on Ciaran's chest to put some distance between them, but the fairy stayed put.

"Or maybe you were waiting for me to tell you what to do?" He leaned down to touch a kiss to the corner of Trent's mouth despite the other man's soft growl. "I noticed how much you liked being made to submit," he whispered against Trent's cheek.

Trent's grip tightened on the chair, but he didn't move. He wasn't about to give Ciaran the satisfaction of knowing how it had made him tremble to be pushed face down on the bed, to feel his lover's tongue on him—he tried to stop that train of thought before he went too far, but he could already feel the heat pooling in his stomach.

"You really want to do this now?" Trent said, not entirely managing to keep his voice from wavering. He hated how the fairy could drop his defenses so effortlessly. "Aren't you supposed to be resting?"

Ciaran let out a low chuckle and slipped his hand up Trent's thigh, gripping him over his trousers and causing him to inhale sharply through his teeth. "I have three days of hot baths ahead of me," he murmured, easily stroking the younger man to almost painful hardness. "I'm going to need some way to pass the time."

Trent tried to answer, but he didn't have any sarcasm left. When Ciaran bent to kiss him, he eagerly returned it, opening his mouth to him and letting the fairy's tongue explore his mouth with aching slowness. He felt Ciaran's hand move away from him and groaned in protest, but then came the soft sound of his zipper, and he sighed into the fairy's mouth in relief as his erection was freed from his pants.

Ciaran gripped him loosely, idly stroking him until Trent was bucking impatiently into his lover's hand. The fairy tutted at him and fastened his teeth onto the younger man's neck, a rumbling laugh in his chest at Trent's sharp gasp. Ciaran worked his way up to Trent's earlobe and gave it a sharp nip before whispering, "Get up."

Trent stood as Ciaran moved back to allow him space, immediately stepping in close to the fairy again to catch him in another kiss. Ciaran pulled away with a soft chuckle and unfastened the soft leather belt around his hips. He gestured with one finger for Trent to turn around, but the younger man scowled at him.

"You're not serious."

"I'm not asking, a mhuirnín."

Trent hesitated, his stomach already fluttering at Ciaran's suggestion. He had been nervous enough to let Ciaran take control before, and now he would be giving up even more. The thought made his heart race, but if Ciaran knew, he would be insufferable. So Trent did his best to sigh with resignation and turned his back on the fairy, holding his hands together behind him. Ciaran was up against him in an instant, gripping his wrists and wrapping the leather strap three times around his hands. Trent tensed as Ciaran tightened the belt and fastened it securely, locking his hands in place.

Ciaran growled in satisfaction and slipped around to Trent's front, his hands gliding smoothly across the soft fabric of the younger man's shirt. He started with a kiss to the hollow of Trent's neck as deft fingers worked at his buttons, exposing his tan skin to Ciaran's eager mouth inch by inch. Trent instinctively pulled against his bonds, desperate to put his hands on the fairy, but Ciaran only chuckled low in his throat.

"You're making no decisions here, a mhuirnín," he purred against Trent's stomach as he crouched to undo the last of his buttons. He gave one single, lingering lick to the tip of Trent's exposed erection, tasting the pearl of liquid there and drawing a guttural moan from the other man.

"You know, it occurs to me," Ciaran began softly as he stood, "that we've been lacking a certain…reciprocation."

"What?" Trent panted. He could barely focus on Ciaran's words—the cool air of the bedchamber drew up goosebumps on his heated skin, and he longed for the fairy's touch, but Ciaran had taken a step back to look at him. He felt flustered and exposed, with his pants undone and pushed down low on his hips, his shirt open to show his flat stomach.

"You're so good at doing what you're told," Ciaran went on with a sly smile. "But there's something I haven't yet told you to do." He reached out to Trent, and a shuddering sigh escaped the younger man as Ciaran drew a single fingertip from the base of his cock to the tip. Trent grit his teeth to hold in the whine threatening to spill from his lips. He wanted to be let loose, to touch Ciaran and hold him and stroke him in turn, but he could feel the trembling of anticipation in his skin as he waited for the fairy to finish his thought.

Ciaran moved close to him and left a sharp bite on his jaw, his lips hot against Trent's skin as he whispered, "On your knees."

Trent didn't even attempt to argue. He spared an uncertain look at Ciaran, but the fairy only raised his eyebrows at him expectantly, so Trent shifted and dropped down to his knees as gracefully as he could without steadying himself with his hands. Ciaran pulled his tunic up over his head and tossed it carelessly aside, and he watched Trent with a slow smirk on his lips as he tugged at the tied strings holding up his trousers.

"Have you ever done this before, a rún?" Ciaran murmured softly, reaching down to caress his lover's cheek with his thumb.

The simple touch sent a jolt straight to Trent's aching groin, and he heard a quiet moan slip from his lips against his will. He couldn't take his eyes off of the smooth skin at Ciaran's hips, the soft hint of dark curls as he pulled the last string free of its knot. He only looked up at Ciaran's face when the fairy tapped a reminding finger on his cheek.

"Don't ignore me," he said in a voice that sounded dangerously low.

"I…haven't," Trent admitted, feeling the flush of embarrassment in his cheeks. His stomach twisted at the sight of Ciaran's smile. It wasn't entirely the truth that he'd never done it before, but the only time he'd tried, he'd managed to choke himself the first time the other boy had thrust. It hadn't been pretty, and Trent had been loath to try again. He watched, his bottom lip caught nervously in his teeth, as Ciaran pushed at the rough fabric of his borrowed trousers. When the fairy was fully revealed in front of him, Trent hesitated just a moment, and Ciaran's sudden tight grip on his jaw gave him pause as he started to lean in to him.

"No teeth," Ciaran advised with a teasing grin, and Trent managed a derisive snort despite the ache in his belly. He was glad that his hands were tied; it was easier to hide their trembling in fists behind his back.

He brushed his tongue tentatively up Ciaran's length, savoring the heat of the silky skin. The fairy sighed, his hand moving slowly up to fix his fingers in Trent's dark hair. He whispered something in Gaelic that Trent didn't understand but took as encouragement, so he shifted on his knees and inched closer. Trent hesitated with his lips at the tip of Ciaran's straining cock, trying to steel himself and catch his breath, and he waited so long that that fairy's grip tightened in his hair in time with a growl of impatience. The noise made his own erection twitch in response, and he pressed forward, taking as much of Ciaran's length into his mouth as he dared.

Ciaran immediately groaned, pulling Trent closer, but the younger man resisted the urging press of his lover's hand, instead letting his tongue run over him with uncertain slowness. Every beat of Ciaran's heart made him pulse inside Trent's mouth, and the fairy's soft moans and pleading whispers bolstered his confidence, allowing him to draw him deeper and taste the salty liquid seeping from him. Even though he couldn't use his hands, Trent could feel his lover's breath hitching with every brush of his tongue, and Ciaran's hand in his hair was gentle and insistent all at once. He never pulled Trent farther than he wanted to go, but as Ciaran's panting grew faster, Trent grew bolder, pressing deep enough to feel him touch the back of his throat. Ciaran swayed on his feet, his free hand blindly searching for the bedpost to steady himself and his grip faltering in Trent's hair. It was satisfying to see the confident fairy suddenly whimpering at his touch, his face flushed and his lips parted, skin trembling from Trent's eager ministrations.

"Stad, stad," Ciaran half begged, "nó ní bheidh mé in ann stad." He tried to retreat and pull Trent away by his hair, and the younger man released him, his breath coming in gasping pants as he sat back on his heels. He looked up at Ciaran in confusion, but the fairy immediately pulled him to his feet and caught him in a kiss. Trent groaned into his mouth as Ciaran tugged frantically at his shirt, pushing it down past his shoulders and letting it bunch around his bound hands.

"Get on that bed," Ciaran growled against his lips, and he turned Trent by his arm and pushed him down onto the blankets without waiting for an answer. He crawled up behind him and reached forward to take hold of the waistband of his pants, and Trent fell face first into the bed as Ciaran lifted him by the hips to pull his trousers down his legs.

"Easy," Trent grumped as he fell back to the bed, but Ciaran pushed him forward until his elbows were at the edge of the bed and leaned over him to bite at his ear.

"Open up your bag," he growled against Trent's neck, "and find that little bottle we packed." He pressed a hot kiss to the younger man's shoulder blade, sending a shiver down his spine as Ciaran unfastened the belt around his wrists. "Because I'm going to fuck you blind."

Trent bit his lip to hide the whine in his throat as he reached out for his abandoned bag, his cheek pressing into the blanket without the support of his elbows. He tried to focus his attention on searching his bag, but it was difficult with Ciaran nipping at his back and pressing his fingers against his entrance. His skin was trembling under the fairy's biting kisses, and once or twice Trent had to close his eyes to steady his breath, but he managed to find the bottle of lubricant at the bottom of his duffel bag and offer it over his shoulder.

"Good lad," Ciaran whispered against the shell of Trent's ear, and he took the bottle and dropped it conveniently near him. He pulled Trent further onto the bed and turned him onto his back, straddling his hips and pinning his arms over his head. He wrapped the belt around each of the younger man's wrists and then around the bedpost, and Trent shuddered at the sound of the softly creaking leather securing him to the bed.

He still desperately longed to touch Ciaran, but the sight of the fairy above him, that smirk on his lips as he pushed his dark hair out of his face, his bottom lip caught in one sharp canine—it made Trent shudder almost as much as actually feeling his skin under his hands.

The fairy took his time opening the small bottle, clearly savoring every shallow rise and fall of Trent's chest. Trent was determined not to squirm, but his hands jerked involuntarily against his bonds as Ciaran reached one slick finger down to touch him, and his cheeks burned as his lover urged his legs open with a slow touch to his inner thigh.

"That's it," Ciaran chuckled. "Let me look at you." Trent bucked against him, biting the inside of his cheek so hard he was certain he'd draw blood. He hated the shakiness of the muscles in his legs as Ciaran teased him into readiness, probing him with slender fingers, and he turned his head away to hide his moan in his bicep when the fairy brushed that secret, sensitive spot deep inside of him. He could feel the smear of wetness on his stomach from his own seeping erection, and he twisted his hips with a whimper, seeking friction. He almost sobbed at the sudden loss of Ciaran's fingers, but found himself lifting his hips impatiently as he felt the pressure of the fairy's cock at his entrance.

Ciaran pushed against him, not quite enough to slip inside, and he hooked his elbows under Trent's knees to keep his hips raised. "Eager little thing, aren't you," he said with a grin, and Trent growled at him and rolled his hips in an attempt to hurry him along. "What is it you want, a rún? You must tell me, or I'll never know."

"Just hurry up," Trent panted, his hands clenched painfully tight around the leather holding him.

"Hurry up and what?" Ciaran inched forward, and Trent's back bowed at the delicious burn of the fairy beginning to stretch him. "Don't mumble, now."

"Please," Trent whimpered in place of a real answer, burning with shame at the begging he'd been reduced to. Ciaran growled and slid forward, burying himself in the younger man until he had no more to give.

"Ah, a rún, conas is féidir liom a dhiúltú duit, when you make that sound," he panted. Trent's head fell back helplessly against the blanket as the fairy began to move, his body feeling flooded and hot, and he pushed back as much as Ciaran's grip would allow him. He couldn't keep in his desperate moans; his shame was forgotten, his skin too alive and electric for his mind to take over. He let the fairy take him, harder and harder until he thought he would break, and when he finally felt Ciaran's hand wrap around his painfully hard cock, he cried out so loudly he was sure the whole hall must have heard him.

Trent rolled and twisted against the fairy's touch, his mouth hung open as he panted, until the coiled spring in his belly snapped, and he spilled hot liquid onto his stomach with a strained cry. Ciaran was relentless, driving into him again and again until suddenly he gripped Trent's thighs hard enough to leave bruises, his own shuddering groan slipping out of him as he finished deep inside his lover.

Both men collapsed after Ciaran carefully removed himself, and they lay together, the sheen of sweat on their bodies making them shiver in the cool air. After he was able to catch his breath, Trent peered down at Ciaran and cleared his throat, tugging pointedly at his bound wrists.

The fairy chuckled. "Sorry," he muttered, and he reached up to undo the buckled leather, the belt dropping to the floor with a heavy clunk. Trent massaged the feeling back into his hands and turned to tuck his head under Ciaran's chin as the other man tugged the blanket up around them to keep off the chill of the room.

"You really are a bit beggy, aren't you?" Ciaran rumbled lazily, and he jumped with a small laugh when Trent flicked him in the stomach.

"Can't you ever just shut up?" he mumbled against the fairy's chest. He hadn't quite reawakened to reality enough to blush, but he didn't want to hurry the process along.

Ciaran inched back and put a hand to Trent's cheek, gently urging him to look up, and he pressed a long, soft kiss to the younger man's lips, lingering close to him even after they parted.

"I love you," he said with an unfamiliar firmness in his voice, like he was trying to make sure Trent knew he meant it.

"I love you too," Trent assured him with a furrowed brow, and

Ciaran drew him close, barely holding in a cough as he clutched him to his chest.

15

Noah had suffered through the fairy woman rubbing his every crevice down with oils that she claimed would keep his fever down and help prevent future flashes of memories that weren't his own, and he had done so with some measure of his dignity intact, he thought. Cu had blatantly stared at him the entire time, which hadn't exactly helped, but the fairy at least hadn't teased him for his embarrassing breakdown.

Airmed gave him hot tea to drink that tasted of ginger, and she had the servants draw him a scalding hot bath and demanded that he get in it. She had left explicit instructions for Cu as to when and what to serve Noah to eat, but before she could scurry out of the room again, Noah stopped her.

"Please, could you..." He hesitated as she tilted her head at him. "The man who was with me—the hunter. They took him somewhere. Could you at least...make sure he's all right?"

She smiled and patted his head like a child. "Get in that bath before it cools. I'll check up on your companion."

"Thank you."

She only tutted at him and went on her way, once again leaving him alone and naked in the room with Cu.

"You heard the lady," Cu chuckled. "Hop in, and let's get you all steamy."

Noah flushed under the fairy's undisguised gaze. "I can manage a bath by myself, you know," he muttered, and he stepped over the rim of the tall copper bathtub and sank into the water with a slight hiss.

"Aye, but I wouldn't be a very good guard if I just let you be, now would I?" Cu lounged on the bed nearby, letting one leg dangle over the side as he picked idly at his fingernails. "What if you've hidden a weapon somewhere on your person, and you've just been waiting for the right soapy moment to strike?"

"If I had any weapons, you sister would have found them," Noah grumbled. His skin was already pink under the water, and the steam created a thin film of sweat on his forehead that he dunked his head to wash away.

"I'd be happy to search you again, just to be sure."

"Ha ha." The bathwater smelled of various oils that Noah couldn't identify and some that he could—it was clearly a cleansing mixture, but he would have liked to know what exactly it was he was bathing in.

"You let me know if you need any help scrubbing, as well."

"Are you this relentless with all of your prisoners, or am I just lucky?"

"Well I don't get many prisoners, to be frank," Cu chuckled. "And the ones I have gotten didn't have little rings in their lips just asking to be bitten."

Noah sank down lower in the deep bathtub until his nose almost skimmed the surface. Being flirted with was not an added bonus that he needed. It was flattering at first, but now it just made him nervous. He was already worried about Julien and miserable thinking about the conversation they'd had right before Lugh had found them. Now they were separated, he had made an ass of himself in front of his captor, and he just had to wait around for…whatever it was they were planning on doing to reverse what he had done. And said captor was now talking about biting his piercings, which totally wasn't something he'd imagined Julien doing a hundred times in the dark of his lonely bedroom. Not at all.

Somehow, Noah's life had gotten off track. Just a few weeks ago, he had been pining over a straight guy, which was nothing particularly new for him, but at least the straight guy had been his friend. They had worked together, and hung out, and Noah had been able to talk to him, tell him stupid stories about the middle aged women who showed up to Noah's yoga classes in pants that were way, way too sheer. He had a job that was satisfying if not financially rewarding, and he got to spend his days doing monster research and going out with his straight crush in the middle of the night. He was able to flirt with Julien sometimes without having to worry that anything would ever come of it. It wasn't bad.

This, all of this—fairies and soul magic and secret entrances and horses that ran on water and memories of a thousand-year-old Irishman—it was too much. He wanted to go back to the way things were. Even if he could have just kept his stupid mouth shut about his stupid feelings, maybe things wouldn't be awkward between him and Julien, at least. That might have been enough to get him through the rest of this insanity. He at least wouldn't have the memory of the hunter's lips on his, of that perfect instant before everything came crashing down.

"Everything all right in there, deas?" Cu called with a chuckle. "You look a wee bit stormy."

Noah ran his hands through his wet hair to push it out of his face and sat up at least enough to speak. "Don't call me whatever you just called me."

"So sour." Cu grinned over at him. "I bet I know a way to make you smile."

"I bet I know a way to hex you into a rash that'll ruin that pretty face," Noah countered, and Cu let out a barking laugh.

"You've a bit of life in you yet, don't you? Airmed does know what she's doing after all."

Noah ignored him. He leaned back in the bath and shut his eyes in an attempt to forget he was being watched and let the hot water relax his aching body. He coughed occasionally, almost sloshing water over the side of the tub, but the quiet flick of a match and the smell of earthy incense soothed his throat. He had almost relaxed again when suddenly he felt a strong hand on his shoulder, and he jumped, definitely sloshing water onto the stone floor.

"Easy, lad," Cu chuckled. "I'm going to fetch you your prescribed meal. Promise not to drown or run away while I'm gone?"

"I'll manage," Noah muttered, shrinking away from the other man's touch. He watched Cu walk out the door, leaving it propped open behind him, and he took the opportunity to step out of the bath and dry off on the cloth left for him. He could at least dress himself without being ogled, even if he only had the one pair of clothes. He slid into his worn jeans and pulled his shirt over his head just in time to be decent for Cu's return.

"Oh, well that's a disappointment," the fairy murmured as he entered with a tray. "Here I am waiting on you hand and foot—you who's supposed to be a prisoner, I might add—and you don't even have the decency to stay naked so I can look at you."

"Sorry," Noah answered without sincerity, and he settled himself on the bed as he let out another round of coughs. Cu managed to keep a polite distance as he set the tray down in front of him, and Noah grimaced as he realized quite how long it had been since he'd eaten. He had to try hard not to swallow down the entire cup of rich milk in one breath, though he did drink a good half of it before stuffing a small, soft pastry into his mouth. He normally didn't like sweet things, but just then, there wasn't anything he would have rather had.

He heard Cu give a soft laugh beside him, but when he looked over at him, it wasn't Cu sitting next to him, but the hard-faced Chinese boy whose apartment he had broken into with Julien. They were on a sofa together with a television flickering just in front of them, but Noah couldn't tell whether the sweet taste on his tongue was real or a memory. He was pressed against the boy next to him, the heat of his body bringing up goosebumps on his skin.

It's too quiet. Too easy. His shirt is open; he couldn't have done it on purpose. If I ran my tongue over that little hollow in his throat, would he push me away, or would he whimper? Even if he complained, he'd get that little blush in his cheeks he gets when he's pretending he doesn't want me to kiss him. If he'd let me, I'd push him down on the sofa right now. But sitting is...nice. His breathing is slow and steady, and he doesn't mind my knee against his. It's easy. Isn't it supposed to be?

Trent looks at me, and for just a moment, I think he's thinking the same thing I am. Shouldn't it always be this easy?

Noah felt his shoulder jerking back and forth—his own shoulder—and then he was back in the guest room where he was confined, with Cu looking into his face with a concerned frown. He fought to catch his breath, but every time he inhaled, it came out in a rough cough, until he was doubled over on the blankets, barely avoiding his tray of food as Cu scooted it out of his way.

The witch's fingers trembled as he gripped the soft furs lining the bed. He couldn't quite sit up yet; he couldn't bring himself to move and disturb the last lingering emotions washing over him. He was nervous, as though he was on the verge of something exciting and frightening, and his skin tingled with arousal. It gave him a warm sensation in his stomach that he didn't want to lose, and somewhere underneath the fairy's memory, Noah himself felt a pang of jealousy. It should be easy. Being with the person you love—even if it's intimidating at first, even if you're afraid of being hurt—you should be able to sit quietly together on the couch and watch television without anxiety. He'd had that with Julien, at some point. But that was before Julien had known how he felt. Julien had been comfortable with him because he'd thought he was just a friend. That thrilling prickling at the back of his neck when the hunter's hand had happened to brush his as he handed him a cigarette—Noah had been the only one feeling it.

Cu's warm hand touched Noah's back, and he flinched. He felt like such an idiot. Even after Julien had told him he cared, tried to let him down easy, Noah had still let hope fester in his heart like a parasite. His best option was to try to complete the spell as quickly as possible. If he succeeded, he would be himself again, and maybe they could escape. If he failed, he would be dead—but he would die if he didn't do anything anyway. He couldn't wait around for his captors and stay at their mercy. Who even knew what they were planning to do, and if it had any chance of working? He had to try.

Noah finally sat up, and Cu watched him with a wary eye but didn't move his hand from the witch's back.

"And what was that?" the fairy asked.

"Your brother," Noah answered. He wrapped his arms around his middle and held his stomach to quell the nausea that always followed his flashes. "It's like he's…in here with me sometimes, or…like maybe

I'm in here with him. I see things."

"What sorts of things?"

"All sorts," Noah shrugged.

"Have you seen me?"

Noah paused. "Sometimes it's...hard to remember what I've seen when it's over."

"Well, that's a relief," he chuckled, and Noah quirked an eyebrow at him.

"Why?"

"Well, if you'd seen me through my brother's eyes, you'd be even less inclined to give in to my advances."

Noah sighed through his nose and shook his head to hide his faint smile. "And it doesn't bother you at all to know that your brother's soul, or spirit, or whatever, is...you know, up here?" He tapped his own temple with one finger.

"But you aren't my brother," Cu shrugged. He leaned in close to Noah with a sly smile, his nose lightly brushing the witch's cheek. Noah froze, setting his jaw and refusing to tremble at the warmth of the fairy's breath on his skin. "If you were, you'd have hit me already."

Noah pushed him away by his chest and pointedly pulled the tray of food back into his lap. "Just stop," he said as he picked at a piece of pastry. "I've got a little too much going on right now, if you hadn't noticed. And even if I weren't on the verge of death and stupidly in love with someone else, I still wouldn't be interested in a fling with a fairy who's supposed to be keeping me prisoner."

Cu snorted out a laugh. "That's fair. Disappointing, but fair."

Noah chewed his pastry and peeked at Cu out of the corner of his eye. Once he'd swallowed, he said softly, "Could I ask you for a favor, though?"

"Cheeky cuss," he chuckled. "Go right ahead, lad, why not?"

"Could I...see him? Julien." He turned to face Cu's thoughtful frown. "I don't even know where they took him. I just...I'd like to talk to him." He could leave out that he'd like to talk to Julien about finishing the spell that would kill Cu's brother and breaking out before they could get punished for it. He didn't like it, but it was their best option. And he could use the opportunity to settle things between him and Julien—tell him to forget about everything Noah had done to complicate things. With time, Noah was certain he could readjust to having the hunter as a friend. Or if not, then maybe it wouldn't be so bad for Julien to move on to a different city. At least they'd both be out of here and safe.

Cu must have taken pity on Noah's pained look, because it only took a moment's hesitation for him to drop his shoulders in a heavy sigh.

"I know where they'll have taken him," the fairy nodded. "But I'm not risking my father's anger. If you can wait until tonight, I'll check—I'll check, you understand—and see if I can get you out for a bit. But it'll be right back again afterward, hm? And don't make me watch any sappy business between the two of you."

"I promise," Noah agreed.

"And in exchange, I get to look at you naked again."

The witch let out a puff of air, but he couldn't decide if it was a sigh or a laugh. "If your sister wants to give me more of her treatment, I'm sure you'll get your wish."

Cu nudged him with his elbow and offered him a smile as he stood. "Go on and finish eating, then, and I'll bring you a change of clothes so you can get some sleep. We'll see about your little love drama later on."

"Thank you," Noah said, making Cu pause on his way toward the door. "I mean it. You didn't have to speak to me, let alone be kind to me, after what I did to your brother. You're being ridiculously accommodating," he chuckled. "So...thanks."

A small smirk tugged at one corner of the fairy's mouth. "I know I'm still unbelievably handsome, but when you're as old as I am, it's hard to find the energy to hold grudges. Especially after hearing pitiful sob stories and having pretty young men cry into your shoulder. Now eat."

Cu left him behind in the room, and Noah sighed as he stared down at his half-finished plate and tried to decide what he would say when he was face to face with Julien again.

Airmed returned before too long—just as Noah was finally able to fall asleep, of course—and stripped him of the soft clothes Cu had brought him. It was barely embarrassing anymore. She chose her oils and applied them to his forehead, chest, and hands with swift, professional movements, a soft song humming in her throat while she worked. She had him chew herbs, though at least this time he was able to convince her that he was familiar enough with magic that he deserved to know what she was feeding him. He admitted when she asked that he had had another flashback, and she'd prescribed him another hot bath full of oils and scented with herbs. She stayed long enough to make sure that he ate his supper and got in the bath, and then she was gone again.

It was impossible for Noah to tell what time of day it was. They had brought him supper, and he was tired, but he'd been tired for a week. There was no sun here—only the light of the lanterns and the luminescent plant life that grew along the roads. Noah frowned in the steam of his bath. He hoped that wherever they'd taken Julien, they hadn't confiscated the many mushrooms and mosses he'd secreted away in the hunter's bag on their way down the winding stair to the city. He'd want to send samples to Sabin when—if—they made it back to the surface.

Cu was singing a quiet song from his place on the bed, his attention focused on a small bit of stone perched on his knee as he carefully scraped and carved it into a vaguely animal shape.

"When can we go?" Noah asked, but Cu only told him to finish his bath before returning to his song. He had a deep, throaty voice that was clearly untrained, but not unpleasant. If Noah's thoughts hadn't been consumed by running over the lines he'd been practicing in his head, he might have found it soothing.

I don't want this anymore, he would say to Julien. I'm glad that you care. I care about you, too. I shouldn't have tried to push you. You shouldn't have used my feelings to manipulate me, either, he would be sure to add. Let's just be friends. Partners. Until it's time for you to move on. Then we'll part on good terms, and maybe I'll see you again someday.

That was definitely the healthiest thing to say. It wasn't what he wanted to say—not really—but it was the right thing. He was torturing himself, torturing Julien, and making things harder on everyone. Still, the little parasite wriggled in his chest, refusing to be squashed by logic.

By the time the bathwater had gone cold, Noah was impatient. He held in a cough as he pulled himself out of the bath and dried off. Cu's little carving was recognizable as a dog now, but he still seemed content to work on it while Noah dressed himself. His clothes had been cleaned at some point, but he wasn't quite sure by whom.

Noah stood staring expectantly at Cu once he was dressed, and eventually the fairy leaned over to look out the window, gave a short sigh through his nose, and nodded.

"Right," he said. "Come along. Quiet now."

Cu led the way down the empty corridor. Though he had a lean figure, Noah was still surprised at how light the fairy's step was as they moved down the hall. He didn't seem like the kind of person to sneak anywhere. Noah did his best to keep up and keep quiet in the silent house, though once he had to press both hands against his mouth to muffle the sound of a cough. They walked through the house, passing through a library, a long dining hall, and a kitchen full of fruit and bread dough waiting to rise. Cu held the door for him into the back garden and led him through the path to the hidden cellar near the wall, but he paused with a hand on Noah's chest when they saw that the door was already open.

"Someone's in there," Cu whispered, and he shook his head. "We'll have to try later."

"But what if they're hurting him?" Noah hissed. "Please."

Cu hesitated, a reluctant frown on his face, but then he seemed to give in. He put a finger to his lips and tilted his head toward the door, and together they snuck down the steps into the dark cellar.

There were quiet voices echoing on the stone, but Noah paused as he heard a different sound from the end of the corridor—a sound he'd heard precious few times before. Julien was laughing. The witch rushed forward as quickly as he dared, straining to see without being seen. Airmed sat on the ground at the door to the last cell, her hands in her lap and her face close to the bars. Noah's heart stopped as he spotted Julien's hands held gently in hers, his face lowered and a relaxed smile on his lips as he said something to her that Noah couldn't hear. He looked—happy? The remnants of a meal were on the floor beside them, clearly long forgotten. She squeezed his hands and leaned forward to whisper to him, and the hunter answered her in a soft voice that Noah had rarely heard him use.

He felt rooted to the spot. Here he was worried for Julien, aching, agonizing over what to say to him to release him from whatever guilt he still felt about what had happened between them, and Julien was holding hands with some woman—a woman. Noah's heart withered into a pit in his stomach, taking his dying parasite of hope with it. She was a fairy, a magical thing—but she was a woman. No wonder she had been so brusque with him earlier. She was in a hurry to get back to the mysterious and handsome hunter. And Julien had apparently been happy to see her. He moved quickly when he wasn't being pressured by stupid, clingy men.

That was it then. If Julien was able to forget so easily, then Noah could, too. He didn't need to give his practiced speech. Julien had decided for him. Good. Noah was cut loose, just like he wanted. He was free. His shoulders shrunk at the pain in his stomach. So why didn't he feel free? He felt more chained than ever.

He couldn't look at them anymore. When Airmed reached up to touch Julien's cheek, Noah turned away and hurried back up the stairs, dragging Cu behind him by the hand.

Once they were outside, Cu allowed himself a chuckle. "I knew Airmed had given herself over to spinsterhood, but I didn't expect she'd make eyes at the first new blood to drop in," he snorted, but he stopped when he saw the look on Noah's face. The witch was clinging tightly to his hand, standing silently in the garden. Cu tilted his head to catch Noah's eyes. "Not what you expected to see, I take it?" he asked softly.

"It's exactly what I expected," Noah answered in a whisper. "Take...take me back. Please."

Cu did as he was asked, leading Noah by the hand back the way they had come. They passed quietly through the house, and Cu shut the guest room door behind them while Noah stood hugging his own arms. It shouldn't have hurt so much. Noah had been prepared to put an end to everything, hadn't he? Julien had just beaten him to it. Maybe if Noah finished the spell, Airmed could speak on Julien's behalf and save him from punishment for what Noah had done. Then everyone who mattered would have what they wanted. But he still felt sick.

Cu approached him from behind with a light hand on his back, and Noah jumped at the touch. Maybe that was the answer. If Julien could forget—maybe Noah needed to forget, too. He turned to face the fairy and took hold of the front of his dark tunic with one hand, looking up at him with his heart pounding in his chest.

"You still want me naked?" he asked in a low voice, and Cu's eyebrows lifted in surprise.

"You aren't a bit...distraught?"

"Are you kidding?" Noah did his best to sound cavalier. "I'm free. And good riddance." He tugged Cu a half step closer to him and leaned close enough for the ring in his lip to brush the corner of the fairy's mouth, hoping his grip was tight enough to hide the trembling in his hands.

"Now do you want me or not?" he whispered, feeling the other man's muscles tense.

Cu didn't bother to answer. He lifted Noah by the waist as easily as if he were a child and took two long strides before depositing him on the bed. Noah let the fairy crawl over him, and he shut his eyes, sucking in a sharp breath as Cu's lips pressed hot against his neck. His hands were under Noah's shirt in an instant, calloused palms caressing the witch's long-neglected skin. He squirmed at the touch, but the fairy's rough hands were too much like he'd imagined Julien's would be. The heat of Cu's tongue sent a jolt down his spine, but he couldn't open his eyes. He fisted his fingers into the blanket, too afraid to put his hands on the man on top of him. He couldn't stop imagining the look on Julien's face when he'd told Noah he trusted him. So gentle and soft, and a little fearful. He felt the fairy's sharp teeth bite into the skin at the base of his neck, and he let out a shaky, startled cry. Cu's hand slipped down the witch's stomach, but Noah could feel tears prickling behind his eyes. He didn't want this. He didn't want Cu to be the one touching him this way.

"Stop," he begged, his throat so tight he could barely get the word out. "Stop, please."

Cu lifted his head, slightly out of breath himself, and he propped himself up to look down at Noah with a furrowed brow. He clicked his tongue and reached out to brush away a tear that had managed to escape and roll down Noah's cheek.

"I asked you if you were distraught," he murmured, and Noah squeezed his eyes shut and shook his head, pressing the balls of his hands into his eyes.

"I'm sorry. I thought...I thought I could—"

"Yes, I thought so," Cu chuckled. He lifted himself off of Noah and sat on the bed beside him, giving the boy time to compose himself.

"I'm sorry," Noah said again with a soft hiccup in his voice, but Cu only shushed him and patted his head.

"Sleep on it," the fairy suggested, and he nudged Noah until he could pull the blanket out from under him. "If you decide you do want to be ravaged, I'll be here." He covered Noah with the heavy fur and moved himself to a chair by the window, humming his low, quiet tune as he picked up his half-finished carving.

Noah hid his face in the down pillow and curled up as tightly as he could, letting out the rest of his tears in silence.

16

Julien wasn't sure how much time passed with Airmed sitting beside him, listening patiently to every story he had about hunts with Noah, about drinking beer while the witch pored over dusty books in other languages, or lazy afternoons cleaning guns while Noah stretched himself into seemingly impossible poses in the living room, both of them meditating in their own way. He told her about Noah always making sure that Julien ate, even when it meant spending money he didn't have.

She reached through the bars to squeeze his hands, barely restraining her wide smile. "Julien Fournier, you are a very lucky man. You're making it so confusing, when it could be so very simple."

Julien allowed her to keep a grip on him, and he let out a faint sigh as he looked down at their joined hands. "It doesn't seem so simple. Saying what I mean is...harder than it should be. I've been alone for most of my life. If I wasn't alone, I was with my father and brothers, training to be the only person I've ever known how to be. And that person—that life doesn't really allow for companionship, or—romance."

Airmed's brow furrowed as she looked up at him, and she scooted closer to the bars and reached out to touch the blonde stubble on Julien's face, urging his eyes up to meet hers. "Do you realize how rare this is, this thing that you have? I am thousands of years old, and I have yet to meet a single person that makes me feel the things you've described. You must tell him. You absolutely must."

Julien found himself faintly smiling. "Then I hope this spell of yours gets over with quickly."

Airmed suddenly paused, and her grip tightened on his hand. "Oh, no," she whispered. She sat up straighter, and her brow furrowed as she leaned in closer to him. "I can't believe I didn't—oh, dear," she murmured. Julien frowned and watched her with a wary eye while she covered her mouth and shook her head.

"If I'd have known—"

"What?" Julien pressed, and she seemed to remember herself.

"Oh—oh dear. The spell they plan to do. If Cian has lost his soul, like they say, there's only one spell they can use to reverse such a thing." She clutched the hunter's hands tightly in hers. "He'll die for certain. Especially with it having been so long already...he simply won't have the strength to withstand the spell."

Julien's brow furrowed, and he pulled his hands away from her and got to his feet to pace the small circle his cell allowed. Lugh had said the same thing, but Julien had assumed—or hoped, perhaps—that the man had been exaggerating the risk. He paused to look down at Airmed's frowning face. When they had first come, his plan had been to allow Noah to finish the spell he had started, but he found himself hesitating. He had no soft feelings for the fairy himself, but he realized with a start that at some point he had allowed himself to think of Airmed as a *her*, rather than as an *it*. He didn't want to take her brother from her, even if that plan had still been feasible with him and Noah separated. "Then we have to find another way," Julien said simply. "There has to be something. Doesn't there?"

"Well we can't simply not—even if they didn't do the spell at all, he would still—" She stopped and suddenly shifted, pulling herself up by the bars of his cell. "You know, there might just be—oh, but he would have to—oh, just wait. Wait here. Please. I need some time."

She rushed down the corridor before Julien could give her an answer one way or the other, leaving him standing alone in the dark cell. He leaned his forehead against the bars with a frustrated sigh. When had he started caring what happened to any of these people—

these things? Julien muttered a curse and thumped his head once against a silver bar. He was complicating things. If he could get Airmed to let him out, perhaps he could get at his bag and his iron, and use her to bargain his way out—but that wouldn't save Noah. It might even get him killed even faster. If he could escape undetected, perhaps they really could finish the spell. But as weak as the witch was, Julien didn't like his odds of surviving it a second time. It seemed that to save Noah, he would have to play by the rules of his captors, and his wavering nerve when it came to kind-hearted fairy women was—thankfully—irrelevant.

He paced his cell for a time, his mind running over every scenario he could foresee. Despite how long he had spent looking for weaknesses, the cell seemed to be made too strong to dig through, and the bars were sunk so deep into the stone that he had no chance of prying them free. His only option was to wait for Airmed and hope that her apparent interest in his relationship with Noah was enough to earn her help.

When she eventually returned, Julien gripped the bars and strained to look down the hall for her. He almost smiled when she appeared, but he took a step back from the bars when he saw Lugh following close behind her. Julien watched the fairy warily as he stepped close to the bars, seeming hulking and stoic even to Julien himself.

"My darling nephew will be the key to saving your love," Airmed said with a slightly anxious smile, and she put her hand on Lugh's thick bicep without a care that he looked strong enough to snap her in half with barely a thought.

"Will he now," Julien muttered softly as he glanced between them. Lugh's scowl didn't make him look very much like a savior.

"Airmed tells me you need passage to Emain Ablach," Lugh said in a curt tone. He folded his arms across his chest and stared down at Julien with an impatient frown.

Julien looked across at Airmed in confusion. "Do I?"

"Yes, you very much do," she assured him, and she stepped forward to put her hands on the bars. "Emain Ablach is the isle of Manandán," she said eagerly. "There you can find Manandán's orchard. His apples are the only thing that might give your witch the strength to survive the spell my father will mean to use. It's impossible to get there for a human—well, unless you're dead, I suppose," she added with a slight purse of her lips. "But Lugh can get you there. Manandán raised him, you see." She patted her nephew on the arm and gave him a bright smile.

Julien looked up at Lugh but only received a slight quirk of the eyebrow in response. "You have cause for a quest, I'm told," the fairy said.

Julien paused. "I…suppose I do." He glanced back to Airmed.

"The best reason for a quest," she bubbled, bouncing on the balls of her feet as she looked between the two men. "Lugh, this is a quest to save his true love."

Julien felt his face grow warm, and his hands balled into fists at his sides as Lugh scoffed. This had escalated rather quickly. He may have been able to admit to Airmed that what he felt for Noah should be called love, but he didn't exactly feel confident shouting it from the rooftops. He wasn't positive that her plea would be particularly helpful to his cause, either—Lugh didn't seem the type to be moved by love stories.

Lugh tilted his head slightly as he looked down at him, but he said nothing, only gave a low, pondering grunt in his throat as he sized Julien up. After a few moments of Airmed fingering her nephew's sleeve anxiously, he finally spoke.

"This is because of your witch?" he asked.

Julien stared back at him. "Yes."

"Emain Ablach is not a place for living men, and Manandán does not part with his treasures freely. It is just as likely that you will die on this journey, and then your witch will die regardless. You still wish to take this risk?"

Julien didn't waver. In his mind, there was no question. "I do. I have to try, and I don't intend to fail."

Lugh gave a small snort. He considered Julien for a moment, and when he nodded, Airmed clapped her hands and let out a small, sudden laugh. Lugh held up a hand to quiet her, and she pressed her fingertips to her mouth and did her best to stifle her excitement.

"I can get you to Emain Ablach," Lugh clarified. "I can present you to Manandán. Presenting your cause and earning one of his apples is something I cannot and will not help you do. If you succeed, I will bring you back here. If you fail, I will ensure you are buried honorably. That is my offer."

Julien almost laughed. It was definitely more help than he expected, and probably more than he deserved. The hairs at the back of his neck prickled at the thought of accepting so much aid from these two fairies, as well as the idea that he would soon be proving himself—whatever that meant—to an unknown entity that was clearly revered in some way by these same fairies. He didn't like putting his trust in Lugh, he didn't like that he was so willing to accept help from Airmed, and he didn't like that he would be leaving Noah behind to be held captive until they needed him. He didn't like any of it. That didn't mean he had a choice.

He spared a glance at Airmed's face, her eyes wide with anticipation, and he nodded. "I accept."

Lugh glanced over his shoulder and snapped his fingers, and the same servant who had locked Julien in came scuttling out of the darkness with his large ring of keys in his hand.

"You understand, my lord," he began with hesitation as he approached, not having the courage to look up into Lugh's face, "that my lord Dian Cecht has insisted—"

"You let me deal with Dian Cecht," Lugh interrupted in a gruff voice, and the servant visibly flinched. "Whatever trouble's to be had for this man's release, let it fall upon my shoulders if your master dares to put it there."

"Yes, my lord," the servant whispered in answer, and he chose a key from his ring and opened the bars to Julien's cell.

Julien stepped out into the corridor and found his hand immediately grasped by Airmed's slender fingers. She looked up at him with a strange mixture of admiration and longing that he didn't quite understand. Before she could say anything about the true love he was defending, Julien looked up at Lugh and spoke instead.

"I want to see him before I go. Noah. If what you're saying is true, and I'm likely to die on this trip, then I want to see him."

Lugh studied him a moment before nodding. "Fair," he decided, and he glanced down at his significantly smaller aunt. "Fetch the witch. I'll get this one ready."

Airmed huffed out a pleased sigh, seeming hardly able to contain herself, and she trotted off down the corridor and disappeared into the dark. When she let herself into Noah's room without even knocking, the witch started from his curled position on the bed and turned to look at her over his shoulder.

"Can't I just rest, please," he begged, his voice hoarse from tears. Even if he hadn't been exhausted, Airmed was the very last person he wanted to see right now. He couldn't get the image of her with her hand so gently on Julien's cheek and the soft smile the hunter had given her in return as she whispered to him. After Noah had left, had they—he hid his face in his pillow again. He couldn't think about it. He was torturing himself.

"You're going to want to get up for this, dear heart," Airmed said, and she rushed to Noah's side to touch him on the arm and urge him upright. She was positively beaming, and it made Noah sick.

"What's happening, Airmed?" Cu asked from his chair, but she waved a hand at him in dismissal.

"Never you mind. I have a surprise for our young witch."

"I don't want it," Noah frowned, but Airmed took him by the hands and pulled him to his feet with ease despite his slumping.

"Believe me, you do. Come along now. Stop this pouting; whatever could be the matter with you?"

Noah wanted to shout at her. He wanted to tell her that she should have known what was wrong, but he knew somewhere underneath his self-pity that that wasn't fair. If she and Julien...cared about each other, then good for them. She couldn't have known that Noah had considered himself in the running for Julien's affection. It was a race that he had never had a chance of winning. Even if it had only been a day and it was absolutely ridiculous that Julien should be so chummy with her so suddenly, he thought bitterly.

Airmed pulled him out of the room by his hand, ignoring how he dragged his feet, and she led him down the stairs and back to the courtyard he had just left a short time ago.

"Where are we going?" he asked, his chest growing tight. He didn't want to see Julien now. He couldn't. He just wanted to curl up in his bed and cry. And then die, maybe.

"Your hunter has something very important to say to you."

Noah's mouth went dry. He couldn't even fight as Airmed led him to the cellar door. Now he definitely wanted to die. There couldn't be anything good waiting for him in that dank prison.

But when they reached the bottom of the stairs, Noah spotted Lugh standing tall and imposing at the end of the hall, and Julien inexplicably out of his cell. Noah thought he saw a sudden tension in the hunter's shoulders as they locked eyes, but it couldn't compare to the anxious pounding in his own chest. This wasn't what he had expected.

"Give them a minute, won't you, my dear nephew," Airmed urged, and Lugh spared a stern glance at Julien before following the woman back up the stairs.

Noah stood a safe distance from Julien, holding his own elbow and feeling impossibly uncomfortable. Julien had decided to go back to Vancouver, maybe, and leave Noah to whatever fate was waiting for him. Or he'd made such good friends with Airmed that he was going to stay with her instead. Noah couldn't even look at him.

"Have you been crying?" Julien asked, his voice soft in the narrow hallway. Noah didn't answer, and he heard Julien sigh. He tensed as the hunter stepped closer to him, Noah's skin prickling with goosebumps as Julien laid his hands gently on the younger man's arms.

"I have something to tell you," the hunter whispered, every word clearly a struggle. "Please look at me."

Here it came. Noah reluctantly raised his gaze to look into Julien's anxious hazel eyes.

"I…have to leave," Julien started, and Noah's heart sank into his stomach. He kept the hunter's gaze but could already feel the tears starting again as his throat constricted. He felt weak and stupid, and he hated it, but he was determined not to look away until the hunter had said his piece, no matter how much it hurt.

"This spell they're going to use to put the fairy's soul back where it belongs…Airmed says it will kill you. So I have to find something that will stop that from happening. Lugh has agreed to take me. He says it will be dangerous. I'll do what needs to be done, but just in case…in case I don't make it back. I wanted you to know where I'd gone."

Noah could barely breathe. His mind was reeling, and his sunken heart suddenly felt like it was about to leap back into his throat.

"This isn't a choice for me," Julien went on before Noah could find the words to answer. "If there's something I can do to...to keep you safe, then I'm going to do it. That's it."

Noah shook his head, which was about all the movement he could manage. "What are you talking about?" he asked in a whisper. "Where are you going?"

"Some island where a sea god grows apples," Julien muttered with a vague wave of his hand. "It makes as much sense as anything else in this damned place. But the where isn't important." He inched a half step closer to Noah and took a slow breath before continuing. "What's important is the why."

Noah didn't dare speak. He looked up at Julien with a furrowed brow, a mixture of excitement and dread bubbling in his gut.

"I've been...unclear with you," the hunter said, and he glanced down at the floor for a moment before looking back into the witch's dark eyes. "And I want you to understand me. For days now, I...I've been thinking. I can't stop thinking. About you," he clarified in a rush. His lips pressed into a thin line, and Noah was certain he saw some color rise in Julien's cheeks. "I thought that you were my friend, Noah. My partner. But I want to—I want to give you more than that. Not because you asked me to, or because I think you just want to...sleep with me. But because I simply can't imagine how I would go on if you weren't there beside me."

All the air left Noah's lungs. This wasn't happening. This couldn't be happening. This sounded like—but it couldn't be. Julien was watching him, clearly waiting for him to say something, anything, but Noah had no words. His heart was beating so loudly that he wasn't sure he could hear anything else. Finally, after an eternity of silence, Noah was able to squeeze out the single word, "Pardon?"

Julien dropped his head and sighed in a dry, humorless chuckle. He squeezed Noah's arms tight and looked back up into his face. "I'm trying to say that I...somehow, and without knowing why or when it happened, I...love you, and I want you to know that I'm going to do whatever it takes to keep you safe and—and happy. Not just now, but...after we've left this damnable place. Always."

Noah felt himself hiccup, and he felt the tears running hot down his face, but he still couldn't bring himself to speak. This was impossible. After all the scolding he'd done, telling himself not to get his hopes up, convincing himself that he'd had no place in the hunter's life—this was impossible. Julien reached up to gently thumb away the tears on the witch's cheek, a soft, uncertain frown on his lips.

"Is that...not what you wanted to hear?" the hunter whispered.

"I just," Noah managed through a tight throat, "I just never thought—"

"I was an idiot," Julien said quickly. "I don't know how to...how to handle these things. I know that I said the wrong things, and that I hurt you. I won't do it again," he promised with such a firm frown that Noah's skin trembled. "And before I go, I...I wanted to make it up to you."

Noah could only look at him in confusion. Didn't he think this was enough? Noah could barely think, let alone argue. This was all too much.

"Before, in the hotel," he began quietly, "I ruined something that should have been...better." Noah could feel Julien's grip on him tighten, and he thought there was a slight shiver in the hunter's hands. "If you'll let me, I want to try again. If you can forget before. You...deserve a better first kiss than that."

The witch was rooted in place instantly, his face burning red. Julien was waiting for an answer, but Noah could only whisper, "Okay."

Julien hesitated, shifting his weight for a moment, and then he bent down close to Noah, stopping close enough that the witch could feel his breath against his lips. Noah knew that he was trembling, but he was surprised to realize that the hunter was trembling, too.

"Dois-je arrêter?" Julien whispered with his nose brushing Noah's cheek, and the witch thanked God for his years of being forced to learn French in school.

"Don't...please don't stop," he answered, and before he could take another breath, Julien's lips were on his, the hunter's strong hands on his back, pulling him close. Noah gripped the other man's shirt in his fists, unable to keep in the shaky moan in his throat as Julien's mouth opened to him, both men lost to the world in a single instant.

As the hunter moved his hand to Noah's hair, tangling his fingers in the witch's dark tresses, Noah's legs almost gave out from under him. He clung to Julien as though he would fall through the floor if he didn't.

When they finally broke apart, both of them panting for breath, Julien let his forehead rest against the younger man's and gently stroked his temple with his thumb.

"I'm going to come back to you," Julien whispered, and Noah nodded just slightly.

"I know you will."

Nearby, in the darkness of the stairwell, Noah heard a tiny, high-pitched sound like a barely restrained squeal of excitement. He turned to look over his shoulder and saw Airmed lurking on the stairs, peeking around the corner at them.

"I need to go," Julien said, clearly not wanting to linger and be stared at. "I don't know how much time I have."

Noah reluctantly unfastened his fingers from the hunter's shirt and took a step back. "I'll...be here when you get back," he answered in what he hoped was a cheerful voice. He still felt lightheaded and more than a little overwhelmed. He was waiting around for his captors to cast a spell that was apparently guaranteed to kill him, but Julien loved him and had kissed him and meant it—so things weren't all bad.

17

Trent's back arched away from the bed as Ciaran ground against him, the fairy's unnatural weight in his lap keeping him firmly in place. Trent was certain he was leaving bruises on Ciaran's waist, he was gripping him so tightly, but the fairy was relentless. Ciaran rolled his hips at an almost violent pace, taking every inch that Trent had to offer and trying to press deeper with every stroke, demanding more and more. His fingers curled into claws against Trent's thighs, his blunt fingernails digging into the skin as his head fell back in an aching sigh.

Ciaran was distractingly attractive, even through the fog of pleasure that clouded Trent's mind, even though he was slightly pale from illness. A tiny bead of sweat ran from the fairy's temple to his cheek, threatening to drip onto Trent's stomach as Ciaran leaned forward in a desperate search for a deeper angle. Ciaran whispered to him in Gaelic, neither of them caring that Trent couldn't understand, and he growled with need as he purposefully moved Trent's hand from his waist to his neglected erection. Trent conceded with a sudden groan as Ciaran began to move faster, attempting to time the movement of his hand with the fairy's demanding pace.

Trent dug his heels into the bed to keep steady, but he was barely helping—he may have been inside Ciaran, but the fairy was undeniably the one taking him. He kept up his rhythm as best he could until Ciaran hissed out a few words that Trent had begun to recognize, and he felt the other man tense suddenly around him as he spilled himself onto Trent's stomach with a shuddering moan. Trent's hips jerked up in response as Ciaran squeezed him, and he was actually able to set his own pace for the brief few moments until he found his own climax.

Ciaran collapsed on top of him, refusing to move. He bit rough kisses along Trent's collarbone and nipped at his chin on the way to his lips. Trent could barely breathe, let alone move enough to shove the other man off of him, so he drowsily accepted Ciaran's kiss. They had hardly left the room since they'd arrived. Every time Trent had tried, claiming hunger or boredom, Ciaran had dragged him back to bed. Now Trent felt on the verge of passing out from sheer exhaustion, and he was more than a little sore from the fairy's constant attention. Ciaran climbing into Trent's lap had been the compromise.

"Think you could...fuck off?" Trent asked breathlessly, Ciaran's body weighing heavily on top of him. Ciaran grumbled and shifted just enough to curl up beside him, but he still clung to Trent and pressed hot kisses to his shoulder.

Trent tried to pry him away, desperate for just a moment spent without being touched. Ciaran bit his shoulder in defiance, and Trent shoved him with more force. His muscles had begun to ache, but he wasn't yet too tired to wrestle against Ciaran's cloying embrace. They had almost made it onto the floor in their struggle when a knock at the door made them both pause.

"Cian Mo Thiarna, is é an béile tráthnóna sheirbheáil," a woman's voice called through the door.

"Ag teacht," Ciaran almost snarled in response, his hands firmly pressing Trent's wrists into the bed.

"Was that for food?" Trent asked. "What time is it even?"

"They'll want a proper dinner," Ciaran muttered. "Teaghlach mór sona. I won't go."

"Ciaran, for fuck's sake," Trent sighed, twisting his wrists until the fairy released him. He sat up and stared across at Ciaran's scowling face. "I'm starving. You need to eat too. Look at you. Feel your hands."

Trent reached out for him and held the fairy's chilled fingers in his hands.

Ciaran clicked his tongue in annoyance and pulled his hands away, tucking them under his armpits like a child. "An mbeidh sí a bheith ann." He looked up when Trent only stared at him expectantly. "She's going to be there."

"Who is?"

Ciaran frowned down at the bed, his brow knit together in irritation or confusion—Trent couldn't quite tell. "Her," Ciaran said again, as though that would explain it. "The...my—woman," he finished, causing Trent to quirk an eyebrow at him.

"Your *woman*."

The fairy snorted in frustration and got to his feet, though the swift movement caused him to sway and hold onto one of the bedposts for stability. "I don't want them with her," he snapped.

"Ciaran, what the hell are you talking about?"

Ciaran stopped, clearly struggling to breathe, and Trent moved to put a comforting hand on his back. After a few slow, shaking breaths, Ciaran finally looked up into Trent's eyes.

"Fine," he said. "You should...you should eat."

"*You* should eat," Trent answered. "Isn't this going to be fairy food, all sorts of sweets and bullshit that you'll like? You won't have to eat eggs anymore."

Ciaran managed a weak smile. He sighed as he reached for his discarded clothes and pulled his brother's black tunic over his head. Trent stepped to the small basin on the shelf to clean the stickiness from himself, and he watched Ciaran with concern as they both dressed. Ciaran was fading fast, and Trent wasn't sure he'd helped the situation by agreeing to be ravaged all day long. He didn't know if it was some weird life-confirming thing, Ciaran wanting to do nothing but have sex, but it was definitely tiring him out. Not to mention how gingerly Trent himself was going to have to sit down at this proper fairy family supper. Good decisions had not been made today.

Ciaran still seemed reluctant to leave the room even when they were both dressed and as put-together as they could be on short notice. He stood at the door with one hand on the carved silver handle and sighed through his nose.

"It's just a meal," Trent said. "You'll survive; I promise."

Ciaran frowned at him, and for a moment Trent wondered if he'd said something wrong, but the fairy just pulled open the door and led the way down the hall to the stairs.

As expected, Ethniu sat at the table with her hands folded delicately in her lap, her glowing ember eyes on Ciaran as soon as he entered the room. Dian Cecht sat at the head of the table with Ethniu and Airmed to his left, but the seat to his right was empty. Cu sat one spot down, and then Cethen, and there was another empty space between Ciaran's brother and Noah. The witch sat with his hands between his knees and his shoulders hunched, as though he knew he didn't belong there. Did they expect Trent to sit next to him?

Ciaran looked back at Trent with a frown that confirmed his suspicions. Whatever kind of weird hierarchy existed in this stupid fairy world, Ciaran's family was clearly important enough to care about things like seating arrangements.

Ciaran's father snapped something in Gaelic, and Cu patted the back of the chair beside him with a bright grin. Ciaran caught Trent's fingertips in his for a brief moment before they were forced to separate, and Ciaran took his place at his father's right hand while Trent grumpily sat in the empty space between Cethen and the witch.

Servants bustled back and forth, filling cups and offering plates. Trent wondered briefly where Lugh had gone, but he supposed the man didn't have any particular affection for Ciaran that would have kept him from going on his way.

Even as hungry as Trent was, he still found the meal presented to him sickly sweet. It wasn't candy, at least, but the bread and its buttery filling was sweet, the honeyed milk was almost too thick to drink, and even the pottage, made up of what looked like barley and various roots and herbs Trent couldn't identify, was sweet. Trent glanced sidelong at Noah while the family chatted in Gaelic at the other end of the table and found him making much the same face down at his plate as Trent had been. At least he wasn't the only one.

Noah caught him staring and looked up at him, opening his mouth with a slight smile as though he was about to make some kind of joke, but then he seemed to remember who he was looking at and decided against it. The witch prodded a lump of root around his bowl with a silver spoon.

"For what it's worth, I am sorry," he said softly.

Trent could only scowl at him. "What, sorry you tried to kill Ciaran, or sorry that now you're suffering for it?"

"Both?" Noah offered with a half shrug, and Trent's grip tightened around his own spoon. "Look, it's done now, right? And they're going to fix him, so you don't have anything else to worry about." The witch lowered his eyes, and Trent got the impression that he wanted to say more, but he stayed silent.

"If we hadn't come here, you would have just tracked Ciaran down and killed him anyway, so don't try to play the pity card now," Trent sneered. "You and that asshole hunter started all of this. If it hadn't been for him—"

"We never would have met at all," Noah interrupted, his brow knit together in confusion as he looked up into Trent's eyes. Something about the witch's gaze looked distant and cloudy, his dark brown eyes almost black in the flickering light of the dining room. He reached out to touch Trent's cheek with his fingertips, and Trent immediately swatted him away, but Noah edged closer to him and took a tight hold of his arm.

"Tá mé buíoch dó anois, a mhuirnín," he said in a voice not quite his own.

Trent leaned away from him and twisted his arm out of the witch's grip so suddenly that he jerked backwards into Cethen and brought a quick end to the idle chatter at the other end of the table. Trent got to his feet and held his arm as though it has been burned by Noah's touch.

"You don't...you don't talk to me that way," he said, trying to contain the trembling of anger and fear in his voice.

"A mhuirnín, tá an-brón orm," Noah tried again, but Trent shouted at him to shut up and moved away from him. Ciaran was already on his feet, his hands on Trent's shoulders to keep him still, but when Trent looked back at him, the fairy was deathly pale, with sweat on his brow and a drawn, dark look on his face.

Cethen stood beside them and laid a gentle hand on Ciaran's back. "A ligean ar dul, deartháir," he said, as though speaking to a child or someone very ill, and he urged both men ahead of him out of the dining hall.

Ciaran looked back at him as he was pushed, seeming bewildered and liable to dart away like a startled animal at any moment. Cethen spoke quietly into Trent's ear as they climbed the stairs back to their room.

"Make him rest," he said. "Try to settle him. Airmed will come to see him soon. He is so far gone; he must save his strength, or he will not last through the night, let alone the spell our father intends for him."

Trent kept a straight face despite the churning in his stomach. He nodded and helped Ciaran into the room ahead of him, letting Cethen shut the door gently behind them. Trent laid Ciaran down on the bed and tugged off his boots before tucking him under the blankets and furs. Ciaran was mumbling to himself, half dazed, but when Trent tried to move away, the fairy's hand snapped out and took hold of Trent's wrist so tightly that he jumped.

"Don't," Ciaran begged. "Stay. Come." He moved over in the bed with some difficulty and nodded to Trent to lie beside him. As soon as Trent settled, Ciaran pulled him close and kissed him, holding him firmly by the sides of his face. His hands were cold, and Trent could feel the fairy's skin shivering, so he broke away as gently as he could.

"I was watching you," Ciaran whispered, keeping his forehead against Trent's. "I was watching you next to him. With him. You talked. Tá sé dom, agus níl mé dom—" Ciaran squeezed his eyes shut and tried to focus. "He's...he's me. I'm not. Not me. Soon. I can't—"

"Hush," Trent shushed him softly, stroking the fairy's trembling cheek with his thumb. "Get some sleep."

"No. I need...I need to—" Ciaran sighed and pressed another hard kiss to Trent's lips, his hand moving down and tugging impatiently on the younger man's belt buckle.

Trent leaned away from Ciaran and held his wrists to stop him. "What are you doing? Are you crazy? You need to rest. This isn't the time for—"

"It's almost gone," Ciaran snapped, but then he softened instantly and reached up to gently cup Trent's cheek and look into his eyes. "It's almost gone."

"What are you talking about? What's almost gone?"

"You," Ciaran said as though it should have been obvious. "Tá mé ag a chailliúint—no. Losing. I'm losing you. I can't...those people down there, I can't...I don't know who they are. My family, my wife, but only because they say so. I've been to Vancouver, but níláit ar bith roimh an. Before that—there isn't anything before you. But I don't...conas a rinne muid le chéile? I don't know. So I need more—cuimhní. I need more memories. I need to make more."

Trent's throat was so tight he thought he might suffocate before he could answer. He'd known that Ciaran had lost a lot of his memories from the spell he was under, but this—to have forgotten his family, to be forgetting Trent—he'd thought the fairy was only fading physically.

"That's why you've been like this?" Trent whispered. "All the sex—it was to try and make more memories with me?"

"You're all that's left," Ciaran answered in a weak voice. "Is breá liom thú." He paused to growl in frustration and tried again. "I love you. Stay, a mhuirnín."

"I'm not going anywhere, Ciaran. I love you, too."

Ciaran tucked his head under Trent's chin and breathed warm, feeble breaths against him. Trent kissed the fairy's hair, holding him as tightly as he dared until he heard the door click open behind them. Airmed let herself in with a bowl of something steaming hot in her hands and a soft cloth draped over her arm. Trent pulled away to stand, his heart breaking as Ciaran's clutching hands reached for him, but he allowed Airmed to take his place. She touched Ciaran's forehead with a tender frown.

"Oh, mo dheartháir, cad a bheith de tú?" she whispered softly to herself, and she let out a short sigh as she dipped her cloth in the hot liquid she'd left on the nightstand. "If only Miach were still here. He would know what to do." She touched Ciaran's forehead, his temples, his lips, and his chest, all while quietly singing a gentle song that at last seemed to lull Ciaran into calm. When he finally slept, she left her soaked cloth in the bowl and stood to let Trent sit on the bed again.

"He's very weak," she said in a hushed voice, her eyes on her brother. "My father's spell can't come too quickly for him." She touched Trent's shoulder and gave it a squeeze of assurance, but he didn't look up at her as she quietly left the room. He held Ciaran's hand while he slept and did his very best not to panic at the thought of the fairy dying before anyone could help him.

Airmed came back again and again through the night to check on Ciaran, each time bringing more and variant herbs and oils and humming softly over him as she applied them. Trent felt useless and out of place, but Airmed smiled kindly at him whenever she happened to catch his gaze.

Ciaran woke up less as the hours went on. When he did, he struggled for breath and looked around the room with wild eyes, as though he was looking for something. Even when Trent held his hands and whispered to him to calm him, he sometimes didn't respond. He was shivering, but sweat dampened the hair at his forehead, and Trent had to urge him again and again to keep the blanket on.

"Don't you know how to fight a fever?" Trent asked Ciaran during one of his swiftly-dwindling lucid moments. "What, fairies don't get sick? Should I clap my hands, and you'll feel better?" he teased with a soft smile, hoping to see even a glimmer of light in Ciaran's tired eyes. At this point, he really would have clapped if he'd thought it would help.

"Cá bhfuil mé," Ciaran answered instead, his brow furrowed as he glanced around the room.

"What?" Trent asked with more patience than he felt. English was becoming more and more rare.

"Ní féidir liom a bhraitheann go maith."

"I don't understand you, Ciaran."

"Cad atá ag tarlú?"

Trent sighed. "I don't know what you're saying. Just try to go back to sleep," he whispered, gently brushing damp hair from the fairy's forehead.

Ciaran reached up and took a tight grip on Trent's wrist, keeping him still. He looked up at him with a pained frown on his lips, his shallow breath rasping in the quiet room.

"Trent," he said.

"I'm right here."

Ciaran's grip loosened. "Trent," he said again. "A mhuirnín. A rún

179

mo chroí. Tá a fhios agam."

Before Trent could answer, Ciaran had slipped away into sleep again. Trent watched him with a sick, hollow feeling in his gut. How much could he really forget?

Trent tried to keep awake to watch over him, but eventually his eyes began to droop, and he laid down on the blanket beside Ciaran and let himself drift off with one hand gently on the fairy's arm in case he shifted. He didn't know how long he was asleep, but when he woke up, Ciaran was out of bed, hunched by the fireplace with his hands gripping his shoulders.

"Ciaran," Trent called as he sat up, "What are you doing?"

The fairy didn't answer, so Trent got to his feet and moved to crouch beside him. Ciaran jerked away as Trent lightly touched his back, falling onto his backside and scrambling away as quickly as his failing strength would let him. Blood stained his chin and shirt, and he'd smeared a puddle on the floor as he'd backed away. His eyes were sunken and dim, and he wheezed for breath as he stared across at Trent. He looked dead already.

"Cé tusa?" Ciaran snapped, his hand moving instinctively to his hip as though he expected to find a weapon there. "Cad é an áit seo?"

"Ciaran, just slow down," Trent tried, holding his hands up in surrender. "You need to get back in bed."

"Céard é sin? Cad atá tú ag rá?" Ciaran edged himself back farther, glancing over his shoulder as though he intended to bolt for the door.

"Everything's all right," Trent assured him. He was trying to sound gentle, but he could feel his voice trembling.

"Cé tusa?" Ciaran demanded again, but he had to stop to cough. Blood spilled from his lips, and he wiped it away with the back of his hand, leaving a smear across his cheek. "Freagair dom!" he shouted as soon as he found his breath.

The door opened behind him, and Ciaran spun to move away, clambering clumsily to his feet and gripping the bedpost for balance. "Fág mé ar m'aonar!" he begged as Airmed entered, his voice sounding panicked.

Airmed touched her hand to her heart with a knowing sigh, and she stood a safe distance from him to answer. She spoke to him in Gaelic, as gently as she could, and when Trent moved to get to his feet, she stilled him with a subtle motion of her hand at her side. Trent saw Ciaran's eyes dart to him even at his slight movement, the fairy's look feral and untrusting. Ciaran answered Airmed with uncertainty in his voice, but he seemed slightly more relaxed to hear words that he recognized. The two of them spoke for a minute or two more, and Ciaran eventually agreed to sit back down on the bed, but when Trent approached him, Ciaran leaned back from him and pulled away from his touch.

"Ná teagmháil dom," he growled. "Níl a fhios agam duit."

"What's the matter?" Trent asked, looking to Airmed with a puzzled frown. "Why is he so upset?"

Airmed seemed reluctant to answer. She wrung her hands for a moment before opening her mouth to speak. "He says...he doesn't want you to touch him. He...he says he doesn't know who you are."

Trent swayed as though he'd been hit in the chest. He looked at Ciaran, searching his face for some sign that Airmed was mistaken, but Ciaran stared back at him with a scowl of confusion and mistrust. Ciaran had warned him. He'd told Trent that he was forgetting. But somehow, hearing Airmed say that Ciaran had actually forgotten him felt like a punch to the gut.

Airmed squeezed Trent's shoulder, frowning as though the gesture was as much for her own benefit as Trent's. "I...we simply can't wait anymore," she said softly. "Just try to keep him calm. I'll go and help my father finish preparing."

She left them alone in the room with a quiet rustle of her skirt, and Trent was forced to keep a polite distance from the man he loved in order to stop him from panicking at a stranger's touch.

18

"Choose your equipment carefully," Lugh advised as he stood in the dark courtyard with Julien's bag at his feet. "Your guns will be of no help to you on Emain Ablach."

Julien knelt by his bag and zipped it open. "What exactly will be of help to me? What am I to expect from this…whatever he is?"

"Manandán is the lord of all the sea," Lugh answered tersely. "He is not a whatever, and addressing him with respect will be the very first way you can keep yourself alive."

Julien pressed his lips together to avoid saying something rude. Lugh was helping him, even if it was somewhat reluctantly, and all of this was to keep Noah alive. He wouldn't do anything to risk failing at that, no matter what he had to endure. He could feel the lingering touch of the witch's lips on his, the younger man's hand gripping the fabric of his shirt. Julien's heart still hadn't slowed to a normal rhythm. If he had taken the time to think about it, he might have felt strange about how quickly he had gone from a solitary hunter with no interest in companionship to the sort of person who gave male witches dramatic goodbye kisses before risking his life to save them. But he didn't have time to doubt anymore. Noah needed him focused. He wasn't going to fail.

"Don't bring your iron," Lugh added. "He'll be insulted. You aren't going to fight him."

Julien sighed and let his hands drop to his knees. "What should I be bringing, then?"

"Whatever weapon you're best at."

"I thought I wasn't fighting him."

"I didn't say you wouldn't be fighting anything."

"Of course," Julien sighed. He picked a long knife from his bag that wasn't made of iron, a few vials of dangerous tinctures that Noah had mixed up for him, and his heaviest set of brass knuckles. Without guns, he was handicapped but hardly hobbled. He would hold his own.

"Time to move," Lugh said as soon as Julien stood, and he led the hunter from the courtyard with a long stride. At the street, Lugh whistled at a waiting driver, who hastily pulled forward to allow them into his carriage. Julien hadn't been exactly surprised to see the beetles when they had first arrived—not much surprised him when it came to the variety of creatures living under the surface of man's notice—but he was surprised at how smooth the carriage ride was. A beetle wasn't really something he would have thought of as graceful.

They took the carriage to the edge of the city, and then they began the long trek back up the stairs to the surface. Julien smiled faintly to himself as they passed the spots where Noah had picked the rocks clean of bioluminescent mushrooms, hunched over the steps and peering warily ahead at Lugh to keep from being caught. What the witch had planned to do with glowing fairy mushrooms, he chose not to think too hard on.

It was barely light out when Julien and Lugh stepped out of the stone corridor of the ancient mound, so there were no tourists to get in their way. Lugh put his fingers to his mouth and whistled sharply for his horse, and the creature's heavy hoofbeats thundered across the grass until the massive animal trotted to a stop in front of them. Lugh thumped it on the neck affectionately and lifted himself into the rough saddle, then offered his hand to Julien to help him up behind him. Before Julien could lament getting back on the horse too soon for his ass to properly recover from their last ride, Lugh had spurred the creature on with a click of his tongue, and the stone mound disappeared behind them within moments.

"Manandán will test you," Lugh said over his shoulder as they rode. "If he decides your cause is worthy, he must then determine that *you* are worthy."

"What sort of test?" Julien shouted back through the rush of the wind.

"That is for him to decide," Lugh answered with irritating ambiguity. "But heroes must possess certain qualities to be considered worthy of my lord's blessings."

"Heroes?" Julien frowned at Lugh's back. He wasn't a hero. He killed things for a living. His brothers might have considered themselves noble and righteous, but Julien was just providing a service. He had the knowledge, the ability, and the means necessary to thin the world's population of monsters, and so he had the responsibility.

"In the classical sense of the word," Lugh answered dryly.

"If I succeed, will I get a nickname too, so that sylphs will talk about me in mysterious whispers?"

Lugh turned his head to stare at Julien over his shoulder, one eyebrow ticked up just slightly. "The Tuath Dé grant titles for many reasons," he said, "but I don't know of any off-hand that are given for sassing people offering to help save your lover's life."

"What's yours for, then?"

"For victories," he said simply, and he returned his attention to the field ahead of him. Soon they were galloping away from the land, the horse's hooves splashing heavily onto the surface of the water. It was still a little unnerving even after their long ride before.

Julien could barely see the coastline behind him when Lugh suddenly said, "Deep breath."

The hunter opened his mouth to question, but as the horse reared back, he wisely chose to take Lugh's advice instead, and the animal dove straight under the water. Julien hung on tighter to Lugh's cloak as the salt water rushed over him, threatening to dislodge him from the horse's back. He didn't dare open his eyes for a moment, but once the ride seemed to even out, he squinted into the dark water, the salt stinging his eyes. He could feel pressure building in his ears as the horse drove deeper into the sea, and his lungs began to ache from holding his breath. Lugh didn't seem concerned; bubbles blew from his nose and disappeared above them as he took breath from the water just as easily as air.

Far below them, so deep that Julien was certain his heart would explode before they reached their destination, he could just make out a shimmering globe surrounding what seemed to be a green field and a tall, spiraling castle.

Lugh's horse let out a bubbling whinny of excitement as they drew close, and just when Julien's vision was starting to shrink into black, the animal burst through the barrier, landing heavily on solid earth, and trotted to a halt in the grass. Julien lost his grip and slipped to the ground, gasping for breath and dripping salt water as he steadied himself on his hands and knees.

Lugh snorted at him as he dismounted much more gracefully, his own clothes and hair dry as a bone. "Not bad."

Julien got to his feet and shook some water from his hands, running a hand through his hair to slick it out of his face. "Couldn't have shared some of whatever magic all this is?" he asked, gesturing vaguely at Lugh's dry self.

"It isn't my magic to give."

"Lugh Lámhfhada, mar mé i mo chónaí agus bás!" a booming voice called out from across the field, and a man appeared in the distance, approaching them with widespread arms. He was thickly-built and taller even than Lugh, with a bushy red beard that was just long enough to sit on his bare chest. He wore rough trousers and a long cloak that seemed to shimmer between white and the palest blue, barely hiding the longsword hanging from his hip by a thick leather belt. He clasped Lugh in a tight embrace and thumped him on the back with force that would have broken Julien's ribs.

"Cé hé seo go atá tú a thabhairt dom?" he asked as they broke apart, finally seeming to notice Julien. The hunter squared his shoulders and stood up straight, though he didn't feel particularly dignified with his shirt still dripping seawater into the grass.

"This man is a warrior," Lugh began in pointed English, and the other man's eyebrows lifted as Lugh tilted his head toward Julien. "He has come to ask for your blessing."

"My blessing, is it?" the man said in a gravely brogue. He looked Julien up and down. "He's a decent size for a human, isn't he?"

"I wouldn't have brought him if I didn't think he was up to the task. He fought me, Manandán."

The man let out a short, barking laugh. "And how did that go, an duine?" he said, a sly crinkle at the corners of his eyes as he looked at Julien. "You've still got your head on, I see. That's more than many men can say."

"And that with a broken arm," Julien answered, and he saw Lugh's nostrils flare in irritation out of the corner of his eye.

Manandán laughed and shoved Lugh by the shoulder, causing the younger man to sway grumpily on his feet. "That's the kind of answer I like! Who are you, human, and why have you come to Emain Ablach?"

Julien bowed his head slightly. "My name is Julien Fournier, and I've come because someone I love will die without one of your apples. I'll do whatever it takes to earn the right to take one."

Manandán hummed and stroked at his beard. "Well, I can't say I've never heard that before. It's a bit of a trite reason, isn't it?" He glanced over at Lugh. "You couldn't have brought someone more interesting?"

"Tell him who you *are*," Lugh pressed with a stern frown.

Julien let out a short sigh through his nose. "I'm Julien Fournier, seventh son of Gérard Fournier, the seventh son of Jean-Michel Fournier. I am a hunter of all things magic that are a threat to man, as my father and my grandfather before me. The man I love will be forced to give his life for the sake of a spell to save the life of a creature who does not deserve it—unless I bring him an apple from Emain Ablach."

Manandán's eyebrow quirked up, and he hesitated, but then he snorted out another quick laugh. "Well that's a bit more like it, isn't it? Oh, it must gall you to come and ask for my help, mustn't it, seventh son?"

Julien tried and failed to keep his hands from balling into fists at his sides. "I need help, and I will take it where I can get it," he answered through a tight jaw.

"This is a treat," Manandán chuckled. "I've known a few of your kind in my time, sealgaire, but none so humble as to come begging for my aid. And who is it you happened upon that brought you into the company of the Tuath Dé?"

"He was hunting my father," Lugh answered for him.

Manandán turned to look at the fairy with surprise. "What, Cian's alive? And being picked on by a human huntsman, no less. You aim high, don't you, sealgaire? Hunting down one of the Tuath Dé is no mean feat." He paused and tilted his head, simply regarding Julien for a moment. "Yes. Yes, I think you should try. My dear ward Lugh seems to think you're up for it, so who am I to argue?"

Julien let out a soft sigh of relief. Whatever he would be up against, at least he would have the opportunity to fight.

"Challenges," Manandán said, suddenly stern. "Four in all, and each one deadly should you fail. I will allow you one and only one opportunity to turn back, sealgaire. Speak now, and I shall send you on your way without injury. Otherwise stay, and either earn your prize or die."

Julien didn't hesitate. His voice didn't waver. Noah needed him, and he had no better option than this. "I choose to stay," he said.

"Excellent. Follow me."

Manandán led them across the field toward the crystalline castle, and when Julien looked up at the reflective spires, he almost stopped walking at the sight of a small group of humpback whales swimming far above them, beyond the shimmering barrier holding back who knew how many tons of water. He quickened his pace to catch up again and chose not to think too much about quite how much water could potentially come crashing down on top of him. Manandán stopped near a towering wall of opaque blue glass that seemed to stretch on farther than the land itself, and when he placed his hand on the smooth surface, it rippled like water and slowly opened into a rounded doorway.

"A hero must be cunning, or he will fall prey to deceit before ever he begins his journey," Manandán said as he turned back to face Julien. He tilted his head toward the opening. "I will see you on the other side, sealgaire."

Julien spared a glance at Lugh, but the fairy only offered him a brief, stern nod, so Julien stepped forward through the rippling door. When he looked back, the opening had already closed behind him without a sound. Ahead of him, a walled path stretched forward, curving off to the right in a smooth turn. He didn't like the look of this. He took a few steps forward, following the curving path until he saw the sharp bend in the wall and confirmed his suspicion—a labyrinth. He hadn't even had a princess to give him a ball of string. No chance of climbing such a smooth surface. He settled for keeping his right hand on the pale glass wall, and he moved carefully down the narrow path.

After only two turns, he stepped around a corner and was faced with a wooden door the width of the passage. Julien paused and waited a moment for something to happen, but it was just a door. He reached out tentatively and put his hand on the knob, then stopped again to listen. There didn't even seem to be a lock on the door. He turned the handle and pushed it open in a rush, ready to move back out of the way of whatever was waiting on the other side, but as soon as the door was open, a disembodied arm appeared from the darkness beyond and hit him in the chest. He stumbled backward, wincing and touching his accosted sternum, as the hand in the doorway made a rude gesture at him and slammed the door shut again.

"Ce qui la baise?" Julien muttered, staring at the door with a furrowed brow. He reached out for the doorknob again and frowned as he slowly turned it. He threw the door open and sidestepped immediately to avoid the reaching hand, but his first step into the darkness earned him a powerful punch to the face. The hand gave him a mocking thumbs down and pulled the door shut with a loud thud as Julien rubbed at his jaw. This went on a few more times, Julien trying new tactics each try to avoid the hand, but every time, he was knocked backwards and blocked off again.

Sometimes the hand hit him hard, and sometimes it only shoved him, but just trying to get by the door's guardian clearly wasn't working. With a huff, Julien took hold of the door handle once more and turned it, but then he paused. He crept the door open only a crack and peeked inside. He flinched when the hand appeared in the narrow space he'd opened, but it only reached through, gently stroked his chest, then waved its finger "no" at him and pulled the door out of his hand to shut it.

That was somehow even worse. He stared at the door in silence for a while. When he tried to open it, it pushed him. When he tried to rush through, it punched him. But when he had been cautious, it had been gentle. The whole thing was ridiculous—what sort of a door was this, and why would a fairy sea god need one in his backyard labyrinth?

Julien scowled at the closed door. If opening the door didn't work, then maybe—ridiculous. He reached up, bypassing the door handle, and he knocked instead. To his surprise, a cheerful voice called out to him from the other side in perfect Quebec French.

"Yes, hello, who is it please?"

Julien faltered for a moment. "Uh. Julien Fournier."

"Monsieur Fournier? How may I help you, please?"

"I need by."

"Oh, I'm afraid we're very busy at the moment."

"What? Busy?"

"Oh yes. Couldn't possibly let you through."

Julien opened his mouth to shout, but he bit his tongue. Whatever magic had made this door, it didn't respond to force. He grit his teeth and made his best effort to be polite. "It would be very kind of you to let me in," he said. "I would be grateful." When the door stayed silent, he spat out a final, "Please."

"That wasn't so hard, was it?" The door clicked and swung open, revealing still more of the very same path he was already on. "Honestly, such heroes these days, all muscle and no guile," the door tutted at him as he passed through.

"Va te crisser," Julien muttered, and the door audibly gasped behind him as though scandalized, then reached out behind him and slapped him on the rear. He jumped, but when he spun to face it again, it was gone, leaving only the empty path he'd come from.

Julien pressed his lips together in irritation and continued through the curving labyrinth, which actually seemed less and less labyrinthine the farther he went. There were no choices, no alternate turns to take—only the single grassy path that he was on. He walked for so long that he grew impatient and quickened his pace until he was jogging down the paths, taking the corners at a tilt. The maze seemed endless, but just when Julien was about to stop and attempt to scale the walls, the path opened up into a round courtyard.

He skidded to a stop just before entering. Standing in front of him, at the far end of the empty courtyard, was Noah—not just one Noah, but several, each standing in front of a door. Julien approached the center of the courtyard cautiously, and each Noah lifted his eyes to watch him.

"What is this?" Julien asked softly. Noah looked healthier than he had in days. He wasn't hunched over to cough or pale with fever. He looked just like Julien knew him—all of them did. It was almost painful to see him like this, knowing that it was a lie, and that the real Noah was trapped and waiting to be sacrificed like an animal.

"A choice," all of the Noahs said in unison. "Several paths, but only one way forward. Choose your path. Choose correctly, and advance. Choose poorly, and die."

"Well, that's straightforward," Julien muttered dryly. He focused on the Noah in front of him, since trying to look at all of them was too confusing. "How am I supposed to choose?"

"Choose your path," they said again. "Choose which of us to save."

"To save?" Julien echoed with a frown.

"That's why you're here, isn't it?" a Noah at his left spoke up. "You came here to save me. So let's bust out already." He gestured to the door behind him, and Julien tilted his head and paused.

"Why should I?" he asked, guessing the nature of the game. "Why should I save you?"

The Noah scoffed. "Uh, because this whole thing is bullshit, and Manandán is wasting your time? Time that should be spent getting your prize and saving my ass, by the way. So come on," he urged, tapping the door behind him with his knuckles.

Julien's brow furrowed slightly, and he turned his attention to the next Noah, earning an impatient sigh from the first. "And you? Why should I choose you?"

This Noah smiled at him. "You've tried so hard just to get here," he said. "You should rest. I'm not going anywhere."

"What if I choose someone else?"

The Noah shrugged one shoulder and gave a soft half-smile. "I know you'll make the right choice in the end, Julien."

Julien paused, and he almost took a step forward, but he stayed put. There were still four more Noahs. He couldn't rush and risk picking the wrong door. He turned and looked at the next Noah instead.

"What if I choose you?" he asked.

"Then we'll go through the door together," the Noah answered immediately. "And if you die, I die. I go where you go. We're partners, right? Together 'til the end."

"Right," Julien murmured. This was getting harder. He looked over at the next witch in the half-circle.

"You really have to ask why you should choose me?" this Noah spoke up before Julien could. "You liked it, didn't you, when I was pressed up against you in bed, begging for you to touch me?" He ran an idle finger down the collarbone exposed by his worn t-shirt. "You wanted to, right? To pin me down, kiss me, feel me writhing underneath you? I wanted it too. I can give that to you. I can give you whatever you want," he added with a predatory smile, catching the corner of his bottom lip in his teeth.

A small shiver ran down Julien's spine at the look on the witch's face, full of promise. He'd never seen Noah so brazen, but he'd felt the witch's need in his kiss, his hunger—Noah was no shrinking violet. Julien pulled his gaze away from the Noah threatening to unfasten his belt buckle and focused on the next to last one in the line.

"What about you?" he asked, and the Noah shut his eyes for a moment before answering.

"I can't make this choice for you," he said. "You have to figure out who you are, Julien. Who you want to be. I know who I want you to be—but the path you're on is your own. The one you go down from here on is yours, too, and you'll reap the benefits or suffer the consequences of your choices. Just like we all do."

The Noah smiled placidly and waited with his hands in his pockets, apparently satisfied to say his piece and wait. Julien frowned at him and looked to the last Noah.

"Why should I choose you?" he said, feeling a bit like a broken record, but this Noah didn't answer. He shrugged and fidgeted and crouched down to pick at the grass.

"Maybe you shouldn't," he whispered at last, so quietly that Julien wasn't sure he'd said anything at all. "Maybe you shouldn't have come at all. You've put yourself through so much because of me, and I—I've only made things harder on you. I've always made things harder on you. You've protected me so many times, and I...I can't do anything for you. I want to. I want to help you, and keep you safe, but I—what if I can't?" he finished in a hushed voice.

Julien hesitated, his heart clenching in his chest. "It isn't your job to keep me safe," he said without thinking. "It's mine to keep you that way."

"You deserve better than me," the Noah whispered.

Julien stepped toward him and reached out to touch his shoulder, but he stopped himself. Noah had been so depressed lately, so resigned—this was the Noah he had left behind. But this wasn't who Noah was. He pulled back and looked at each of the duplicates in turn. Noah could be quiet and uncertain. But he was also reckless and kind. He was brave, and sexual, and he never judged.

"I can't choose," Julien muttered to himself. He shook his head. "I can't choose," he said aloud. "There isn't just one right version of you. They're all you."

Behind him, he heard a sudden, heavy thump, and he turned to see a seventh door click itself open.

"No man has only one side," the Noahs said together. "No man sees only one path. Proceed."

They vanished before Julien could answer, taking their doors with them, and Julien let out a long sigh before stepping through the last remaining door.

19

As soon as Julien stepped through the door, he found himself in front of Manandán's castle again, with the smooth labyrinth wall behind him.

"I'm glad to see you again, sealgaire," Manandán said, clapping him on the shoulder so hard that he almost stumbled. "Are you ready to proceed?"

"There's more than that?"

Lugh scoffed nearby, but Manandán answered. "Oh, of course. Four trials, remember? I can't give one of my precious apples to a one-sided hero, now can I?"

Julien held in his sigh. "Then what's next?"

"I'm so glad you asked. You must be tired, walking through that long labyrinth of mine. For your next test, just stand...oh, right over there." He moved Julien by the shoulders to stand near the castle wall. "Yes, that should do. Oh, hold these for me, will you?"

Manandán snapped his fingers, and Julien suddenly jerked forward from the weight of a filled water bucket in each hand. Manandán tapped his elbows to urge him to hold his arms straight out at his sides and then stood back to look at him.

"Yes, just like that. Very good. You've done this before, I can tell. Were you naughty in school, perhaps?"

"What is this?" Julien asked, gripping the rope handles of the buckets tightly to avoid spilling any of the water.

"They're buckets," Manandán said slowly, his eyebrows lifted as he nodded at Julien like a small child.

Julien bit his cheek to avoid snapping back. "What am I supposed to do with them?" he asked instead.

"You're doing just fine." Manandán turned to look at Lugh. "Do you want anything? A drink. You need a drink! I haven't seen you in ages."

Lugh allowed the larger man to lead him to a small gazebo just within Julien's line of sight. There were sturdy seats underneath the roof, which spiraled upwards into swirling blue waves. Servants took Lugh's cloak, and the two men settled into their seats and were instantly provided with soft footrests and silver cups. Julien stared in tight-jawed disbelief as Manandán cheerfully raised his cup at him. Servants carefully adjusted the footrests and kept the cups full of fresh mead while Julien stood nearby with outstretched arms.

"So how have you been, my boy?" Manandán asked. "What's this business about your father? This sealgaire was giving him trouble?"

"It isn't a story worth telling," Lugh said into his cup.

"I just want to know how this human managed to even put a hand on a Tuath Dé," Manandán said with a boisterous laugh. "Well, the benefits of being a seventh son, I suppose," he sighed, shrugging one shoulder. "When you have that kind of lineage handed to you, I don't imagine your own skill matters so much."

The muscles in Julien's arms slowly began to tremble with effort, but he gripped the rope handles tighter as Manandán spoke. He'd been teased enough by his brothers for "inheriting" his abilities and coasting effortlessly into his father's favor, but that couldn't have been further from the truth. His father had pushed him harder, kept him awake longer, and expected more of him than he ever had of Julien's brothers. *Don't get complacent*, he'd said. *Don't think you're special. Being born last just means you have more to catch up to.*

Julien kept his eyes forward, refusing to give Manandán the satisfaction of glaring at him. He managed well until he felt something sharp hit his cheek. He looked over at the pair of lounging men and spotted Manandán lining up another shot with a small chip of ice in his palm. He squinted one eye for a moment before flicking it at Julien's face, and the hunter had to flinch to keep the chip out of his eye.

"You're doing well, sealgaire. Much better than I expected."

"How long do you expect me to stand like this?" Julien ground out, trying to hide the shaking in his arms.

"Until I tell you to move," Manandán answered with sudden sternness in his voice.

"They aren't that heavy," Lugh muttered, and he drained his cup and passed it into the hands of a waiting servant. He glanced up at Manandán. "You did give him the human ones, didn't you?"

"Well his arms are still on, so I must have."

Julien snorted and set his jaw, refusing to allow his elbows to droop. He wasn't sure how long he stayed there, the buckets of water seeming to grow heavier by the moment, but the time wasn't made easier by Manandán's constant pestering. He pelted Julien with ice and chatted pleasantly with Lugh about how unbelievably long it had taken the hunter to make it through the labyrinth.

"There were only the two obstacles, after all," he had laughed, and Julien had gripped his buckets tighter.

Finally, Manandán stood from his seat and took a few steps toward Julien. The buckets vanished from the hunter's hands, the sudden loss causing his hands to jerk upwards. He hid his sigh of relief as best he could and rubbed at his reddened palms. Manandán moved to stand in front of him with a faint, satisfied smile on his face.

"A hero must have fortitude, or he will turn back before his journey's end," he said. "Are you ready for your next challenge?"

Julien almost bit back with sarcasm, but he held his tongue and simply nodded. "I am."

"Oh, but you've been through so much already," Manandán said with what Julien suspected was mock sincerity. He looked over his shoulder and gestured at a nearby servant. "Why don't you have a rest for a while, and we can pick this up later?"

"I don't have time to wait," Julien objected even as the servant put a hand on his arm. "Noah doesn't have time. Give me your trials; I don't need to rest."

"That's a sweet sentiment, sealgaire, but you really must. Go on now."

Julien scowled as the servant turned him by the arm and led him through the towering doors of the castle. They walked down the broad hall and turned down a short corridor, but as soon as the man pushed Julien into a room behind a heavy door, the hunter swayed on his feet and his vision went black.

Julien felt the soft ground under his cheek before he was fully awake. His eyes were open, but there was nothing to see in the pitch blackness. When he tried to pull himself up, he realized with a jolt that his hands were tied securely behind his back. He shifted onto his side and immediately found his back against a wall of earth, and when he stretched out his bound feet, he hit the opposite wall before he could move more than a few inches. He jerked against the rope binding his wrists and hit his shoulder against the wall of his narrow tunnel.

He was trapped. No light, no space, no freedom to move—his heart began to race as the full measure of his situation dawned on him. He could feel cold sweat forming on his brow, and his stomach twisted. Trapped. Julien's chest shook with shallow, panicked breaths. He squeezed his eyes shut in an attempt to ignore the thick darkness surrounding him. He had never been afraid to fight, never been afraid to be hurt—but being trapped was something else. He could still feel the tight threads of the spiderweb crushing his chest, keeping him motionless and barely able to breathe. The pale silk had covered his mouth, his eyes, everything—and he had laid in the creature's nest for hours before his brother had killed the thing and cut him loose. Here, in his little tunnel of earth, the air felt stifling and hot, and Julien had to force himself to breathe more slowly.

Manandán wouldn't just leave him in here to die. He hoped. This had to be a test. There had to be a way out. But Julien couldn't focus on anything but the scratching rope around his wrists and the press of the earth against his shoulder. There might not be a way out—there certainly wasn't any that Julien could see. He would die here. He would die here, and Noah would die waiting for him, and Julien's body would be hidden in this grave until he turned to dust.

The hunter clenched his fists and shook his head, puffing away the dirt near his mouth as he sighed. This wasn't helping. He couldn't panic. He couldn't afford to panic, and Noah wouldn't survive if he did. There was always a way out. Though his stomach churned, and his heart barely slowed despite his deep breaths, Julien forced himself to shift and test the strength of his bonds. The rope was thick, but that meant it wasn't as tight as it could be. Julien pressed his lips together and took one last, calming breath, and then he began to work the knots on his wrists, angling himself to scrape the rope against the knife hanging from his belt.

When he was finally loose, he was able—just barely—to move his arms from behind his back. The narrow space left very little room for maneuvering. Now he had a decision to make. He stretched one arm up past his head and reached with his fingertips, but he couldn't feel anything but more dirt and darkness ahead of him. He pushed downward with his bound feet and found no barrier there, either. He was in the center of a tunnel with no way of knowing which direction would lead him to the surface.

Julien curled as much as the space would allow as fear tightened his gut, but he let out a soft swear and grit his teeth. He wasn't a child anymore. No one was going to come and save him, and he had someone relying on him. So he made a decision and started to scoot himself forward as best he could, testing the tunnel ahead of him with his hands as he went. He couldn't even see his own arms in front of him, let alone anything that might be waiting for him farther down the tunnel. He paused as he thought he heard a slithering, hissing sound from behind him, but he forced himself to focus and quickened his pace through the tunnel. He just hoped the distant sound meant he'd made the right choice.

He crawled for what felt like years, inching his way down the tunnel and only pausing now and then to wipe the sweat out of his eyes with his sleeve. Finally, when every muscle in his body ached, he reached out a hand to pull himself forward—and touched earth. He pressed his hand against the dirt wall, panic pumping through his heart as he scratched into the soil in search of—anything. He dug at the dirt with his fingers, seeking anything that might have led to a way out. But the only thing he found was more earth. He'd gone the wrong way, assuming there was a right way at all.

He struggled for oxygen and heard himself panting in the narrow space. No. There wasn't time for this. Who knows how long he had spent down here already? Noah was waiting for him. So Julien steeled himself, snorted out the last of his fear, and started back down the way he had come, toward the slithering sound.

Before he could move more than a few feet, a sudden blinding light hit his eyes, and he instinctively flinched to cover his face with his arms. It took him a few moments to realize that he had the space to hide his face in his arms. He slowly squinted into the light as he lifted his head, and he found himself back in Manandán's garden, curled in the grass.

"A hero must have courage, or he will tremble when he is needed most," Manandán's voice spoke from above him.

Lugh offered Julien a hand up, and the hunter took it and was pulled easily to his feet. His hands and arms were filthy—the tunnel had been real enough.

"Part of the test was lying to me about getting some sleep?" Julien grumbled, but Manandán only smiled blithely at him.

"A hero must also expect the unexpected, and will find that very rarely does any good come of trusting any magical hosts he might encounter on his journey. Don't you read your Homer?" Julien only snorted and didn't answer. It wouldn't benefit him to speak his mind. "In any case," Manandán went on, "you're almost finished now. You've done very well. You may even enjoy your last test."

Julien looked up into the bearded face of his would-be benefactor. "I'm ready."

"Good. For your final test—a hero must be strong to lift his arm against his enemy. You must find and kill the Beisht Kione."

Julien didn't like the way Lugh's eyebrows lifted in surprise. The fairy looked over at Manandán with a curious frown.

"I thought you were giving him the human version?" he asked, and Manandán paused.

"What, you think it's too much?"

"You sent me after that thing, and it nearly killed me. Play fair or don't play at all."

"Bah, fair," Manandán grumbled, but he gave a pensive hum as he looked the hunter up and down. Julien could only imagine what he looked like, but if it was anything like he felt, he probably wasn't cutting a very imposing figure. "Very well," Manandán said at last. "A Dobhar-Chú." He looked over at Lugh as though for his approval, and the fairy nodded.

"Where do I find it?" Julien asked.

Lugh spoke up before Manandán could. "Allow me to offer a gift," the fairy said, and he turned his head to whistle. His mottled grey horse trotted up and nuzzled his shoulder. Lugh stroked the animal's nose and frowned down at Julien. "A loan," he clarified. "If the Enbarr will have you, you may ride her. She will take you to your destination." He looked over at Manandán. "And I'm sure my lord will grant you his blessing for your journey, since he has chosen to assign a task to a human that necessitates being completed hundreds of feet below the surface of the sea."

"I may as well do it for him," Manandán sighed, but he reached out a hand and pressed his palm over Julien's mouth, softly muttering a quick incantation that left Julien breathing easier than he had since they'd arrived.

Lugh took hold of his horse's reins and held them out to Julien. The hunter hesitated just a moment, eyeing the creature's dinner plate-sized hooves, and then he took hold of the leather straps and reached out a hand to touch the Enbarr's nose. The animal snuffled his palm, only seeming mildly disagreeable, so Julien moved to its side and lifted himself into the blanketed saddle with more difficulty than he hoped showed. The horse snorted and dug one hoof into the grass, but it didn't try to throw him.

"Good luck, hunter," Lugh said with a curt nod, and he swatted the Enbarr's rear and sent it forward with a burst of speed that almost made Julien lose his grip. The horse ran straight through the glistening barrier separating the castle grounds from the sea, and Julien instinctively held his breath, but the horse kept galloping with no sign of heading for the surface. When he was forced to exhale, he gasped for breath and found that the water filled his lungs as easily as air. Manandán's blessing, he supposed. Julien allowed the horse to lead the way, gripping the reins in one hand and his knife in the other. He had never heard of a Dobhar-Chú—Noah would have known—but whatever it was, he didn't want it to catch him unawares.

The Enbarr reared back when it reached an underwater cove, beating its hooves on the ocean floor and creating clouds of sand at its feet. Julien frowned and stroked the animal's neck, giving it a comforting pat as he peered into the darkness of the cave.

Without warning, something long and sleek darted out of the mouth of the cove, rushing past Julien in a flash of slick fur and sharp teeth. It was easily the size of a bear. The creature had four limbs and a long, finned tail, and when it turned to face Julien again, he saw its strange face, broad and doglike with powerful, snapping jaws. It rushed at him, clawing at him with webbed feet as it passed, and he slashed out with his knife, managing to nick its flank. The Dobhar-Chú let out a hissing growl, easily heard even through the muffle of the water. Dark blood swirled in the water from its wound, and it snapped at Julien once more and darted forward through the Enbarr's legs, forcing the horse to rush upwards through the water to avoid being knocked down.

The Dobhar-Chú was fast, but the Enbarr was faster. Julien urged the horse closer with every strike, each cut of his knife drawing a bit more blood into the water. He wished he'd had a slightly longer weapon, as he was forced to draw dangerously close to the monster to do any damage, but he hadn't accounted for having to fight ugly dog-otter-creatures underwater. Still, it was almost comforting to be doing something he knew he was good at—to forget all the magic and focus on the kill.

When Julien had done enough damage to noticeably slow the Dobhar-Chú, the monster snarled at him and swam away in a flurry of teeth and fur. Julien urged the Enbarr after it, following the creature upwards through the water until they both broke the surface. Real air almost felt strange in Julien's lungs after breathing so much water, but the transition was instant and painless, so he could keep his eyes on the monster ahead of him as it darted along the surface. The Dobhar-Chú vanished under the water again, but before Julien could get the horse to follow, the creature burst out of the water and leapt easily over the horse, catching Julien's shoulder in its teeth and dragging him from the Enbarr's back into the water.

Julien's cry of pain came out in a stream of bubbles as he was pulled deeper. He could feel the Dobhar-Chú's teeth scraping his collarbone and saw his own blood dissipating into the salt water above him. He wasn't going to let this beast kill him. Not after all he'd done. Julien struggled against the creature's grip as they sank, kicking out and reaching to get a grip around its neck. When he finally found purchase, he dragged the blade of his knife across the Dobhar-Chú's throat, forcing it to release him. He didn't give it the opportunity to flee again. Julien held on tightly to the monster, hooking his legs around its middle, and he found the back of its skull with the tip of his knife and buried the blade as deep as it could go.

The Dobhar-Chú thrashed wildly, snapping backwards at him, but after a few short moments, it went still, and Julien was left floating with one hand on the creature's smooth fur, watching his blood cloud red around him. He was losing too much, and the salt water seeping into his wound was excruciating. He tried to pull his knife free and could barely budge it.

He glanced around, hoping he'd be able to at least tell which direction he'd come from, but the Enbarr approached him from below, lifting him onto its back and carrying him effortlessly back toward Manandán's castle. They went more slowly than they had come, as Julien was unwilling to release the Dobhar-Chú. He held it tightly by the scruff of its thick neck and let the Enbarr pull it along behind them, though the horse didn't wait long enough for him to shift the corpse to his uninjured side.

The creature's weight almost pulled his arm out of its socket as they broke through the barrier and landed on solid ground again, but Julien slipped down from the horse's back rather than release the body.

"Not bad time," Lugh commented from nearby. "Not good, but not bad." Julien managed to find the strength to scowl at him as Manandán approached.

"Look at you, sealgaire," he chuckled. "Not the cleanest of kills, was it? You've made a mess of its hide."

"I didn't plan on having it mounted," Julien grumbled.

"Took a bit of a scratch, too, didn't you?"

Julien stood up as straight as he could to look up into Manandán's face, and he tried not to wince at the pain in his shoulder. "Have I earned what I came for or haven't I?"

"I suppose I should have expected that Lugh would have brought me a serious sort of a hero," Manandán sighed. "Very well. Seventh son, you've proven cunning, resilient, brave, and strong. Let my servants tend to your wound, and you'll have your prize."

"I don't need tending," Julien answered impatiently, though he was growing lightheaded from blood loss. "I need to get back."

"You'll get there, sealgaire," Manandán promised. "It wouldn't be fair of me to put you through all this and then let you die on the trip back." He snapped his fingers for a servant, and Julien was led into the castle despite his protestations. This time there was no sudden blackness and no tricks; the servant stitched his shoulder with silver thread and bandaged it with shimmering blue gauze, then bowed and left him alone in the room.

Manandán appeared shortly, carrying a bundle of brown fur with a small silver apple nestled gently in its folds. He placed it in Julien's hands and gave him a smiling nod.

"That creature you killed will do you a favor yet, sealgaire," he said. "The Dobhar-Chú's fur is a good guard against magic. I took the liberty of having it fashioned into a cloak for you. Consider it a parting gift. And you have your apple, of course. Use it wisely."

Julien ran his hand over the smooth fur for a moment before looking up. "Thank you."

"You're a good sport, Julien Fournier, even if you are a little grumpy. Come back sometime if you want to try your luck again. I'll come up with even better challenges for you."

"I'll keep that in mind."

Lugh pushed open the door and poked his head inside. "Time to go," he said, leaving no room for argument. "Your witch is waiting."

Julien stood, clutching the fur and the apple it held tightly to his chest, and he offered Manandán a small bow before following Lugh out of the castle and mounting the horse behind him. Noah was waiting.

20

Noah would have paced the room for hours if he'd had the strength. He had barely been able to stomach his supper, and his awkward attempt at reconciliation had only made things worse. He didn't know why he'd tried; there was no chance Trent would ever forgive him, and Noah didn't blame him. If someone had done to Julien what they'd done to Ciaran—he didn't know how he would respond. But it was still hard to think of Trent as his enemy when he had so many memories in his head of the boy smiling at him, or with his brow knit into such a soft, worried expression that he felt Ciaran's urge to kiss him, or with his head thrown back in ecstasy, baring his throat to hot and biting kisses.

Noah buried himself under the blankets of his borrowed bed. He didn't want those memories. He focused on himself and not the fairy lurking in his brain, and he felt his cheeks burn hot at the memory of Julien's kiss. The hunter was out there, somewhere, right now— risking his life for someone else, just like always. But this time it wasn't for the greater good, or for the general safety of the city at large. It was for Noah. Just Noah. Because Julien loved him. Noah could still hear the hunter's softly rumbling voice, deep and hesitant and perfect. Julien loved him.

Cu nudged his shoulder through the blanket and pushed a cup of steaming tea at him when he poked his head out.

"Airmed says you need to keep drinking this," he said, and Noah slowly sat up and took the cup from him. The tea was dark and bitter, but Noah was used to it by now. Cu leaned back on his hands while Noah drank.

"So your hunter's gone to Emain Ablach," the fairy chuckled. "Not the easiest place to come back from."

"He'll come back," Noah said without looking up. Julien was many things, not all of them great, but he never gave up once he put his mind to something. If he told Noah he loved him and was coming back to him, it was true.

"I hope you're right. It would be a shame to lose such a handsome young witch to a spell just to save my wastrel of a brother."

"You really don't give up, do you? The whole trying to seduce you and then bursting into tears thing wasn't a deterrent?"

Cu scoffed. "I'm not so easily dissuaded."

"Yeah, it's getting creepy now."

"But you're immune to my charms," Cu sighed. "You're a taken man, it seems."

Noah looked down into his cup, suddenly embarrassed. "Well I mean, we didn't—it's not like we discussed—"

"Just drink your tea and try not to leak any of that new love sweetness into the furs."

Noah did as he was told, glad for the heat of the tea to calm his stomach. Julien was risking his life, and stubbornness might not be enough to see him through. Noah tried to remind himself that it wasn't all his fault—Julien had begun the whole thing by asking him to cast the spell on Ciaran to begin with. By hunting Ciaran at all. If Julien hadn't been so—Noah bit his lip and fidgeted with his cup. Trying to place blame was pointless. What mattered was that Noah had done everything he'd done because he loved the hunter, single-minded and oblivious as he was—and Julien was putting himself in danger now because he loved Noah too. All that stupid had to balance itself out, somehow.

He finished his tea and fell asleep with Cu humming a soft tune from the far side of the room, but his nap was restless. He couldn't get comfortable. He kept coughing, and his head ached, and he couldn't find a way to lay that eased the pit of worry in his stomach. He hid his face in the pillow and shut his eyes, but the beat of his heart was suddenly in time with his racing feet hitting the sidewalk in Vancouver. He ran at a sprint, weaving through the crowd and pressing forward despite the lingering ache in his gut.

Trent's waiting. I got him into this, and now that hunter has him. Because of me—I turn onto the right street and head for the building down the block. Because of me. If he's hurt, it's because of me. I didn't mean for it to happen like this. Run faster. I take the steps two at a time on my way to the apartment door. That hunter is going to regret ever seeing my face. Please be okay. Please be okay.

Noah opened his eyes and panted wearily against the pillow, his fingers tangled in the blankets. His heart pounded in his chest, and he couldn't tell if the pain in his stomach was his own worry or Ciaran's. He took a few slow breaths to calm down and tried to stay still under the wave of nausea flowing over him, but he knew how Ciaran had felt all too well. Noah's chest grew tight at the thought that he had helped Julien come between them at all. Monsters were one thing. Ciaran wasn't a monster. At least Ciaran had been able to go after Trent when it mattered. Noah just had to lie here in bed and wait, and it felt pathetic.

Julien wasn't going to die. He knew that. Whatever some sea god or whatever it was could throw at him, Julien would survive. But Noah had seen the look on Ciaran's face at supper. He was fading. Noah was seeing memories that weren't more than two weeks old. If Noah had them, did Ciaran still? Or was he losing every bit of himself that Noah gained? Neither of them had much time left.

Noah sat up in bed and looked across at Cu, who was perched by the window looking down at the courtyard. "Can I ask you something?" he said softly, startling the fairy into attention.

"Hm?"

"If I...if Julien doesn't make it in time—would you do something for me?"

"What's that? You want me to give him a goodbye kiss for you?"

Noah didn't laugh. "There's...a boy. His name is Sabin. He's just a kid—he wouldn't like to hear me say that, but he is. And he's counting on me. He used to write me letters, but I've been kind of on the run for a little while, so…he's probably getting worried. If I don't…make it, could you…send him some things? I've been trying to get him some ingredients, a little bit at a time, you know. He needs them. And he'll want to know what…happened to me, so…could you tell him that too?"

Cu frowned at him. "What sort of things?"

"I have a list," Noah answered immediately. "I can write it down. I just—he's somewhere I can't get to him. I want to make sure he gets what I promised him."

"If you can't get to him, how are you sending him things?"

"He gets my letters," Noah shrugged. "Sometimes when I get letters back from him, there's stuff marked out like with a black marker, you know? Like someone is censoring them. He says he's safe where he is, but…he's not happy. I need to get him the things I promised."

Cu watched Noah with a knitted brow. "You're a strange one. Why do you care so much about some kid you can't even see?"

"He's not some kid," Noah protested. "He's like my little brother. I told him I'd take care of him, teach him. I just want to make sure he'll be okay if I don't make it."

Cu rose from his spot by the window and fetched a parchment and quill from the desk, then offered it to Noah. "Write me a list," he said. "I'll get it done if you can't. I promise."

Noah tried to still the trembling in his fingers as he took the paper. "Thank you," he said earnestly.

"I hope it won't be needed," Cu answered with a faint smile.

Noah tried to sleep again once he'd given the fairy a complete list of ingredients, but he still tossed and turned and alternated throwing the blankets off of him and pulling them up around his chin. He could only tell that the night had passed by the distant sound of people on the street outside, but even that was starting to fade now. Airmed came and brought him tea periodically, and he could see deeper lines of worry on her face with every visit.

"Have you heard anything?" he asked her quietly to avoid waking Cu, who had drifted off to sleep in a chair.

"It isn't a short journey to Emain Ablach," she offered with an encouraging smile. "He might be on his way back even now."

"But you haven't heard anything."

She sat down at the edge of the bed beside him. "I haven't, no."

"How is your brother?" Noah asked, knowing he didn't really want to hear the answer. Airmed wrung her hands in her lap and wouldn't look up at him.

"He...isn't well, I'm afraid. We're running out of time," she whispered. "My father is almost ready to perform the spell, and I don't know how much longer Cian can wait. I'm so sorry," she said, and she reached out to clutch Noah's hands tightly. "No matter who started all this, both of you have suffered so much to be here, and the thought of it all being for nothing is just—" She sighed. "I'm sorry."

"I was angry at you, you know," Noah said instead of answering. "I tried to sneak down to the cellar, and I saw the two of you—I thought you were—but it's because of you that he said what he said, isn't it?"

Airmed's face flushed, and she pulled her hands away from Noah's with an embarrassed laugh. "Oh, I just...it does get dull down here, you know, and I can't resist a good love story." She peeked back up at him. "Yours is a very good love story, Noah. It's going to end well. You have to believe that."

"I do," Noah said honestly. He was still worried for Julien, but a sort of warm calm had finally settled in his stomach. Julien would come back. Julien always came when Noah needed him.

Airmed glanced back at the door with an anxious frown. "I need to get back. Try to get some rest," she added in a gentle voice, and she lightly touched Noah's hair before rising and slipping out of the room.

Noah had just managed to fall asleep when he heard the door open again. Airmed stood in the doorway with her father, looking much more sorrowful than he did.

"It's time, cailleach," the man said, and Noah's blood ran cold. Cu helped him out of bed and he followed in a daze, finding no comfort in the fairy's warm grip on his arm. It was fine. This was fine. Julien would be waiting for him, or maybe he would show up dramatically at the last minute and save him. That would be like him.

Noah was led through the hall and down the stairs into the cellar, where Trent and Ciaran already waited. Ciaran was wrapped in a thick blanket and still seemed to be shivering, the opposing mirror to Noah's sweaty brow. Trent stood nearby, but not too close, and he had a sad, heavy look on his face that made Noah ache for him. He could feel Ciaran's mind at the back of his own, longing to touch Trent's face and kiss him and promise him that everything would be all right, but the physical Ciaran in front of him looked pale and hollow.

Airmed laid her brother down on a long stone table, whispering to him in calming Gaelic, and then she turned and offered her hand to Noah. Julien would be there any minute, he told himself. He let Airmed help him up onto the table opposite Ciaran, the tops of their heads almost touching as Noah settled.

"Just shut your eyes," Airmed whispered, squeezing his shoulder gently, and Noah did as he was told. Julien would come. He'd burst through the door and demand that they wait, and he would hold Noah and apologize for being late.

He could hear the older man humming in a hoarse voice above him, and he felt Airmed's oiled hands on his forehead and the heat of the candles they placed around him. Thin ropes were tied around his wrists and ankles, pinning him to the table. The room grew almost painfully hot as Airmed's soft voice joined her father's, the song running prickling tingles along Noah's skin. Julien would come.

Noah's body tensed, his mouth falling open as his back arched away from the table against his will. A dark cold ran up his spine, pulling him inside out, and his fingers scraped helplessly for purchase on the smooth stone table. Julien would—

21

Julien held onto Lugh's cloak with one hand as they rode, keeping his parcel tightly to him for fear of losing it. They hadn't been gone that long. Hours, certainly, maybe even a day—but it would be enough. He was grateful for the thumping of the Enbarr's hooves on solid ground as they reached land, because it meant that they were almost there. Julien dropped down from the horse as soon as they were at the entrance to the stone mound, and Lugh kept pace with him as he pushed his way through tourists and moved to the back of the dark passage. Lugh opened the way for him, and both of them hurried down the winding stairs to the gates of Tír na nÓg. Lugh whistled for a carriage as soon as they were in the city, and he urged the driver on toward the house where Noah waited. In a quieter moment, Julien would have to thank Lugh for his help. Human or not, this person had treated him fairly and had made it possible for him to save Noah. He would remember to thank him.

Julien ran through the estate courtyard before the carriage could fully stop to let him out, and he threw his shoulder against the heavy front door to push it open without bothering to knock. He rushed by a servant who tried to shout at him and entered the study, pausing in the doorway to look around the room. The fireplace was burning brightly, giving the room a warm orange glow, but Julien's heart went cold at the sight of Ciaran lounging casually on the settee with a book on his knee. The fairy looked up at him with a slow, easy smile, and he flipped his book shut and set it aside.

"Welcome back," Ciaran said, but he made no move to rise from his seat.

"Where is he?" Julien demanded.

"You know, Julien," Ciaran began, and the hunter grit his teeth at being addressed so informally. "Timing is everything in life. A person can be in the wrong place at the wrong time—maybe know the wrong people," he added with a slight sneer. "But they get themselves into trouble, and before you know it—gone, without a person in the world to care for them."

Julien charged toward the fairy in a fury, his precious bundle falling to the floor as he caught him by the front of his dark tunic, but Ciaran only stared up at him.

"Too late, hunter," the fairy whispered.

"Where is he?" Julien shouted, shaking Ciaran by his shirt.

Ciaran stood then, swatting the hunter's hands away from him with careless ease. "You should be more careful," he said. "You're in Tír na nÓg now, and you have nothing else of use to me."

Julien stood numb as Ciaran brushed past him, swaying as the fairy bumped his shoulder. Too late. He was too late.

"Who the hell is yelling?" he heard Trent call from the doorway, but he didn't turn around. A soft rustle of skirt followed as Trent moved into the room, and then Airmed's hand was on Julien's arm, squeezing him tightly as she looked up into his face.

"I'm so sorry," she said, tears already filling her eyes and falling onto her cheeks, but Julien couldn't bring himself to move even as she fastened her arms around his waist and held him in a crushing hug. "We waited as long as we could," she whispered against his chest.

All for nothing. His trip, Manandán's trials, his injury—for nothing. He'd failed. He'd failed Noah. The witch—his witch—was dead because of him.

"And you," Airmed said suddenly, pulling herself away from Julien to glare across the room at Ciaran. "How can you be so cold? Julien's suffering, and Noah gave you back your life, Cian."

"After he stole it to begin with," Ciaran scoffed. "Thus hunter tried to kill me. He kidnapped Trent, then brought his witch to try to kill me again. I'm supposed to feel sorry for either of them?"

"I heard him at supper, Cian," Airmed countered. "I heard what Noah said—what you said through him. Without Julien, you never would have met Trent at all. You said you were grateful."

Ciaran scowled at her, but there was a hint of red in his cheeks. "I hardly think I'm responsible for things a witch says while he's got my stolen spirit inside of him," he grumbled. "Let the hunter go, then. I don't care." He took Trent by the hand and led him back up the stairs, leaving Julien to drop heavily onto the settee and stare helplessly at the floor.

"You know, his friend did just die," Trent pointed out as Ciaran shut the door behind them. "He might be a dick, but you don't have to be a dick back."

Ciaran pressed him into the wall and held his face in both hands as he kissed him. The fairy let out a soft sigh and touched his forehead to the younger man's. "I don't care about him," he whispered. "I only care that you're still here."

Trent felt a faint smile touch his lips, and he let his hands rest on Ciaran's waist as the two of them stood still and quiet. Whether or not it made him a good person, Trent would have traded a dozen strangers for the moment he had seen Ciaran open his eyes and known that he was himself again. Ciaran had hardly left his sight ever since, but Trent hadn't minded at all. It was a relief to hear him speaking confident English, talking about things he wouldn't have remembered at all a day ago.

Ciaran touched another kiss to his lips and pulled him toward the bed, but the fairy wasn't rough anymore. He lay with Trent's head in the crook of his shoulder, his nose buried in the younger man's dark hair.

"So what do we do now?" Trent murmured into Ciaran's shirt, fingertips toying with the embroidery on his collar.

"Whatever you want," Ciaran answered without hesitation. "Wherever you want to go, we'll go. Whatever you want to see, I'll take you. I don't care. I want to make a hundred thousand new memories with you."

"A hundred thousand?" Trent chuckled. "Let's start with a number you can count to."

"Ach," Ciaran scoffed, but there was no malice in his voice. "I haven't even been well a day, and already you're so cruel to me."

Trent smiled at the gentle touch of Ciaran's thumb brushing his arm. "I'm just glad you're coherent enough to bully," he chuckled.

"Good to know," Ciaran mumbled. "I was wondering how long this syrupy Trent would last. I'm rather over it, to be frank."

"I'm going to smother you with a pillow if you don't shut up."

"Ah, there it is. Good to have you back, a mhuirnín."

Trent peeked up at Ciaran to see his smile, and he tugged the fairy down to him to kiss him. They lay together for a while, Trent thinking out loud as he listed a few places he'd always wanted to see. Ciaran didn't answer him, and when Trent sat up, Ciaran seemed distracted.

"What's the problem? You don't want to see Greece?"

"Hm?" Ciaran frowned up at him and shook his head. "Sorry, I— Airmed was quite upset, wasn't she? She said I was cold."

"I didn't know she was so friendly with that hunter," Trent shrugged. "I mean, I feel bad that someone died, but she seemed really torn up. Why does she care so much?"

"Airmed has always had a soft spot for tragedy," Ciaran sighed. He drummed his fingers idly on his stomach. "Maybe the hunter was closer to his little witch than they let on." He let out a tortured groan and rolled over onto his belly. "I can't stand it when she looks at me that way."

"Wait, are you feeling guilty about something? Are you sure you got the right brain back?"

Ciaran reached out and shoved Trent's hip, almost pushing him off of the bed. "Fuck off," he grumbled into his pillow. "She's my little sister. What am I supposed to do? She's always had me right around her little finger—all three of us."

"So go apologize to her if you feel bad."

"It won't be her she wants me to apologize to." He sat up on his elbows and looked up at Trent. "But I'll be damned if I'm apologizing to that hunter."

"Then just sit here and feel bad about it, I guess."

"You're a great help, love." He paused, and his brow furrowed in thought as he pulled himself up onto his knees. "There may be something I can do, actually." He got to his feet and padded out of the room, leaving Trent to trot after him.

Julien stood at the door to the cellar and tried to will his arm into lifting to touch the handle. Airmed waited patiently at his side, but he stood still for so long that she reached out to squeeze his hand.

"You don't have to, if you don't want," she whispered.

"I do have to," he answered, his voice subdued. He put his hand on the door and pushed it open, taking a slow first step into the room. Stubs of candles still burned around the stone table, where a dark sheet lay covering a shape Julien didn't want to recognize. Airmed let him go as he moved farther into the room, and the hunter hesitated at the edge of the heavy table. He knew what he would see if he lifted the cloth. He knew, and he didn't want to see it.

He hesitated with his hand at the edge of the cloth, but he pressed his lips into a line and pulled it back. Noah lay still on the table, his head fallen to one side and his eyes gently closed. Someone had folded his hands over his stomach, but it didn't look like sleep. He was pale, and when Julien reached out a hand to brush the skin of the witch's cheek, it was cold. This wasn't right. Noah was supposed to be smiling at him, laughing, teasing him about being serious. Julien was supposed to have gotten there in time. Noah was waiting for him, and he'd come too late. He was supposed to save him.

Julien felt a crushing weight on his shoulders, and he struggled to stay on his feet. Noah was too still, too quiet, too cold. Julien leaned against the table and squeezed his eyes shut, but he couldn't keep in the tears that burned his eyes. He had done this. He had drawn Noah into this entire mess—he'd used him, manipulated him, and he'd finally gotten him killed. Everything was Julien's fault.

He bent to touch his forehead to the witch's pale cheek, his shallow breath shaking. "Je suis tellement désolé," he whispered. "Je l'aurais été ici. I should have been here." He let out a single, broken sob, and he felt Airmed's gentle hand on his shoulder.

"Well this is a sight," Ciaran's voice sounded from the doorway, making every muscle in Julien's body tense. "What a fearsome hunter you are, weeping like a child."

Julien turned on the fairy instantly, his voice a ragged growl as he shouted, "You get out! You've taken all you can from him, so leave him in peace!"

"Cian," Airmed scolded, keeping a firm hand on Julien's arm to stop him from rushing forward, "must you do this? Be more respectful of the dead."

Julien's throat clenched painfully at hearing Noah referred to as 'the dead,' but he bit his tongue. He wouldn't start a fight with Noah's—Noah's body two feet from him.

Ciaran gave a short, irritated sigh. "Airmed, I came to make a peace offering, hm? This...person," he said, gesturing vaguely at Julien, "clearly has endeared himself to you in some way. Now it's naught to me if he wallows in his own guilt until he dies, but you—yes that exact face, thank you—I don't like it when you make that face at me."

Airmed frowned at him, still tightly gripping Julien's sleeve. "Just say what you've come to say, Cian, if you can stop being so cruel."

"I just thought," Ciaran began with a shrug, "that if your dear hunter feels up to it, and if you can convince our father to try, you might be able to make use of the well at Sláine."

Airmed gasped audibly and shook Julien's sleeve so hard that his whole body wobbled. "The well," she half squealed. "Oh, but without Miach, how can we—" She lifted a hand to cover her mouth.

"He's a seventh son," she and Ciaran said together.

Airmed looked up at Julien and pressed her hands against his chest. "Oh, Julien, the well—the well can bring him back! Oh, we must hurry. I'll fetch father, you—you just wait here." She gave a few more "oh"s on her way out of the room, but her excited smile had made a small twisting of hope in Julien's chest.

He looked over at Ciaran, who lifted his hands in surrender.

"This isn't for you," the fairy said. "But if it pleases Airmed for me to forgive you, then it's done. You aren't going to carry on trying to kill me, are you?"

"What is this well?" Julien asked instead of an answer.

"Before our father murdered our youngest brother during one of his temper tantrums, it was a place where the Tuath Dé could heal themselves of any injury, even death. Without my father, sister, and brother together, it's useless, but you—the seventh son of a seventh son, aye? You've a bit of magic in you whether you like it or not."

Julien frowned. "What do you mean, magic? I can't do any magic."

"Ever tried?"

"Why would I? I'm human."

Ciaran sighed as though being forced to argue with a small child and folded his arms across his chest. "There's a reason men like you have been noted through history. A seventh son is strong; he can see through any illusion or glamour; he has the power to heal. Now how that manifests exactly, I don't rightly know, but with my father and sister singing at the well of Sláine, it may just be enough to bring back your witch. I doubt it'll be free, mind."

"I don't care what it costs," Julien said immediately. "If it brings Noah back, I'll do whatever it takes—even if it kills me."

"That would be just fitting, wouldn't it?" Ciaran chuckled, but Julien ignored him. He turned back to Noah and brushed the hair from his eyes, frowning down at his motionless face. Any chance at all was worth any risk.

It apparently took some convincing before Dian Cecht would agree to help, but it seemed that all the men in Airmed's family were susceptible to her displeasure.

Julien saw Lugh on his way out of the courtyard, but the larger man only gave the hunter a curt nod and said, "Good luck, an duine."

Airmed climbed into a carriage with her father, promising to keep Noah's body safe during their travels, but Julien was forced into a seat alongside Ciaran, Trent, and two other men. Apparently Dian Cecht refused to share a ride with a human.

"Where is this well exactly?" Julien asked.

Ciaran slipped his fingers through Trent's and brought his hand up to brush a light kiss over his knuckles. "It's the well of Sláine, so it's at Sláine, unsurprisingly." He grinned sidelong at Trent as the younger man shook his hand free with an irritated frown.

"Sorry I haven't got such a firm grasp of Irish geography," Julien muttered.

"Was that sass, hunter?" Ciaran chuckled. "I haven't yet heard a thank you for my grand idea."

"I'll thank you if it works," Julien snapped back.

"You should thank me for not killing you the second you showed your face back here, after all you've done."

"You looking for more iron in your gut, creature?"

"Wow," Trent said dryly before Ciaran could answer. "Do you guys want to just get your dicks out and measure them now, or are we waiting for a special occasion?"

Ciaran sighed and sat back in his seat with what almost passed for an apologetic smile. Julien turned his attention to the window to avoid scowling at his companions and watched the city go by instead. They rode until the city faded behind them, the massive beetle pulling the carriage smoothly through low tunnels that left the magic blue lanterns of the streetlights as nothing but pinpricks in the distance.

Tír na nÓg was much larger than Julien had anticipated—the whole of Ireland might have had a fairy world just under its surface, filled with nobles and peasants and merchants and servants going about their lives, with the humans above none the wiser. It was an unsettling thought. The things Julien had seen these past few days were well beyond his depth as a hunter, and he suspected that the best thanks he could give his hosts would be making sure that his brothers never found out about this place. Although seeing the great Edouard Fournier humbled by someone like Lugh would be entertaining.

The man across from Julien nudged him with his knee, drawing his attention. They hadn't been introduced, exactly, but as he seemed to be a slightly more disheveled version of Ciaran, Julien suspected it was one of the mentioned brothers.

"An duine," the fairy addressed him with a tilt of his chin, "has anyone mentioned to you what it is you'll be doing?"

"Other than Airmed thinking I can use magic, not really."

"Cu, don't spoil the surprise," Ciaran chuckled.

"You're out of trouble now, dearthái," the other brother said softly from the far end of the seat. "Have some compassion for a man who stands now where your love may have stood. It wouldn't have taken much for it to be Trent mourning your loss today."

Ciaran puffed out his cheeks in a sigh but said nothing more. He only reached out for Trent's hand, and the younger man didn't pull away this time.

"You'll need to take him into the water," Cu went on, leaning forward in his seat to catch Julien's eye. "My father and sister can help, but you must have the will to bring him back from the dark. Do you?"

A faint frown tugged the corners of Julien's lips. "I do."

"I hope so," Cu answered sharply. "He's a good one. He doesn't deserve to meet his end in Tír na nÓg."

Ciaran slouched in his seat and gestured out at his fellow passengers. "So did the whole family fall in love with these two humans while I was ill, or is it just you and Airmed?"

"Not everyone holds your grudges, Cian," Cu answered. "I'm just trying to give him a chance."

"What is it I have to actually do?" Julien asked, but Cu shook his head.

"I don't know that anyone has ever used the well this way. Our brother Miach would have known, but as he's dead, I suppose you'll have to make do with improvisation. Just make sure that you don't promise anything you aren't prepared to give."

Julien's brow furrowed. "Promise to whom?"

"To anything that finds you in the bottom of that well," Cu answered gravely.

Julien went silent. It didn't matter. Whatever asked him for payment, and whatever payment it asked for—it didn't matter.

The carriage rocked to a stop near the entrance to a sloping tunnel, and they filed out to make their way to the surface. Julien gently scooped Noah up, the wrapped body feeling too heavy and limp in his arms. Airmed walked beside him with her hand on his arm as they followed Dian Cecht up the tunnel.

They walked a worn path through the trees, the mottled moonlight showing the way, and Julien momentarily wondered how the tunnel entrance went unnoticed, as out of place as it looked in the woods. But most people probably simply couldn't see it.

The well was a rather unimpressive stone ring in the ground, the surface of the water almost covered over with jagged brown rocks. Julien peered down at it with a wary frown.

"I'm supposed to get in that?" He glanced over at Airmed. "Aren't I too big?"

"They were just telling you that," Ciaran piped up, but Julien sighed through his nose and ignored him.

"You just worry about Noah," Airmed said softly, patting his arm. "You let us take care of the magic. Stand just there."

Julien did as he was told. He waited while Airmed and her father took their places on either side of the well, and he held Noah tight against his chest as the pair began to hum, soft and low at first, and then louder, until their tuneless droning became a chanting song. Julien could feel the thrum of something unfamiliar in his chest, close and loud and beating in time with his heart. He knew it without having to name it—this was what Noah meant when he talked about feeling magic.

Julien saw Cu approach his sister, and he took her hand in his and added his voice to the chant, as did her other brother. Cu held out his hand, gesturing expectantly, and with a slight groan of resignation, Ciaran stepped forward to take his place in the circle.

While the song carried through the wood, the well shifted at Julien's feet, the slick rock scraping against itself and moving to reveal the full mouth of the well. The water was dark, but iridescent, shimmering blue just like the water that surrounded the island city. Julien caught Airmed's gaze, and she lowered her eyes to the water, so Julien stepped to the edge of the well.

The price didn't matter.

Julien moved forward, taking a step down onto the only remaining ledge just below the surface of the water. The surface glowed brightly at the intrusion, swirling around Julien's feet, and as soon as he moved again, he was pulled downward into the dark water. He clutched Noah's body tightly to him as the water rushed over his head, and he squeezed his eyes shut as the cold drove straight to his bones.

There was nothing but darkness around him, but Julien couldn't focus. He couldn't breathe this water. He couldn't move upwards no matter how he kicked his legs. Bring him back from the dark, Cu had said. Noah needed him, and Julien wasn't going to fail him again. He buried his face in Noah's cloth-wrapped neck. He was never going to fail him again.

Hours might have passed in that darkness, for all Julien knew. He stopped trying to swim upwards. He stopped trying to breathe. This was where Noah needed him.

He could feel more than hear the voice as it gathered around him. It wasn't saying anything that could be called words—Julien understood without having to listen. A trade, it said. A payment. Nothing for free.

Julien didn't have to tell it to name its price. The darkness knew he would pay anything.

A seventh son's greatest gift, it said. Just a portion of this magic, and have what you seek. A fair trade, it decided without waiting for Julien to agree. It didn't matter.

Julien held Noah by the shoulders, his grip clenching as a sudden, burning pain shot through his head. The hunter cried out into the heavy darkness of the water, his body twisting as his back arched. Before he knew what was happening, he was back at the top of the well, both he and Noah collapsed over the edge. Julien looked down at the wrapped body underneath him, his hair dripping water into the grass along with what he barely recognized as blood. He tore away the cloth covering Noah's face, but the witch still lay silent and pale.

The hunter held his breath, ignoring the pain pounding through his skull, until Noah suddenly jerked beneath him with a sharp gasp. Julien touched his face and pushed his hair out of his eyes, letting out a weak laugh of relief while Noah coughed and caught his breath. He whispered a prayer of thanks and bent to clutch Noah close to him. The witch's soft whisper of Julien's name as his hand lifted to his hair was the sweetest sound the hunter had ever heard.

"You came," Noah said, his voice little more than a cracked rasp.

"Sorry I'm late," Julien answered into the witch's shoulder. He leaned back to look down into Noah's face, but the younger man stared up at him with a pained expression.

"Julien, your—"

"Oh, it worked!" Airmed called out from behind them, and she dropped to her knees in the grass beside Noah, her skirt puffing up around her. "You're—oh, mo laethanta!" she gasped with her hands to her mouth as she caught sight of Julien's face. She reached out to touch Julien's cheek and drew away blood on her fingertips. The pain was too great for Julien to take notice of much else outside of Noah, but when he reached his own hand up to his face, he realized that there was blood pouring from the wound where his right eye used to be.

Airmed tried to pull Julien up, but he wouldn't release Noah. He lifted the witch in his arms and carried him back to the carriage at her urging, refusing even to let him sit in a separate seat. Airmed rode with them and did her best to clean and tend to Julien's injury, but between the rocking of the carriage and Noah laid drowsily against the hunter's chest, it was difficult.

Noah slipped off to sleep against him, but Julien took comfort in the younger man's soft breath warm on his neck. He looked over at Airmed and whispered, "Thank you," but she only smiled at him and wiped a bit of blood from his cheek with her handkerchief.

Airmed took them back to her modest house rather than subject either of them to any more of her brother's vitriol, and she settled them in a cozy bedroom. A servant started a fire while Airmed rushed around fetching oils and herbs, but Julien never let go of Noah's hand.

"He'll probably sleep for a while," Airmed said softly as she curled her legs underneath her on the bed beside Julien. "But he should be fine." She smiled brightly and squeezed Julien's arm, apparently not having the words to express her excitement. "Now let me take care of you."

Julien sat as still as he could while Airmed cleaned his face, flinching as she applied her oils and warm packets of soaked herbs.

"It could have been worse," she said with a sympathetic smile as she leaned closer to him to get a better look at his eye. "Does it still hurt?"

"I'll manage."

"I'll find you something to...you know, to cover it. If you want me to."

A low chuckle rumbled in his throat. "Why, isn't it dashing?"

"Very dashing," she assured him. "But I'll find you something just in case." She gave his hand a final squeeze and let herself out of the room.

Julien sat listening to Noah's slow breath for a while. His head did still hurt, but he considered it an easy price to pay in return for the young man sleeping beside him. When Noah rolled over onto his side and forced Julien to release his hand, the hunter stood and stretched, gingerly touching the tender skin around his eye. He bent to look into the polished mirror near the bed, though he misjudged the distance and bumped into the table, scrambling to keep a silver pitcher from hitting the floor. The impaired depth perception was going to take some getting used to.

His eye still looked a bit red, but he supposed it was as clean an injury as he could hope for—his eyelid looked sunken and only opened halfway, and when he lifted the skin with his fingertips, he grimaced at the sight of the pink tissue and muscle underneath. Maybe it really would be better to cover it.

By the time Airmed returned, Julien was fast asleep in the bed beside Noah, so she left the small strap of leather on the table by the bed and slowly shut the bedroom door behind her, smiling to herself and peeking through the crack until the door clicked closed.

22

"So is this going to become a regular thing with you, little fairy magic drum circles?" Trent asked as soon as he was alone with Ciaran again. The carriage ride back into the city had been awkward and silent, with Trent squeezed in between Ciaran and his brother, who seemed not to understand the meaning behind Trent's subtle wriggling every time the fairy had 'accidentally' brushed his thigh.

"You just saw us literally bring a man back from the dead, and still all you have is smart-assed remarks," Ciaran grumbled. He pulled Trent's duffel bag up onto the bed and dug through it in search of any clothes he could use to replace the tunic and trousers he'd borrowed from his brother. Being back in this house with his full faculties was somehow even worse than losing his memory.

"No, no, I think it's adorable. Maybe you can sing me your song of the forest or whatever as I drift off to sleep."

"You are such a shite," the fairy laughed, and he tugged the boy down by his collar and gave him a swift, biting kiss. "Does nothing impress you?"

"I'm impressed by how you aren't all fat living off just bread, butter, and weird fruit jellies."

"Someone was unkind to you when you were a child, weren't they?"

Trent smirked faintly and reached past him to tug a v-neck shirt from his bag. "This one might be small enough."

A knock on the door interrupted them, but Ciaran snatched the shirt out of Trent's hand before calling out, "Dul isteach."

A woman opened the door and gave a brief curtsy before speaking. "My Lord, the Lady Ethniu has requested your attendance at her estate at your very earliest convenience."

"At her estate?" Ciaran sighed. "She had to send someone after me instead of just coming herself?"

"The Lady...suggested you might say that, my Lord, and asked me to remind you that she is, in fact, only telling you to come home." The woman bowed her head as though she'd said something impertinent, but Ciaran only huffed and dropped his newly-gained shirt back onto the bed. He looked over at Trent apologetically.

"I'm sorry," he said in English. "Ethniu wants me. I'm sure she just wants to give me hell about disappearing now that I'm fully here to shout at. I won't be long." He squeezed Trent's hand in an attempt to ease the boy's frown and started for the door, but the servant spoke up.

"Uh, my Lord, actually, the Lady Ethniu asked for your guest as well."

"Oh, for pity's sake," Ciaran sighed, and he turned to look over his shoulder at Trent. "Sorry. You're on the hook too. Come along; I won't let her tease you too much."

"You don't actually have to drop everything and go just because she snaps her fingers, you know," Trent grumbled.

Ciaran softened slightly. He knew that it must have been a shock for Trent to find out the lover he'd risked everything for was already married. But without a life-stealing spell hanging over his head, Ciaran would have plenty of time to make it up to him.

"It'll be quick," he promised. Trent hesitated, his lips pressed into a thin line, but he stuffed his hands into his pockets and followed without answering.

Trent didn't even find it strange anymore to get into a carriage pulled by giant, bristly beetles, which in itself was probably strange. They rode down the lamplit streets with the curtains drawn, and Ciaran kept well away from the window. Trent didn't know who he thought was looking for him after all this time, but he was clearly still wary of being seen. When the carriage stopped, Ciaran peeked to see how close they were to the estate's entrance before he climbed out.

The gate in front of him was smaller than the one at the castle they had just left, but it was strung with the same leafless vines, and rows of mushrooms and softly luminescent flowers lined the path to the door. The home seemed modest compared to the place they had just left, but it still rose two stories above the surrounding wall. It was built of the same dark, slick stone that seemed to make up the entirety of the city, with heavy wooden doors and glassless windows open to the cool air.

Trent spotted half a dozen servants as he was led through the house, which seemed warm and well-lit, a stark comparison to the city outside. There were rugs on the floors and soft furs draped over the furniture. It looked like a home, which Trent hadn't expected for some reason.

Ethniu let them wait in the sitting room for a while before appearing, and she entered without a word, taking her place across from them and gesturing to a nearby servant. She didn't look quite as stern as she had when Trent had seen her before—her long hair was tied in a simple braid that hung over her shoulder and pooled in her lap, and she wore only a simple pair of spiraled silver earrings. Her dress looked comfortable and soft, without the corseted middle she'd had before. She looked prettier this way, Trent thought—or at least less on the verge of violence.

A servant brought a tray of tea and placed it between them, filling their cups with milk and sugar without even asking. Trent's stomach gave a quiet rumble. Maybe he could drink it quickly and get a cup of untainted tea before the servant could do it for him.

"Feeling well, darling?" Ethniu asked as she lifted her cup and saucer into her lap. "All yourself again, hm?"

"Hale and hearty, my treasure," Ciaran answered easily, and he leaned back on the settee to rest his arm across the back, circling Trent without touching him.

Ethniu's eyes followed the movement with idle interest. "You needn't put on a show for me. I believe everyone here is well aware of the situation—unless it's your newest love you're trying to convince?"

Trent felt a pinprick of irritation at being called Ciaran's "newest love." He'd known the fairy had had countless lovers before him—he wasn't an idiot, and he'd been reminded all too often during this little trip—but he didn't like thinking of himself as just the current link in the immortal's chain.

"I'm not the one he faked his own death to get away from, so I'm not exactly worried," Trent said, and Ethniu ticked an eyebrow at him in response.

"Well, this one is charming, isn't he," she mused. "You always did like the spiteful ones."

"Did you ask me here just to try to make him uncomfortable?" Ciaran sighed, though he did relent and lean forward to take his cup of tea.

"I asked you here because I wanted to make sure you weren't doing anything stupid just when you've been given your life back," she answered. Before Ciaran could reply, she turned her attention to Trent with a poised smile. "Would you mind terribly showing me that trinket you're wearing—Trent, was it?"

Trent sensed Ciaran tense beside him, and he frowned as he reached up to touch the amulet through his shirt. Ethniu nodded at him, so he pulled the leather strap and freed the pendant, letting it rest against his hand so that she could see it.

"Yes, I thought so," she said with a slight purse of her lips. "A nice little gift," she added with a pointed stare at Ciaran.

"It's none of your business, Ethniu," Ciaran snapped.

"What's none of her business?" Trent asked, unable to keep his voice from sounding accusing. He had had quite enough secrets revealed over the last couple of weeks. If Ciaran was keeping yet another, Trent might not be able to stop himself from hitting him.

"Do you know what that is?" Ethniu asked him, nodding towards the pendant in Trent's hand. "That mark of the goddess you wear?"

"Ethniu, please," Ciaran said. He leaned forward to put his cup back on the table and stared at her with a furrowed brow that made Trent nervous.

"What is it?" he asked. "Ciaran said it was just a symbol."

"The mother of the Tuatha Dé Danann, yes." She paused to glance at Ciaran's frowning face. "Do you know what Tír na nÓg means,

Trent?" She waited only a beat before continuing, clearly not expecting him to know the answer. "It means the Land of the Young. Here, the Tuath Dé do not grow old or die, except by violence from their fellows."

"Ethniu, it isn't your place—" Ciaran interrupted, and she snapped her eyes to him with such a hot glare of orange that he went silent.

"You are my husband and my friend, and this man is your chosen lover," she said gravely. "Do not think that it is your place to make decisions for any of us."

"Ciaran, what the hell is she talking about?" Trent frowned at him, feeling like he ought to tear the amulet from around his neck.

"That token is a gift from the Tuath Dé's mother goddess," Ethniu began again, "to keep her children safe when they must venture from home. Outside of Tír na nÓg, you see, these creatures age the same as any other—slower, perhaps, due to their nature, but they will become old without the mark of the goddess to keep them close to her."

Trent opened his mouth to speak, and then shut it again. He held the amulet tightly in his fingers and looked over at Ciaran, who couldn't meet his eyes. "Is that true?" he asked through a tight jaw. "Was this thing keeping you...you know, immortal? And you gave it to me?"

Ciaran sighed and turned to face him better on the settee, attempting to remove Ethniu from the conversation. "I gave it to you *because* it was what was keeping me immortal," he said.

"You told me it wasn't magic. I asked you if it was, and you lied."

"I was going to explain," Ciaran said. "I just didn't want to—" He stopped as though having trouble finding the words and gave a short sigh. "Trent, I gave it to you because I was afraid. Of...of leaving you behind." He reached up and put his hand on Trent's, his thumb brushing the gold amulet. "With this, wearing this, you—you'll slow down. You won't wither away while I stay the same as always."

Trent shook his head slightly, but all the breath had left his lungs. He'd been wearing the thing for—at least a couple of weeks, he thought. And it had been stopping him from aging? Slowing it down? What did that even mean? He stopped and looked down at the fairy's hand on his. It meant that Ciaran was giving him literally everything he had.

"But without it, you'll—"

"I'm not worried about me," Ciaran cut in. "Who knows? Maybe like this, we'll match up. Maybe not. But any chance is better than having to just watch you grow old and die."

"No," Trent said without thinking. "This is too much. You—you should have told me. You should have asked me. You can't just...do this."

"I'm sorry," Ciaran said immediately. "You're right. I shouldn't have. But say you'll wear it. Please. We'll leave here soon, and then we can go to Greece, like you said, and we can spend ten years there if you like and still have years and years to spare."

Trent pried his hand away from Ciaran's, and he shook his head and untied the leather strap around his neck, dropping the amulet into his palm. "You don't know that," he said quietly. "Without this, I might be the one having to watch you wither away. I won't do that."

"But you'd have me do it?" Ciaran answered in a whisper so soft that it broke Trent's heart.

"If I may offer a counter proposal," Ethniu spoke up, interrupting the couple's tense stare. "You might simply stay here. Your father may not want you, but you could stay here, I suppose—or I'm sure Airmed would take you."

"And hide forever? I'm not living in Tír na nÓg," Ciaran frowned. "I can't. And I won't. This isn't my life. Not anymore."

Ethniu sighed as though he was being overly dramatic, but she didn't press the issue. "You could always go and see the Morrigan."

Ciaran shook his head before Trent could even open his mouth. "Absolutely not," he said.

"I've never known a race of men so afraid of a woman's power as the Tuath Dé," Ethniu sighed. "It remains an option." She waved a hand dismissively at Ciaran's scowl. "Alternatively, don't you have a human witch very much in your debt at the moment? Perhaps he will have a solution for you."

Ciaran scoffed. "You really think I want that witch's help, after all of this?"

"I think you ought to pull your head out of your arse," the woman answered. "You're willing to give up eternal life for the sake of this boy, but you aren't willing to ask for someone's help?"

Trent sighed, turning the pendant in his fingers. "We should at least ask." He looked up, feeling Ciaran's disbelieving stare on him. "I'm not going to wear this. Not knowing it's keeping you alive. And maybe he knows something. I don't really want to see him again either, but we should check all our options, right? Or, I mean, I'm only nineteen—we've got a while before we really have to worry about me getting old."

A soft growl formed in the fairy's throat, but his gaze dropped to the amulet in Trent's hand. "Fine," he said at last. "We'll ask." He turned to look at Ethniu, who seemed completely nonplussed by his rising temper. "And I thank you for your intrusion, treasure."

The woman idly brushed at her braid, smoothing a few stray hairs. "Just saving you an argument later, darling. Airmed took those humans with her, didn't she? Of course she did. I'll have them sent for, and you can get what you need from them and be on your way. I assume you won't be staying in Tír na nÓg any longer than you must, of course."

"No," Ciaran answered.

"No, I thought not." Trent thought he saw the pair exchange a sad, lingering look, but then Ethniu rose to her feet, apparently ending their little meeting, and she looked down at Ciaran as he stood with her. "Well. Although you've been nothing but trouble since you arrived, it is nice to know that you're still alive, I suppose. Nicer still to know that you're alive somewhere far, far away."

Ciaran smiled and tugged her impertinently by the braid, drawing her down low enough to allow him to kiss her cheek. "I'll write this time."

Trent caught a faint smile on the woman's face before she remembered herself, but it didn't bother him as much as it should have. He took Ciaran's offered hand and stood with him, and he was forced to stop immediately by Ethniu's hard hand on his shoulder.

"Give me a moment, darling," she said. "Go and wait in the carriage, would you? I'll send your little love along in a moment."

Ciaran paused, looking between them for a moment, and then he frowned up at her. "Be nice, Ethniu."

"I'm always nice."

Ciaran hesitated, but he gave Trent a reassuring nod as he released his hand, and then Trent was left alone in the sitting room with a woman a head taller than him and easily as broad. He looked up at her warily, silently cursing Ciaran for leaving him.

"My husband is a very silly creature," she began coolly, folding her hands in front of her with delicate politeness. "But he is selfish above all else. He always has been. You should know that even when he was here in Tír na nÓg, he took many lovers. He must have taken countless more in the world above."

"Is this a pep talk, or...?"

"What I'm saying, Trent, is that you seem to have beaten out the rest of your race. My husband does not bare his heart easily. He will snipe at you, and he will lie, and he will hide things—but I suspect that you are much the same, or you wouldn't have come this far with him, hm?" She tilted her head. "My husband is reckless, and spiteful, and he can be cruel in the way of his kind, but he has a heart that is tender and romantic. If Cian has decided that you are the one he wants to spend his eternity with—however long that may be—then I count you lucky, for I doubt you'll find a more loyal companion in this world or the one above."

Trent stood speechless for a long moment, only staring up at her. He hadn't expected this kind of talking-to.

"Take care of him," she said when he didn't answer. "He needs someone to keep an eye on him, and he's made it no longer my job." She lifted her hand to guide him out of the room, and she followed him to the heavy front door in silence. Trent turned to look at her as he stepped outside, still not certain what to say.

"I'll do my best," he said, and she nodded as though this was an acceptable answer.

"And if you even breathe to him a single word of what I just said, I'll have you strung up by your small hairs and fed to the crows," she said mildly, and then she shut the door in his face.

Trent felt a small smile touch the corners of his lips. He would make sure Ciaran wrote to her.

23

When Noah finally woke, Airmed brought her guests more food than they could possibly eat and helped Julien fit the eyepatch she had brought him over his head. The dark leather had been carved with thick, curling lines, and it fit perfectly over his empty eye.

"I hope you don't mind," she said, "but I put a charm on it. I know you're leery of magic, but it's just a simple protection spell. It'll make me feel better," she added with a smile. She paused to look at him for a moment, apparently satisfied, and then she got to her feet with a quick clap of her hands and told them to make themselves at home and get some rest.

"If you need anything, you just call for Lenora or I, hm?" she said, already backing toward the door. "You've both had...rather a long day. You just relax and...make yourselves at home," she said again. She bit her bottom lip in a smile and shut the door.

Noah looked over at him and let out a slightly nervous chuckle. Neither of them knew what to say, and it seemed too strange to just eat their supper like everything about the day was normal.

Julien shifted slightly so that he didn't have to turn his head as much to return Noah's gaze. "Do you...feel all right?" he asked after a few awkward moments.

"One of your eyes is missing, and you're asking me if I'm all right?"

"Well, you did...die," Julien finished more bluntly than he meant to. "That's a bit more serious than an eye."

"You know, it's a little unfair. You'd think I could at least answer some age-old questions or something, but..." Noah trailed off and shrugged one shoulder. "It was just...sort of dark, and...I want to say there was more, but it's like when you wake up from a dream, and it's just gone."

"Maybe it's better you don't remember."

Noah looked down and fidgeted with the blanket. "Probably." He tried to break the awkwardness by reaching out for one of the trays Airmed had brought, but he put the bread down as soon as he took a bite—it was the same sickly sweet filling he'd had before.

"God, I would kill for some pad thai right now, you know?"

"It's not so bad," Julien answered around a mouthful of bread.

"For you," Noah chuckled. "I've seen those packs of Reese's you keep in your bag." Julien paused and stared at him, and Noah laughed. "You don't have any secrets from me, Mr. Hunter."

"Apparently not."

Julien ate his fill while Noah picked at the meal, and he set aside the tray when they were finished. The house had gone quiet around them, and the streets below the window were silent. Noah fidgeted and tucked his feet under the blanket, suddenly hesitant to look over at Julien.

"So I guess we should...get some rest, right?"

"Sure," Julien answered softly. "Do you want me to go somewhere else?"

"No," Noah said immediately. "No. Unless you—unless you want to."

"I'm fine here." Julien stood to pull off his coat and sat down on the bed beside Noah, leaving the coat tossed over a chair. Both of them hesitated, but Julien cleared his throat and climbed under the blankets, hoping he could lead by awkward example. Noah shifted next to him, avoiding his gaze, and eventually the two of them lay side by side in the dim room, tense and silent.

Noah picked at his fingernails, holding his hands nervously by his stomach. "It feels good to be...just me again," he whispered. "It's...a little empty, but it's a good empty. All things considered, I feel pretty good," he added with a quiet, anxious chuckle. He peeked over at Julien in the darkness. "Do you...feel good? About...you know, things?"

Julien turned his head to look at the younger man with a furrowed brow. "What are you asking me, Noah?"

The witch turned onto his side to face Julien. "Just...what do you want to do now?"

Julien's stomach tensed as Noah's fingertips touched his bicep. He could hear Noah's nervous breath beside him, just barely louder than the pounding of his own heart. He shifted to face the younger man and reached out a hesitant hand to brush his cheek.

"I want to keep you safe," Julien whispered, "and I want to keep you with me always. If you'll let me."

"That...sounds pretty good," Noah answered with a shy smile, and for a moment the two of them just watched each other in silence. Then Noah inched forward, his fingers curling into the front of Julien's shirt, and he hesitated a breath away from the hunter's lips. Julien met him tentatively, barely brushing his lips over Noah's, and a spark ran up his spine at the younger man's quiet gasp. His heart threatened to break his ribs, it was beating so hard, but he still hardly dared to move. They exchanged a few more timid, chaste touches of lips, but when Noah's tongue ran a light line across Julien's upper lip, he clutched the witch to him and held him close with a hand in his hair, groaning as Noah opened his mouth to his kiss.

Noah's hands pulled frantically at Julien's shirt, and the witch whined impatiently at being forced to break the kiss to remove it. He almost trembled to press his hands against Julien's firm chest, to finally feel the heat of the other man under his palms instead of in his daydreams. He had spent so long pining, hopelessly hoping for something he knew he could never have—but now Julien was here, with him, promising to keep him safe. Noah arched into the touch as the hunter's fingers brushed the skin at his waist, catching his lips in a kiss again, but he paused when he felt Julien hesitate.

"What's wrong?" Noah panted against the other man's lips, his fingernails scraping Julien's scarred torso as he reached for the top button of the hunter's pants. He stopped suddenly at Julien's uncertain frown. "Oh God, it's too fast, right? Too—I'm sorry. I shouldn't—"

"No," Julien cut him off, his grip tightening on Noah's waist. "I just don't...really know what to do. I've never been—I've only ever—"

Noah's heart felt ready to burst at the embarrassed flush in the hunter's cheeks. "Because I'm a man?" Noah finished softly. He smiled when Julien nodded. "Well, just...do whatever you feel like, okay? We don't have to do anything you don't want to do. I'll be gentle with you," he promised with a sly grin, and he caught Julien's bottom lip in his teeth.

Julien let out a rough groan and tugged Noah tightly against him, making the witch shudder to feel the press of his erection through his pants. The hunter's body wasn't shy, at least. Julien pushed him onto his back and pressed hot kisses down his neck, his hand finally slipping up underneath Noah's shirt to brush his stomach. The hunter's thumb brushed over Noah's nipple experimentally, and the witch hummed his approval and moved to shimmy out of his own shirt as quickly as possible. He hissed and gripped Julien's hair as the hunter's mouth closed over his nipple, his hips rolling up against him.

Noah could barely breathe. This was Julien over him, kissing his chest, squeezing his hip, pressing his hard cock against his thigh. Julien, the straight one, the oblivious, the untouchable. Noah swore under his breath as Julien looked up at him with a deep flush in his cheeks, and he bent to kiss him, drawing the hunter up closer to him and savoring the shudder in the other man's skin as he slipped his tongue into his mouth to taste him. He reached down to fumble with Julien's zipper, tugging it down too quickly and slipping his hand inside to feel him through the thin fabric of his boxers.

Julien gasped into Noah's kiss, his hand tightening painfully on the witch's hip, but Noah didn't mind. He pressed his palm closer to feel each throb that followed Julien's heartbeat, and he shifted a bit to be able to touch him with both hands. He slid his hands beyond the waistband of Julien's boxers, desperate to feel the silky skin under his fingertips. The hunter's back arched upward at the sudden touch, and he broke the kiss to mumble a low string of curses in French.

"Now—now it's too fast," he whispered with an embarrassed smile hidden in Noah's shoulder.

"What's the matter?" Noah slowed his pace, as requested, but he kept his fingers wrapped around Julien's erection, stroking him agonizingly slowly. He really didn't mean to tease, but it was so satisfying to know that Julien really did knit his brow and bite his lip just the way Noah had always imagined. He looked so timid.

"It's been—" Julien paused to grunt as Noah ran his thumb over the seeping slit at the head of his cock. "It's been a while."

Noah hummed sympathetically and peeked out his tongue to lick a slow line over the hunter's upper lip, drawing a shivering moan from him that shot straight to Noah's groin. "For me too," he admitted softly, "but I don't know how slow I can go."

Julien grit his teeth as Noah squeezed him again. He shook his head and reluctantly pried Noah's hands away from him, taking just a moment to catch his breath. He tried to speak once or twice and apparently couldn't find the right words.

"Je ne veux pas te décevoir," he said at last, resting his forehead gently against Noah's. "I don't know what I'm doing."

Noah smiled and tilted his chin up to press his lips to the hunter's. "How about this," he whispered, his heart racing as Julien's weight pressed him into the bed. "If you're worried…we can just get the first one out of the way."

"The first—"

Before Julien could finish, Noah had slipped out from under him and pushed him by his shoulder onto his back. The witch hooked his fingers into Julien's waistband and urged him to lift his hips, allowing Noah to tug his pants down his thighs and toss them onto the floor. Julien swore as Noah bent over him again and nipped a sharp kiss at his hipbone.

"Is this okay?" Noah asked softly, but he had to take Julien's nervous swallow as a yes, because the hunter's voice seemed to have completely left him.

Noah hesitated now, wetting his lips and letting his hands press into the tight muscles of Julien's thighs. He'd imagined so many times pinning Julien against the wall and dropping to his knees, unzipping him slowly, grazing him with his teeth through the cloth, teasing him until he begged—but now that he had the hunter completely naked underneath him, he suddenly found himself hoping he was as good at this as he liked to think. If Julien's first ever man-given blowjob was disappointing, Noah would have to throw himself off a cliff.

He bent down and first touched a soft kiss to the sensitive skin, smiling to himself as Julien jumped. He ran his tongue slowly up the full length of him, letting the hunter feel his breath against his wet skin before he took him into his mouth. Julien's grip twisted into the blanket beside him, and he reached up a hand as though he wanted to touch Noah's hair but was too afraid. Noah hummed softly around him and helped him along, guiding his hand to the back of his head with a reassuring moan.

He lowered himself until he could feel the tip of Julien's cock touch his throat, and he pushed just a little farther, groaning as he felt the hunter's fingers tighten in his hair. He heard Julien gasp and hollowed his cheeks to draw him deeper. Noah circled him with his fingers to touch what his mouth couldn't reach, finding a steady rhythm that made Julien tremble under him. Noah fought the urge to touch himself through his still-buttoned jeans, determined to focus. He kept up his pace until Julien panted out a breathless warning, and he moaned his encouragement as the hunter's grip pulled at his hair.

Julien's shoulders lifted from the bed as he tensed, a rough growl escaping his throat as he emptied himself into Noah's eager mouth. The witch shifted with the helpless movement of Julien's hips, and he swallowed everything the hunter gave him, squeezing him slowly and giving him a delicate lick as a final drop pearled at his tip.

"Tabarnak," Julien sighed. He finally seemed to realize how tightly he was holding Noah's hair, and he quickly released him as the witch climbed up to straddle his hips.

"See?" Noah purred with satisfaction as he bent to kiss Julien's collarbone. "Now you can take your time."

He lifted himself out of the larger man's lap and dropped onto the bed beside him, sighing in relief as his erection was finally freed. He almost tore his jeans in an attempt to get them off faster. He saw Julien's amused smile as he wriggled out of his pants, but he didn't care.

Julien reached up to cup Noah's cheek, his thumb brushing the younger man's lower lip. He was still catching his breath, and Noah longed to trace each and every scar on Julien's torso with his tongue.

Before he could try, the hunter sat up with Noah in his lap and drew him close for a kiss. He ran calloused hands down Noah's slender back and pressed slow kisses down his jaw to his neck. He paused with his lips at Noah's left ear, and the younger man shuddered as Julien touched a soft, purposeful kiss to the wine-colored stain that marked Noah as a witch.

If Noah had any doubts about Julien still being wary of his magic, they vanished in that instant, and he felt suddenly that he understood what it had really meant for the hunter to say he trusted him.

Julien still hesitated with his hand on Noah's hip, inching toward touching him but seeming unsure of how to proceed.

"It's not complicated machinery, Julien," Noah panted. His fingers dug into the hunter's shoulders and he bit his lip, not wanting to rush him but desperate to feel his hands on him.

"I'm sorry—"

"Like this," the witch urged, and he guided Julien's hand around his cock and squeezed, unable to hold in his trembling gasp. He kept his hand on Julien's and helped him set a pace he liked as he balanced himself with one hand on the hunter's shoulder. He let his head fall back, his breath coming in short pants, and he ground down against Julien's hips. His bottom lip caught in his teeth as he felt Julien begin to stir again beneath him.

Noah didn't want to leave Julien's touch, but he was also impatient. He reached up and pulled the hunter down to him as soon as he was free, kissing him and gripping him tightly to stroke him back to readiness. He couldn't wait anymore.

"Touch me, Julien," he begged with his lips against the other man's ear, "Please." When Julien hesitated, Noah rolled his hips against him and pushed the hunter's hand between his legs, guiding him shamelessly to where he ached to be touched. "Here."

"I—I don't want to hurt you," Julien objected, and Noah groaned impatiently.

"You aren't going to hurt me," he promised. He murmured softly to himself and arched his back as he slipped his hand into Julien's, spreading slick oil over the other man's fingers. Julien started at the sudden wetness and looked down at Noah in confusion.

"Practical magic," Noah smiled slyly at him, the flush of embarrassment in Julien's cheeks making his stomach pleasantly twist.

This shy, nervous Julien wasn't like the hunter he knew, but it was a nice surprise.

He lifted his hips to remind Julien to focus, and Julien obliged him, but he was so tentative and slow that Noah wanted to pin him down. When Julien finally pressed beyond the barrier and slipped a finger inside him, Noah whined and pushed back against his touch. He told himself not to rush, but it was impossible. This was Julien. It was still a little hard to believe the whole thing wasn't a dream.

Without warning, Noah turned over onto his hands and knees and reached between his legs to make sure Julien understood his intentions. "Please," he groaned. He felt Julien's weight shift on the bed behind him, and he shuddered as he felt the soft pressure of the hunter pushing close to him, but Julien wasn't moving.

"Please," Noah said again. His skin shivered as Julien's hands ran over his waist and back. He ground against Julien's hips and savored the other man's rough groan. "Please hurry."

Julien was clearly trying to do as he was told, but for every centimeter that he pushed forward, he stopped and tilted his head to try and look at Noah's face as though checking on him.

"Julien, you aren't going to hurt me," Noah assured him with as much patience as he could manage.

"Are you sure?"

"I'm so sure. I'll tell you if you do, I promise."

Julien bent over him to place a soft kiss between his shoulderblades, and he finally centered himself with a hand on Noah's hip and eased slowly into him, both men's breath catching in their chests. For a few moments, they could only stay that way, Noah's hands twisted desperately into the blankets and Julien's panting breath against his back. Then Julien began to rock against him, and Noah let him set the pace. He tilted his hips to help Julien hit that weak spot inside of him, and he cried out with every thrust of the hunter's hips. Julien's hands were hot against his skin, his every pant and groan sending shivers down Noah's spine.

Julien gripped him tightly, all shyness forgotten, and they moved together easily, going faster and faster until Noah had to put a hand up to keep from being pushed into the headboard. When Julien noticed, he shifted slightly and tugged Noah back to him with one strong pull to give him more room.

The witch swore into the pillow, supporting himself on his shoulder as he reached down to stroke his neglected erection. He pulled and squeezed at the rhythm Julien set until he began to tremble. When he felt Julien's weight on top of him, the hunter pressing soft, achingly loving kisses to his back and shoulders, Noah had to let his head drop, overwhelmed with relief and longing and everything that he'd been keeping pent up inside for the past months. This was Julien—Julien kissing him, holding him, loving him. He felt on the edge of a chasm that he was afraid and eager to fall into.

Each of Julien's kisses was like a brand on his skin, marking him with every heated breath. He let out a string of begging whispers as the hunter rolled into him, his own slick fingers working quickly on himself, and finally he tensed, grinding back helplessly against Julien as he spilled his climax onto the bed.

Julien slowed, but Noah reached back to grip the hand on his hip. "Don't stop," he begged, "please." He swallowed hard and squeezed Julien's fingers. "Please, I want you to—" The thought was lost in a moan as Julien pushed deep inside him again, quickly finding his former rhythm.

A growl formed in Julien's throat as Noah whined and twisted against him, pleading and panting. Julien wrapped an arm around the witch's waist and held him tight, his forehead leaned on Noah's shoulder, and he dug his fingernails into the younger man's skin as he finished again with a ragged moan.

Noah's legs gave out from underneath him, but he managed to let Julien remove himself without injury before collapsing onto the bed. The hunter dropped down beside him, and Noah shivered at the other man's light touch on his back. They lay in silence except for their slowly steadying breath until Noah turned his head to peek up at Julien's face in the darkness.

"I never knew you had tattoos," the hunter said softly, and Noah smiled lazily at him.

"Surprise," he answered with a tired chuckle.

Julien traced the intricate marks with his fingertips, and Noah shuffled closer to the larger man's warmth and nuzzled his face into the blonde hair on his chest. Noah let out a long, satisfied sigh and craned his neck to press one final kiss to Julien's collarbone.

"This is for real, right?" he whispered after a moment. "I'm not still dead, am I?"

Julien chuckled, and the rumbling sound made Noah smile. "You're not dead." He shifted to let Noah lay his head on his shoulder and bent to kiss the witch's temple. "You can even go to sleep, and I'll be right here when you wake up."

Noah's face grew warm. "You did so much for me," he whispered. "I never even asked what it was like when you went—wherever it was you went."

"I'm here," Julien said. "A bit sore, and down one eye, but I'm here."

"And this...this was okay?"

Julien paused. "What, you mean—this this?" He ran a hand tenderly down Noah's back. "You?"

Noah shivered at the light touch and hid his face in the pillow. "Yeah, me. I know how it is to be, you know...caught up. But if you're straight, you're straight, I mean—"

"Noah," Julien interrupted him, slipping gentle fingers through the witch's hair and urging him to look up at him. The look in Julien's eyes was so serious that it ran a chill down Noah's spine, and he chewed his lip as Julien brushed a thumb along his temple. "I may not be good with...saying what I mean. But if it puts you at ease, I'll tell you I love you a hundred times a day, every day, for a hundred years."

Noah wanted to have a witty retort, or to brush aside the sentiment with a joke, but he could only state up at the hunter with his heart in his throat.

"I'm only sorry I was too blind to see it sooner," Julien whispered, and then Noah did laugh.

"You mean it took you losing an eye to stop being blind?"

"It's not a little too soon to make jokes about it?" Julien frowned, but there was no malice in his voice.

"Why, are you feeling tender?"

"In places," Julien chuckled.

"Poor dear," Noah said with a smile, and he leaned up to touch the hunter's scruffy cheek and to give him a slow, patient kiss, reveling in the simple fact that he could do it just because he wanted to.

24

Noah would have stayed in that bed forever, wrapped in warm blankets and tangled in Julien's arms. It still felt like a dream—the hunter's confession, his kiss, how much he had risked for Noah's sake. He found it impossible to think that not so long ago, he had felt afraid just because Julien had raised his voice. This man wasn't Travis. Even when he had shouted, it had been out of concern. He knew that now. Julien had touched him so timidly, whispered so softly to him. Julien was—despite all evidence to the contrary—gentle.

A sleepy groan rumbled pleasantly under Noah's cheek, and he smiled into the soft hair on his hunter's chest.

"Of all the times to be out of cigarettes," Julien mumbled, his arm tightening around Noah as he stroked the witch's bicep with his thumb.

"They probably don't have a Mac's we can run to, huh?" Noah tilted his head up at Julien's face. "What do you think they use as money here, anyway? Anything? Or do they just trade?"

"Maybe they use those mushrooms you pilfered," the hunter chuckled.

Noah sat up on his elbows with a sly grin. "I knew you were only interested in me for my money."

"You're onto me."

"Not yet," Noah purred, relishing the slightly delayed widening of Julien's eyes and the faint flush in his cheeks. But before Noah could climb on top of Julien as planned, there was a knock at the door, and he paused at the sound of Airmed's voice.

"Sorry," she called through the door, "but are you...up? Decent?"

"Now she cares about seeing me naked," Noah muttered as he reluctantly sat up.

"What? Why were you naked?"

"Fairy magic. Don't worry about it."

Julien reached down to snatch his abandoned shirt up off of the floor and dressed himself just in time to avoid being caught without pants. Noah only cared enough to make sure the blanket was covering the important bits.

"Sorry to bother," Airmed said with an apologetic smile as she stood in the open doorway. "I know you two must still be exhausted."

"It's fine," Julien said in a slightly gruff voice, and he cleared his throat pointedly when Airmed bit her bottom lip in amusement.

"They're asking for you at my father's house," she went on, politely taking Julien's embarrassed cue. "You ought to see them before you're on your way, I think." After a beat, she let out a small noise and held her hands out. "Oh, not that I'm meaning to kick you out, of course!" she added in a rush. "You'd be welcome to stay as long as you like, only it's not good for humans to stay too long in Tír na nÓg."

Noah tilted his head at her. "Why not?"

"Well, usually the humans that we get here are...well, they're stolen, mostly. Not by me," she said hastily, "but, you know, some of the other Aos sidthe are...well, our city isn't the darkest place in Tír na nÓg."

"Stolen?" Julien asked, a growling scowl growing on his face. "What do you mean, stolen?"

"They give them back, mostly," Airmed said with a chagrined smile. "Some things humans are just better at, so they...use them. It's been the way of things for a thousand years, Julien."

Noah could see the gears turning in his hunter's head, so he quickly spoke up. "Hey, so before you declare war on the whole of fairy kind, why don't we hear why it's bad for us to be here?"

"Yes, right," Airmed agreed. "The thing is, for you...it's difficult to explain. Time may seem to you to be passing normally, but you aren't actually aging while you're here. The problem with that is, of course, that you'll do all of your aging as soon as you leave. It shouldn't be so bad, since you've only been here a few days, but...you may not want to linger."

"Jesus," Noah chuckled. "This place has fucked up rules."

"Yes, rather," Airmed admitted after a moment.

"Why are we being asked for at your father's?" Julien asked.

"I'm not sure," she said. "I think Cian wants to talk to you. Maybe all of you can make amends, in light of everything that's happened?"

Julien's face said "no."

"Let's at least hear him out," Noah cut in before Julien could voice whatever murderous thoughts were on his mind. "They did help us. And when we leave, you can go kill a few werewolves or something to make yourself feel better."

Julien frowned at him, fully aware that he was being placated, but Noah smiled at him with such a pleading look that the hunter gave a short sigh and nodded.

"Fine," he said. "Let's go hear him out. But," he added, "if he tries anything, I'm going to make him wish he'd died."

"I'm sure there won't be any call for that," Airmed said with a nervous laugh.

They were welcomed at the estate of Dian Cecht with all the warmth of a funeral home, but as they were led into the sitting room to meet their host, everyone at least seemed relaxed and unarmed.

Ciaran sat beside Trent near the cold fireplace, and he gestured for Julien and Noah to take their places across from him.

"Why are we here?" Julien asked bluntly, and Ciaran smiled at him, nonplussed.

"Well, as usual, nobody actually needs you, hunter," he said. Noah could feel Julien coiling beside him and put a firm hand on his knee to remind him that they were here to talk.

"I...need to ask a favor of you," Ciaran went on with reluctance in his voice as he turned his eyes to Noah. "I never actually got your name."

"Oh. Uh, I'm Noah. What kind of favor could you possibly need from me?"

"A magic one," Ciaran answered simply.

"What?" Noah laughed despite himself. "But you're a fairy, right? I'm sure your magic is a hundred times stronger than anything I could—"

"My skillset is a bit specific," Ciaran interrupted. "I'm hoping you know something I don't."

"Well, you guys did kind of bring me back from the dead," Noah chuckled. "After killing me in the first place. But that was because I— well I'll give it a shot, anyway," he grinned, deciding to abandon that train of thought. "What's your problem?"

"The problem," Ciaran sighed, pausing briefly to glance at an uncomfortable-looking Trent beside him, "is that one of us is human, and the other is not. One of us is immortal, and the other not."

Noah frowned at them for a moment, not understanding, and then his eyebrows lifted. "Oh. Well, uh…I guess the most important question would be which way you want to go," he said. "I mean, do you want to be human, or…?"

"I would prefer not dying within the next fifty years," Ciaran answered.

"Then you're looking for a way to be immortal?" Noah asked, nodding toward Trent.

"It's on the list of 'problems I never thought I'd have,' but yes, apparently I am," the boy said.

Noah leaned on his knees and drummed his fingers on his bottom lip. "Well I mean, there are a couple of standard things that you're probably not going to want," he said with a shrug. "Vampires are immortal, and that's pretty easy to do. Comes with a lot of strings, though. I've heard of a few successes with phylacteries, but that's super risky, and I don't know too many people who've used them and been okay, you know…upstairs." He tapped his temple for emphasis and looked back at Ciaran. "You don't have any way to just make Trent what you are?"

"Only one," the fairy answered grimly, "and it's very much a last resort."

"Why?"

"The price can be…prohibitively high," Ciaran said. "Do you know of a way or don't you?"

Noah puffed out his cheeks in a sigh and sat back in his seat as he frowned across at Trent. "I assume you *don't* want to be a vampire, or something easy like that."

"It wouldn't be my first choice."

"Yeah, mine either." Noah smiled, but Trent didn't smile back. Noah wouldn't have blamed him for still being pissed about the whole situation, but he knew well enough by now that Trent was just sort of a grumpy person in general.

"Anyway," he went on, "if you don't want to be turned into a blood-drinking creature of the night, phylacteries are a stupid idea, and whatever the fairies can do is a non-option, then I don't—" He paused. Ciaran looked at him curiously, but Noah hesitated before speaking. "I might...know one thing. But full disclosure, I've never actually done it, only heard about it—and it means a pretty big commitment from both of you."

"What is it?" Ciaran pressed.

"I've heard that there's a way to...connect you, kind of. It's a Vajrayana principle. But when I say connect, I mean irrevocably. It's a way to bind your souls together—for better or worse. That means that Trent will live as long as you do, but he'll still be human. If he gets killed for whatever reason, you'll die too, and vice versa."

"Well," Ciaran chuckled, "that is fairly well commitment defined, isn't it?" He looked over at Trent, who was frowning down at his own hands. "What do you think, a mhuirnín?"

"You said you've never done it," Trent said after a moment, glancing back up at Noah.

"I haven't," the witch admitted. "But it's not the sort of thing that's going to kill you if I fail. I don't think." He paused, pondering. "No. No reason it should kill you," he decided.

"Reassuring," Trent muttered.

"Hey, magic is uncertain science, okay?" Noah frowned defensively. "You asked for my help, and this is the best option I know. You're free to find something else."

Trent went silent, and he hesitated a long while before looking over at Ciaran. "I'm in if you are," he said softly, and Noah felt a little flutter in his heart at the gentle smile the fairy gave Trent in return.

"Then I'm in," Ciaran answered.

"This is a quick process, right?" Julien interrupted, fixing Noah with a pointed stare.

"Well...no, not at all, actually," the witch chuckled. "But we don't have to do it here. In fact it's probably better if we don't."

"You really want to help them?" Julien frowned.

"I don't hold grudges," Noah shrugged. "Especially after everything we've all been through. If they're willing to ask for my help, then I'm willing to give it. This is some true love stuff here, Julien. I want to help. You could go back to Vancouver and wait for me if you want; I'm a big boy."

"Absolutely not," the hunter said immediately.

"Then I guess you're helping, too."

Neither Ciaran nor Julien seemed happy about that prospect, but neither of them said anything.

"I'll need to do some reading," Noah said. "I don't suppose either of you have a laptop here. We were sort of forced to leave most of our crap in a hotel in Vancouver. It's probably been pawned by now. I'll need supplies too, but we can do that back in the real world."

"You can use mine," Trent offered, "but there's no Wi-Fi down here."

"Shocker," Noah laughed. "Then whenever you guys are ready, we can leave."

"We're more than ready," Ciaran answered with a frown.

Airmed tearfully hugged everyone as they gathered near the door of her father's estate, even Trent, who looked supremely uncomfortable in her embrace. She kissed Ciaran's cheeks until he was forced to pry her away, and he hugged his brothers and shook his father's hand before hiding himself away in the dark carriage to wait for the rest of his company.

"A moment," Cu whispered in Noah's ear as he stepped toward the door, and the fairy gently led him back into the hall by his arm.

"You really are relentless," Noah said with a teasing grin, but Cu only smiled at him.

"I have a gift for you," the fairy said. He picked up a box from a nearby table and offered it to Noah. It was heavy in Noah's hands, about a foot wide, and covered in silver carvings of Celtic knots and what looked like pairs of dogs. Noah frowned curiously up at Cu.

"I'm glad that I don't have to finish your list for you," Cu said. "This will make it easier for you to do it yourself." He tapped the top of the little trunk. "This is one of a pair. Anything that you place in this box will appear in its twin within a few moments. It works the other way too, of course; you may find unexpected things in it that have been placed in the other box." Cu smiled slyly down at him. "I took the liberty of having the other delivered to a boy you know in America."

Noah's mouth dropped open. "What? How? How did you find out where he is?"

"I entrusted the package to a spirit I know," he said with a shrug. "It will find him. You may want to put a little letter of explanation in your box to pass to him."

Noah clutched the box to his chest, not knowing that to say. To be able to communicate freely with Sabin again, to be able to send him the things he needed—it was an impossibly perfect gift. "Thank you," he said simply.

"Make sure that hunter takes good care of you," Cu answered, and he bent to peck Noah's cheek before turning him back toward the door and sending him on his way.

The four of them rode in the carriage in silence, Julien and Ciaran exchanging stony stares the entire way, but Noah smiled and held his silver box in his lap like a child might cling to a longed-for Christmas present. He could send word to Sabin. Julien was beside him and was going to stay that way. He was going to be able to test his skill for the sake of what was really an almost sickeningly romantic endeavor. All in all, dying had turned out to be a pretty good deal for him.

BECAUSE YOU NEEDED ME

ABOUT THE AUTHOR

Born and bred in the South, T.S. (or Tess) started writing young, but began writing real novels while working full time as a legal secretary. She's a chronic researcher, a lover of all things villainous and gruesome, and a giant nerd for history, video games, classic novels, and comic books.

Find me around the Internet!

tsbarnett.com
Facebook: Tess Barnett
Twitter: @TS_Barnett
Instagram: @tsbarnowl